In an uncertain time in the future, Kaya More uses her gift of second sight to lead LUPO - the Let Us Play Organization - a group of rebels as they fight the unjust laws that ban rock and roll music. In the United States their opponent is Judah Arnold and the People Against Rock and Roll, otherwise known as PARR.

Some of LUPO's members are descendants of a legendary rock band that were the last to oppose PARR on the fateful night that rock music was wiped out. The band, Mystique, disappeared, never to be heard from or seen again. Such was the fate of many rock musicians.

As the rebels race from the streets of New York City to the tops of the Canadian Rockies to the beaches of the California they find adventure, music and love. Yet the story doesn't really explode until the rest of the world takes a stand and joins in the struggle.

ISBN: 978-1-84728-519-5

Cover designed by Richard McQuire

To Kathy

Enjoy

LET US PLAY

A Rock 'n Roll Love Story

DEDICATIONS

To my family and friends for putting up with my insanity and supporting me all these years. You know who you are; there are too many to mention.

To Micheline and all those at KBD for their support.

Thanks goes to Richard McQuire for designing an awesome cover. I am totally blown away.

Special thanks to Caro, Tammy, Regina, Joyce, Kim and other online writers who are always there for me when I need them.

To Bret and the boys whose music inspired me to write the first draft of this book years ago and who I still listen to whenever I get stuck for just the right words.

To Paul Laine; the greatest singer, songwriter, musician to ever emerge from the rain sodden shores of western Canada. Thanks for believing in me when very few did.

And last but not least, to all the musicians who make this world a better place by filling our hearts with the sounds we love. No matter what genre it is.

PART ONE

The End and the Beginning

PROLOGUE

People ran from the concert hall, screaming in reaction to the horror they had just witnessed. Their clothes bloodied, assorted limbs broken and their minds numb by the massacre they had just seen, many fought their way to the ambulances that were just pulling up.

Appearing much calmer than the fleeing concert attendees, several identically black clad individuals emerged holding various assortments of weapons. Those waiting for services of the ambulance attendants cowered at the sight of these imposing figures and anyone who would manage to retain their sanity knew that they would never forget this horrific night.

In addition to their confusion, the earth began to shake violently. Buildings shook on their foundations; people struggled to maintain their balance as they attempted to assist those in need. Suddenly, a crevice in the ground began to form around the auditorium. Rapidly, it widened and the concert hall began a slow descent. Before the horrified eyes of the onlookers, the building slowly disappeared from sight and the ground sealed itself around the buried structure.

The earth stilled but was replaced by a forceful wind that seemed to approach tornado proportions. The gusts were so strong that people were thrown from where they stood and deposited a few feet away; trees were uprooted and vehicles were overturned. Sand from the nearby beach was lifted by the winds and created a sandstorm that was blinding.

As quickly as this chaos had started, it stopped with what many later claimed sounded like a great sigh. Two events of importance happened that night: Rock and roll music ended and a legend was born.

CHAPTER One

Twelve Months Previous

The new offices of the government agency 'The People Against Rock and Roll' were packed with reporters, waiting to interview the head of this controversial organization.

"Hey Graham!" A young newscaster asked a veteran newspaperman. "Do you think that this is for real? Can this guy really stop rock and roll?"

The aging reporter shrugged.

"Doubt it." He muttered. "I've heard it all before and I am sure we will hear it until the end of time."

Further speculation was interrupted by the arrival of a tall man dressed in black and accompanied by two others in similar uniforms carrying weapons.

"Ladies and gentlemen of the media." The baritone voice was in sharp contrast to the man's almost anorexic stature. "We are PARR, 'the People Against Rock and Roll' and we are hear to put an end to the decadent music that has caused so much turmoil.

"Rock and roll music is created by people in the hands of Satan and is destroying the minds and moral fiber of our young. We intend to put an end to this atrocity so that our country can once again be strong."

"Mr. Neils, have you any proof that the music is causing the harm you say it is?" One reporter asked.

"It is obvious. Since the emergence of rock and roll music, teenagers have been more rebellious and have committed more crimes than ever before. And when heavy metal and thrash metal music made their appearance, the situation became worse. The lyrics in these songs speak of such sinister things as suicide, death, illicit and promiscuous sex and a score of other things that any self-respecting citizen would find offensive. The youth, especially, must not be subjected to this."

"But, according to the law, if the Washington State Superior Court judges a record obscene, it will be labeled adults only and therefore cannot be displayed where it can be seen by minors." Another reporter pointed out. "Don't you think that this is enough government control over the music industry? After all, we are supposed to have freedom of speech in this country."

"It is the duty to the government to protect the people of this fine country. It is our duty to ensure that the youth of today, the future, are given the chance to become well-adjusted adults. "

"You aren't protecting the people! You are trying to control the people" Someone angrily interjected."

"The PMRC tried much the same thing back in the nineteen eighties. All they did was create more publicity for the musicians and all you are going to do is to drive the music underground where there won't be any chance for control. At least now, if something is overly offensive the government and the industry have a chance to regulate what gets heard. Why do you think you can accomplish a total banishment of the music and that the underground scene won't occur?"

"Very good question." Peter Neils remarked. "We will show the people just how harmful the music really is and how beneficial to the moral good of the country it would be if the music no longer existed. That way, I am sure that our goal will be realized." At a signal from one of his many aides, Peter Neils nodded.

"But I am afraid that this meeting is now over with. I am sure that I can count on your support in the future." With that, he disappeared behind the partition, leaving a group of sceptical reporters.

"Do you think he is really going to do it? I mean can he really bring an end to rock and roll?"

"Ever since Elvis Presley first gyrated, they have been trying to stop rock and roll. Quite frankly, I don't think it will ever happen."

Peter Neils waited until the office had been cleared before buzzing his secretary.

"Have Judah Arnold come to my office immediately." Within a few moments, Judah stood at attention before his supervisor.

"You wished to see me sir."

Peter looked up from his papers and studied the young man intently.

"How far do you want to advance in this organization, Arnold?"

"As far as I can, sir."

"Can you be trusted to carry out a very special mission, one that must be kept in complete secrecy?"

"Of course."

Peter regarded the officer before smiling grimly.

"Many of the activities of PARR will be considered illegal but they have to be done in order to ensure the end of rock and roll music. It is necessary for us to break the laws in order to protect the people. Do you have any difficulties with committing illegal acts?"

"No sir."

"What do you feel has to be done to end the music? How will we stop the musicians from playing the music and the people from listening to it? What do you feel would be our most effective weapon?"

"Fear." Judah Arnold answered simply.

Peter Neils nodded.

"Right. And fear is what we will use."

CHAPTER Two

The impressive Capitol Records building in Los Angeles was the first to fall under the hands of PARR. Late one night, several identically black clad individuals illegally entered the building. Within moments of their leaving, the structure exploded from within. The midnight housekeeping staff died in the explosion or in the blaze that followed as well as a few junior executives working late. The culprits were never found.

Other recording houses hired extra security but still expensive and sometimes irreparable damage was inflicted. It was extremely difficult to record new releases and, even if they managed to be produced, getting the music out to the public was almost impossible.

Shipments of the product were lost in transit. Mysterious individuals in black uniform raided the shipments, often seriously injuring or killing those handling the transferal of the product.

Radio stations that specialized in any form of rock and roll music suddenly began to lose sponsors. Transmissions were tampered with; disc jockeys were mysteriously injured when outside of the stations; one by one, stations began to shut down or change format.

Nightclubs that played rock and roll were raided on a constant basis. Musicians that were hired to perform would arrive before the show to find their equipment damaged beyond repair.

Anyone involved with rock and roll music was suffering. The big corporations found that their rock and roll acts were losing money; many fans were frightened away from concerts; musicians were being beaten by unnamed figures but still they held on. The supporters were determined that rock and roll would never die.

At the PARR offices, Peter Neils and Judah Arnold were in a late night meeting. Judah had advanced rapidly through the ranks of PARR and, in less than a year, he was now Peter's aide.

"You would think that these people would realize that the music is finished." Peter grunted. "But they still hang on."

"Perhaps what we need is something drastic. Something that will convince them of the harm of listening to rock and roll." Judah commented.

"And what would you suggest?"

"On December 31, Mystique is playing to a sell out crowd at the club Rocker's Paradise. Mystique has been very vocal about their disapproval of PARR and they should be taught a lesson."

"And?"

"And we will be able to show the people just how harmful rock and roll is."

Peter looked into the flat, emotionless eyes of Judah Arnold and shivered. Without a doubt that would be an evening that no one would forget.

CHAPTER Three

An uncertain time in the future

"Thank you for coming." Kansall Morc surveyed the group of people. "And I would like to thank Calo for allowing us to use this room.

"This is a meeting of the Let Us Play Organization, more commonly known as LUPO. Our goal is to wipe out PARR and bring back rock and roll music. But I will let Brent explain more."

Brent stood as Kansall took his seat.

"One thing I would like to point out immediately is that it isn't just the fact that rock and roll music has been eliminated which we object to. It is a question of our rights that we are fighting for.

"We don't feel that everyone has to listen to rock and roll. Just that everyone should have the opportunity to choose for him or herself.

"To put it bluntly, what we are doing is illegal. It is dangerous and our activities must be kept secret. If there is anyone here who is having any doubts, then you should leave right now. This is a cause that will require your total commitment. " Brent waited a moment but everyone remained seated so he continued.

"OK. Now down to business."

A child stood under the neon lights and shivered in the night air. Her head turned slowly from side to side and her grayeyes searched the faces of passers-byes. Across the street she saw her father, illuminated by the interior lights of the diner he stood outside of. A feeling of foreboding engulfed the girl but, though she tried, she was unable to call a warning or move.

A loud crack of a rifle shot sounded amid the other noises of the city inhabitants and she watched her father fall, blood staining the front of his white shirt.

"No!" She screamed. Eight-year-old Kaya More sat up in bed, the events of her nightmare coming back to her with perfect clarity. "I have to help him!" Quickly, Kaya got up and put on a pair of jeans and a sweatshirt. As she was tying her running shoes, she listened intently for any noise that would indicate that her mother was still awake but all was silent. Cautiously, Kaya slipped quietly and quickly out of the house. She began running along the street, not knowing where she was going, yet being drawn by some unknown force. Following this force, she kept on running; hoping to reach her unknown destination in time to save her father.

Kaya ran along the brightly lit streets, pushing past the hookers, drug dealers and other people in her way. The panic was growing inside her and Kaya feared that she wouldn't reach her father in time.

Kaya stopped when she saw Kansall standing under the lights of the Underground Cafe. He was in conversation with another man but all Kaya saw was her father. Tears of relief at finding her father alive trickled down her face. She opened her mouth to call to him when he jerked back, as if hit by something. He started to fall and the nightmare that had brought Kaya here merged with the reality of what was happening.

Oblivious to the traffic, Kaya ran across the street. At the sound of car brakes screeching and horns blaring, Brent turned to see the child running purposefully towards him. He tried to block Kaya from her father but she slipped from his grasp.

Although she saw the blood staining the front of her father's white shirt and instinctively knew that he was dying, a part of her refused to believe it.

"Daddy! You will be all right."

Kansall lay on the sidewalk, his heart pumping away his life. But he managed a weak smile for his daughter.

"What are you doing here, Starlight?"

"I wasn't too late! I know you will be all right! You will tell me bedtime stories and take me to the park. I know you will!"

Kansall coughed, spraying Kaya with blood.

"I don't think so."

"Daddy!" Kansall didn't answer and Kaya shook him, gently at first then with more force. "Daddy! Answer me!"

Brent Mitchell tried to take the girl in his arms but she stubbornly clung to her father's lifeless form.

"Daddy, please don't die. Please don't die!" She sobbed.

The lights of the diner shone on the little girl crying over her dead father as the curious and morbid gathered around to watch.

Everyone's attention was on the horror and they didn't notice the man, dressed in a PARR uniform and carrying a rifle, slip quietly away into the darkness. That is everyone except the child weeping over her dead father. Suddenly she was quiet and stared, past the onlookers, into the night. Unknown to the PARR agent, she saw his face clearly.

CHAPTER Four

Sixteen year olds, Kaya More and Krista Andrews entered the cafeteria, discussing their latest history class.

"That test was a killer." Krista moaned. "I think it should be against the law for teachers to give tests like that!"

"Or better yet, against the law for teachers to give us any tests!"

"Right! The only thing worth gaining from school are the guys. If it weren't for them, it wouldn't be worth coming here at all."

"Well, some of the classes aren't so bad. I guess it depends on who's teaching it."

"You mean if someone like Mr. Jayce taught history, you would enjoy it?"

Kaya blushed.

"Yeah, I guess so." The two girls collapsed in giggles. Mr. Jayce was a young, good looking English teacher and, for the first time in her scholastic career, Kaya was excelling in English.

"So what do you think of that new guy, Paul Nelson?" Krista asked Kaya as they sat at a table.

Kaya shrugged.

"He's OK, I guess. I prefer older men."

"Hello Kaya, Krista." Mr. Jayce chose that moment to walk by the two girls and once again both collapsed with laughter.

Kaya abruptly stopped when a strange chill enveloped her. A horrifying premonition flashed through her mind. Krista was lying, beaten and bloody. Her petite body was motionless but Kaya was certain that her friend wasn't dead. There was a feeling that something unspeakable had happened but she wasn't certain what.

"Kaya?" Krista's voice broke into Kaya's haze.

"How are you getting home?" Kaya asked quickly.

“I'm walking. How else would I get home?" "I had better skip band practice today. I don't want you walking home alone."

"What? Are you crazy?" Krista was perplexed. Kaya was a serious person, true, but she was always so calm. The note of hysteria in Kaya's voice was very alarming.

"I mean you can't miss band practice. I can walk home by myself. After all, I am old enough and I will look both ways before crossing the street." Kaya didn't catch the attempt at humor in Krista's statement. She was too concerned about the horrifying vision she had just had.

"I just don't think you should walk home by yourself today." Kaya was at a loss. She had kept her gift of futuristic visions (or was it a curse?) a secret from everyone so she couldn't explain to Krista why she shouldn't go home alone but she had to do something.

"You are going to stay for your band practice, Kaya More and I am going to walk home. I'll see you tonight at the party." Krista continued even though she had a feeling that Kaya wasn't really paying attention to her.

"At least have someone walk home with you." Kaya saw Krista go to interrupt so she held up a hand to stop her. "Please? It would make me feel better."

"All right." Krista conceded. "But who is going to walk me home?" Kaya surveyed the cafeteria then smiled.

"Just leave it all to me."

"So you don't mind?" Kaya asked.

Paul grinned.

"Mind walking Krista home? Of course not! "

"Great! I'll see you at the party tonight."

"Kaya asked you to walk me home?" Krista asked. She was secretly pleased about this turn of events and the faint stain spreading across her cheeks proved the fact.

"Of course!" Paul huffed comically. "What other strong, young man would she ask?"

A number of teasing retorts came to mind but Krista bit them back. Instead she smiled sweetly and, adopting a southern drawl, said,

"Why thank you kind sir. I'm sure that I will feel safe with you by my side." Krista closed her locker firmly and waited for Paul to make the first move.

Paul grinned, also holding back some remarks and took her arm to lead her out of the school.

For a few blocks Krista and Paul walked in silence. Neither knew what to say to the other. Since they were so involved with each other neither of the teens noticed the black car pull up alongside them. Before Paul or Krista could react, they both had sacks thrown over their heads and were heaved unceremoniously into the back seat of the vehicle. As the vehicle started to move, both Krista and Paul feared for their lives.

Kaya's mind was floating in another time. For numerous reasons, she couldn't seem to concentrate on the band practice. Part of her mind was concerned about Krista while another part was seeing music scores she had never seen before. The music from another time and without realizing it, her fingers were flying over the keyboards, playing this strange melody and generating an exhilarating feeling of excitement that she had never felt before.

As she finished playing Kaya gradually came back to the present to realize that the entire music room was staring at her with varied emotions. Some of the students looked confused while others looked pleased. However the music teacher, Mr. Chay, was furious.

"Miss More!" He bellowed. "What was that noise? Do you realize that I can have you thrown in jail for playing whatever that was? Where in the world did you find that music?"

Kaya was shocked.

"I'm sorry, Mr. Chay. My fingers just started playing."

"Just started playing?" Mr. Chay was purple with rage. "I ought to expel you from school for this!"

A slow but deep anger started to burn within Kaya. Her mind flashed back to when her father was alive. She remembered, more clearly now than ever before, the speeches about the injustice of censorship. Even more unjust was the way that people were punished for listening to the music. In her mind's eye, Kaya could see the battles of other rebels, and people like them, had gone through. Her father had died trying to stop people like Mr. Chay. People with narrow minds.

Keeping a tight rein on her anger, Kaya pulled up her head to face the music teacher.

"Expel me? Jail me? For expressing myself through music? For being creative and original enough to play something besides that boring crap you give us? I didn't realize that this band was run by a person with such a narrow mind." Kaya's voice was bitter. "If this is the way you are going to run this band, I don't think I want to be in it." Saying this, she proceeded to dismantle her keyboards and pack them up.

A quiet murmur had begun to run through the students as everyone was commenting on Kaya's words. Although the impulse to look up was strong, Kaya kept her face down and continued the task she had begun. Once everything was ready to go, she straightened up and looked her stunned teacher straight in the eye. The room was silent as all waited expectantly for Kaya's next words.

"Men and women have died because of people like you. People who were more than willing to enforce laws that they didn't understand or even agree with just because that was what they were told to do. People who thought that the narrowness of their thinking was the only way to think." Kaya's voice rang strong and clear in the eerie stillness. "Those men and women fought against the injustices brought on by people like you. We all have a right to make our own decisions and not have the government or teachers make the decisions for us."

Once more, Kaya paused to survey the group that was mesmerized by her speech. Shaking her head in disgust, she walked to the classroom door. Once there, she paused. Turning to look at the occupants of the room, she continued,

"Right now, I stand behind those men and women who died. I would rather die than live in a society that restricts my freedom to express myself and be an individual." With one final look at the people who sat in stunned silence, she left.

A chilly autumn wind caused Kaya to pull up the collar on her light jacket. She felt strangely relieved after her antics in class. She didn't regret a word of what she had said or how she had said it. Though she knew there would, more than likely, be repercussions from her actions; she didn't fear them. Rather she welcomed them as a validation of the injustice of present day society. Confident, Kaya continued to walk home.

Wind More glanced at the clock as she hung up the phone. Smiling grimly to herself, she contemplated what Mr. Chay had told her about Kaya's actions that afternoon. She felt a chill of fear crawl up her spine. Would Kaya meet with the same fate as her father had? That night, eight years ago, when Gleven had woken her to inform her that her husband was dead, still remained vivid in Wind's memory. Perhaps the most frightening revelation of that evening was the fact that Kaya seemed to have physic powers. Many times during the last eight years Kaya had stated amazing facts, both bad and good, that had come true. Bringing her mind back to the present, Wind ran her fingers through her ash blond hair and sighed.

"What is going to happen to Kaya now?" She mused inwardly. A small part of her feared the consequences of her daughter's actions but a larger part admired Kaya for what she had done. Though Wind knew that Kaya's outspoken comments concerning her views on censorship could cause the two of them to be once again hounded by PARR agents, she felt a secret satisfaction that Kaya had made such a stand. Chuckling to herself, she waited for Kaya to return home.

Krista and Paul lay, bound hand and foot, side-by-side in a dingy dark room. They had been dropped there a few moments before one of their kidnappers had said to another that they had to get Judah. With their heads no longer covered, Krista and Paul were able to gaze at their dismal surroundings.

"What am I doing here?" Krista wondered to herself.

"A fine bodyguard I turned out to be!" Paul groaned inwardly.

Their musings were cut short by the arrival of Judah Arnold. Judah was an impressive sight as he stood 6'5" and, though he was starting to turn flabby, his build gave the impression of immense strength. Judah stood in the doorway for a moment, letting his appearance intimidate his young captives then he moved steadily forward.

Krista shivered: Judah reminded her of a predator stalking its prey. Both Paul and Krista were seized by a chilling fear that engulfed them totally.

Judah smiled grimly to himself. The stark fear on both teens' faces was just what he wanted. Standing close to Krista, he reached down and, grabbing a handful of hair, he savagely yanked her head back.

"Miss Andrews. So nice to see you." Judah's teeth bared in a gruesome semblance of a smile, "You have two choices: You can either do this my way and give me the information I need or... "

Here Judah paused and pulled harder on Krista's hair. "You can make this difficult on yourself and your friend by not telling me what I want to know." He waited to see if his words had the desired effect and saw by the raw terror in Krista's eyes that they had.

"Good! I see that you have got my meaning. Now, my first question is: where does LUPO hold its meetings and when?" Krista's mind went blank

"LUPO?" She asked hesitantly.

Judah's eyes narrowed.

"The Let Us Play Organization of which your father is a founding member." Judah spoke as if talking to a dim witted child. "Once again, where and when do they meet?"

"I don't know." Krista's answer was simple and truthful. "I have never heard of LUPO." Judah's free hand came down in a blur to deliver a hard slap across Krista's face that sent her head spinning.

"Quit lying to me! " Judah growled menacingly. "I will not stand for it. Now you either tell me what I want to know or I am going to turn you over to those men who brought you here and believe me, they won't be as patient."

Krista's eyes filled with tears. Up until this moment she had never heard of LUPO so she couldn't tell him anything.

When Krista didn't say anything, Judah muttered something then, letting go of Krista's hair, went to the door. The three men who had brought her and Paul there were motioned inside. They looked inquiringly at Judah, Judah turned to leer evilly at Krista and Paul

"Do with them what you want then return them to where you got them. Just make sure they are alive. I want them to be able to talk of the experiences they had. " With that Judah closed the door and walked away to the sounds of Krista's terrorized screams.

Kaya walked into the apartment to see her mother gazing at pictures of Kansall. With a flash of intuition, Kaya knew that the school had called.

"Mom?" She asked hesitantly. " Are you angry with me?"

Wind tore her gaze from the mementos of her dead husband with tears in her eyes.

"Of course not, baby. I have always taught you to stand up for what you believe is right." Wind chuckled. "And when you decided to make a stand, you made sure that everyone was aware that you were doing so! Your father would have been so proud of you." Wind patted the sofa beside her to indicate that Kaya should sit beside her. Once Kaya was seated, Wind opened one of the photo albums that were placed beside her.

"I think it is time for me to tell you a story." Wind opened the album to reveal pictures of a very young Kansall and herself. For a moment, Wind recollected past events before beginning her tale.

"When I met your father, I was sixteen years old and he was eighteen. We were both attending one of the meetings put on by PARR. Now they only hold their meetings a few times a year but back then, they were held weekly. Anyway, your father was sitting on the grass just away from the crowd. He was wearing a cap that didn't hide the fact that his hair was longer than what was socially acceptable. I think that was when I started to fall in love with him. He was a rebel and did things his own way.

"When the leader of PARR started to speak, I noticed that Kansall seemed to signal to someone. To the casual observer, he seemed to be lost in his own thoughts but since I was watching him so intently, Kansall looked as if he was on edge.

"Suddenly, all hell broke loose. The guy that Kansall had signalled to had climbed up a tree and was yelling through a bullhorn that PARR was wrong and that they had no right to censor the music. When the officers went to go to this guy, they had to walk by Kansall. Well, he came alive. As quick as a flash of lightning, his leg shot out and tripped the guy then Kansall was running. He positioned himself under the tree where his friend was." Wind's eyes were glazed and unseeing as she looked back into the past.

"Kansall looked like a warrior from long ago as he stood there with his legs spread wide, hands on hips and his silver hair blowing in the wind. Defiance was clearly stated in the manner that he stood. I think that, at that moment, I knew I would follow Kansall to the ends of the earth."

Kaya was engrossed in her mother's story. In her mind's eye, Kaya could see the scene as her mother was. She was about to encourage Wind to continue when the phone rang. Kaya raced to answer it, talked for a moment, then came back to her mother.

"I'm afraid your story is going to have to wait, Mom. That was Gleven and Krista is in hospital. He asked if we could come immediately. "

Shocked, Wind turned to face her daughter.

"What happened? Is it serious?"

Kaya's eyes filled with tears.

"Someone kidnapped her and Paul. Gleven says that she has been raped and beaten and that he thinks the same thing has happened to Paul.

Paul won't say anything and Krista just keeps crying." Here Kaya broke down and sobbed. "I saw it Mom! Today at lunch. So I asked Paul to walk her home. I should never have asked him!"

Wind put her arms around her daughter.

"It's not your fault. There was nothing you could do to stop it. But right now, Krista and Paul need you to be strong. You are not going to do any good if you walk in there with your eyes all red. So why not go wash your face then we'll go."

Seeing the wisdom of her mother's words, Kaya nodded and went to do as she had suggested, her heart still breaking as she blamed herself.

At the hospital Kaya was trying to talk with Krista. She still had not been able to find out who had done this to Krista since the other girl still refused to say anything. And Kaya wasn't pushing it. Just knowing that Krista wasn't seriously hurt physically and, with a little time, should come out of this, made her feel a bit better.

"Krista?" Kaya's voice was soft as she noticed that the tranquilizer that the nurse had given her friend was beginning to take effect.

"They wanted to know when and where LUPO meets." Krista said softly, almost asleep. "But I don't even know what LUPO is, do you?"

Kaya's mind flashed back to that day that her father had been killed. Someone, she recalled, had said something about LUPO but she couldn't remember exactly what. Answering Krista wasn't necessary however, since the girl was already asleep. Kaya looked at her friend for a moment then went into the hall. The first person she saw was Gleven.

"How's Paul?" She asked.

Gleven looked concerned.

"He still hasn't said anything. I think he has gone to sleep. How is Krista?"

"Asleep. May I talk to you Gleven?"

Gleven looked startled at the tone of Kaya's voice. She was determined, her tone not leaving room for any opposition or argument. For a moment it was as if Kansall had been reincarnated.

"Of course. Why don't we go into the lounge where we can have a bit of privacy?"

Kaya nodded and they both went, in silence, into the lounge.

"OK, what's up?" Gleven asked.

"Who or what is LUPO?" Kaya didn't waste any time with preliminaries. She got right to the point

Gleven was taken aback for a moment. He was at a loss for words.

"Why do you want to know and what makes you think that I know?" Gleven hedged for time.

"Krista told me just before she went to sleep that the men that had kidnapped her asked her about it. I remember someone saying something about it the night my father was killed. So come on Gleven! I know that you know."

Gleven's face was white.

"They asked about LUPO? My God! I never thought they would stoop so low as to rape my daughter."

Kaya was getting impatient "So? Are you going to tell me or not? I think that I do have a right to know. My father was killed for whatever this is and now my best friend has been terrorized! I deserve to know." Gleven knew that there would be no more hedging. Wind had told him what had happened with Kaya at school today so he knew Kaya's feelings on censorship. Taking a deep breath, he started to explain.

"LUPO stands for the Let Us Play Organization. It is an organization founded by your father, Brent Mitchell and myself. Brent is now in California running that end of it and I am running this end. It is an organization to bring back rock and roll music.

"Who were those people that kidnapped Krista and Paul?"

"I think that that would be PARR but I can't be certain. PARR, as you know, is a government agency that was set up solely for the purpose of making sure that people don't listen to rock and roll music. Though we have no proof, we think that they are also the ones responsible for Kansall's death."

Wind came into the lounge just then, extremely distraught.

"You two have to come quickly. Paul just hung himself." Wind ran out of the room but as Gleven went to follow her, Kaya stopped him.

"I want to destroy PARR for all the evil they've done. How can I join LUPO?"

CHAPTER Five

The late afternoon sun was slowly sinking behind the ocean, setting the water aflame and illuminating the surfers coming towards the shore with fiery halos. With waves breaking around his ankles, Brent Mitchell watched his eighteen-year-old son, Boyce, handle his surfboard with the grace and ease of someone that had been doing it for years. The blond hair billowed behind him as Boyce rapidly approached solid ground.

After Kansall had been so tragically murdered, Brent, his wife Sheila, and ten year old Boyce had left New York for California. For four years, Brent and his family had enjoyed life and the challenges of starting the Western chapter of LUPO.

Then, when Boyce had been fourteen years old, Sheila had passed away suddenly. The exact cause of death had never been found though all assumed it was from natural causes. Although neither Brent nor Boyce were overly concerned anymore about how or why she had died, the pain of losing her still resided in their hearts.

Without his mate, Brent had focused all his energies on LUPO and Boyce, making sure that neither of the two was ever in want of anything. Though this should of caused Boyce to be extremely self centered and spoiled for some reason he wasn't. However, Brent occasionally found Boyce's casual approach to life and its hardships somewhat disturbing.

For Boyce, life had always been easy. Schoolwork had never required that much extra application and neither had sports for this natural athlete. Friends, both male and female, gravitated to Boyce and his carefree nature so that Boyce was never without people around. He was not consciously aware of having to struggle for anything and he had never, in his entire life, felt lonely or without friends. Having never actually been in love, Boyce didn't comprehend the doubts, uncertainties and hard work that are generated by that overwhelming feeling. All these factors had developed Boyce into a carefree, likable young man who got along with everyone. Especially his father.

"Hi Dad!" Boyce hollered as he came loping across the sand. "What's up?"

Brent smiled fondly at his only child, vainly trying to recall how he had been himself at that age.

"I want to talk with you and I knew that this is where you would be." Brent answered. 'Do you mind if I steal you away from your friends?"

"No problem!" was Boyce's cheerful reply. "I'll just say goodbye and get Chuck to take care of my board." Boyce sped away, talked to his friends for a moment then returned.

"So where to?"

"Why don't we just walk for a little while? Then I can be sure of complete privacy."

Boyce shrugged his agreement as he struggled into a sweatshirt then adjusted the sweat pants he had put on earlier.

"Sounds serious. Have I done something wrong that I don't remember?"

Brent smiled slightly.

"No. What I have to talk to you about is something that could affect you indirectly." Brent paused, concern for the possible events of the future showing clearly on his face. "Or perhaps directly."

Boyce was going to retort with a joking remark but, when he saw the seriousness of his father's expression, quickly changed his mind. Whatever was on his father's mind was of a very important nature and this did not seem like the time to make jokes. Together, the two men walked silently along the cooling sand.

“I’m trying to think of a way that I can tell you this but I'm having difficulty finding out where to begin."

"Try the beginning. That is usually the best place to start."

"Right you are. OK, have you heard of a government agency called PARR?"

"The People Against Rock and Roll? Yeah, a guy from there came down to the beach one day."

"What did you think of their ideas?"

Here Boyce exploded. "We would have run him off the beach but he had a couple of guys with guns standing there so I didn't want to try anything."

"Good thing you didn't." Brent remarked dryly. "Those guys are trained to shoot first and ask questions later."

"What he was saying really made me angry. I have never, in my life, had the opportunity to listen to the music he was talking about so his threats were absolutely ridiculous. It's funny though, ever since I heard that guy, I have been thinking more and more about what he was saying. What right did they have to ban the music? The government shouldn't have the right to tell me what I can listen to! Now I really want to hear what that music, rock and roll, sounds like."

Brent was silent for a moment, contemplating his next words.

"Perhaps that can be arranged. But I'm getting ahead of myself." Brent sat on a large piece of driftwood and motioned for Boyce to join him.

"We aren't really sure when it all started. Through the use of murder, destroying almost all the evidence that ever existed and maintaining a policy of silence on the subject, PARR has managed to keep the existence of rock and roll music a mystery to most people. As well, they have managed to convince almost everyone that the music is a bad thing so they should stay away from it and keep their kids away.

"But they haven't managed to convince everyone and through finding articles that PARR missed and talking with a few people, we do know that rock and roll was making quite a stir in the world. Ever since its beginnings, many had criticized rock and roll. It had always been a sign of rebellion that I think managed to sometimes frighten some of the older generation. The musicians got weirder each year, the music got louder and it was something that was totally alien to some people's way of thinking.

"So this group of people got together and started passing laws to stop the sale of the music. At first, no one paid any attention to them because, as I said before, the music had always had its critics. But when the fans found they couldn't buy their favourite CDs any longer since they weren't allowed to be sold, the uproar began. That is when PARR started erasing people's memories, controlling their lives and murdering others.

"The organization that opposes PARR is the Let Us Play Organization, LUPO. A man named Kansall More founded it in New York City about twenty years ago. At least it was his idea to begin with. You see, Kansall More and I had family members that were involved with a legendary rock and roll band that was in existence around the time of the formation of PARR. As are you. Kansall and I were in college together and one day, we were sitting around our room complaining about the injustice of it all when Kansall said that we should do something about it. So, we got together with another guy we knew felt the same way, Gleven Andrews, and started LUPO.

"The first couple of years were rough, especially when you were born. Suddenly, I had a family to take care of and a cause to fight for."

"Is Kansall More still running LUPO from New York?"

"No." Brent shook his head sadly. "He was shot about eight years ago." Brent was silent for a moment, remembering Kansall, before he continued.

"So after Kansall was killed, we had to have a quick regrouping. Remember that LUPO was ten years old by that time and – in a way - we were still fairly new. We could not openly oppose PARR since that would mean instant death for all of us so we had to do everything secretly. Also we had to be careful whom we told so our membership was limited."

"It's still that way though, isn't it? I mean, no one I know has ever heard of LUPO."

"Yes it is. And I have to ask you not to say anything to anyone about me being involved with it. "

"I won't Dad." Boyce vowed. "Now tell me more about our relatives and about this LUPO. Imagine my father being a rebel and me not even knowing it!"

Brent laughed.

"Sure. But why don't we go and get something to eat? I'm starved and I know this little restaurant near here that is owned by a supporter of LUPO."

Boyce quickly agreed.

"That was good." Boyce said as he finished his meal.

Brent agreed with him then motioned the owner of the restaurant to come and sit in.

Steven Went, the owner of the restaurant had been with the Western Chapter since its formation in this area. In fact, he had been the first person to join forces with Brent Mitchell.

In another era it was quite likely that Steven Went would have been considered an aging hippie. His greying dirt brown hair was long and straggly, tied back from his face with a simple elastic band. His thick beard and moustache also touched with grey, framed a set of sensual lips. Small, circular glasses encased intelligent brown eyes and Steven was a man who loved other people but, more importantly, firmly believed in freedom for all. Now he looked with interest at Brent's son whom he had seen around the restaurant and on the beach but had never actually met.

"Boyce I don't think that I have ever introduced you to Steven Went. Steven, this is my son Boyce."

The two men shook hands as Brent glanced around the restaurant.

"I think I will lock up now." Steven commented when he saw Brent's face. "It's not that busy at the moment and I'll send the staff home."

Brent and Boyce sipped their coffee while they waited for Steven to return. Once he returned to their table, Brent began immediately. "I have told Boyce a little about LUPO, mainly since I wanted to warn him because of what happened to Gleven's daughter and now he wants to know more."

"Are you interested in stopping the censorship of music?" Steven asked Boyce.

Boyce thought a moment.

"I don't agree with it if that is what you are asking. I do not know enough about LUPO to say at this time that I want to join but I guess that is why I am here."

Brent smiled approvingly.

"Then first Boyce, I suppose you should hear what we are fighting for," Steven said. Steven then led the way down a flight of stairs to a soundproof room. Shutting the door, he went over to a CD player and turned the power on. He went over to a hidden safe and, after unlocking it, withdrew a very old looking CD. Smiling at Boyce and Brent, he put it on and turned up the volume.

Within moments, Boyce heard the music start and experienced the thrill of his lifetime. The music unlocked feelings within him that he had never before felt. It was if he could do anything he wanted to.

"This is great." He yelled at his father. "Who is it?"

Brent motioned for Steven to turn down the volume and hand him the cover of the CD. Boyce was astonished to see that one of the musicians looked exactly like him. In wonder, he turned to his father. "Yes Boyce. He is one of your relatives. His name was Bradley Mitchell and he played lead guitar for the band Mystique."

Boyce looked puzzled.

"How is he related?"

"We really don't know." Brent sighed. "All family records had to be destroyed and all I know is that he did once exist and that he is related. For all I know he could be a cousin, a brother or a grandfather. We just aren't able to discover that information at this time."

Boyce grinned.

"I think I would like to join LUPO and fight PARR."

Brent and Steven smiled across Boyce's bent head at one another. Somehow they had always felt that Boyce would be interested. LUPO was taking on its next generation of rebels.

PART TWO

THE REVOLUTION

CHAPTER Six

Two years later
New York City

The night air was dense - the pollution eating away at a person's very life breath. Across the street from a luxury apartment building, a lone figure stood and carefully watched. Clothed in an evening dress covered by a dark cloak, the female figure watched intently until the person of her attentions left the building.

Crossing the street, the female figure walked seductively up to the security desk where a young guard sat. Flicking her platinum blond hair over her shoulder and letting the low cut silver lame gown gape open slightly, she leaned over the desktop to bat her grey eyes at the astonished young man.

"Excuse me," she breathed, "I was wondering if you could help me."

The young guard blushed under her intense gaze and stammered a reply.

"I, I hope so." He prayed with all his might that he could. "What is your problem?"

The woman lowered her eyelashes demurely, as if ashamed that she had to ask for assistance.

"I have made a terrible mistake." Her eyes opened wide and the guard saw embarrassment and a little fear hidden within their depths. "I was supposed to meet Mr. Arnold here and I totally forgot."

"Well, he just left the building."

The woman let tears fill her eyes.

"Oh dear! " Her voice cracked with terror on those two words. "He probably went out to find me. What am I going to do now?"

The panic in her voice touched the guard and he offered a solution to her problem.

"You could wait here." He began then saw the disappointed expression in this young woman's beautiful face. "Or I could let you in his apartment and you could wait there."

She immediately brightened.

"Could you? I would so like to surprise him!"

The guard's heart warmed at the expression of joy that illuminated the woman's face. At this moment, he would do anything for her.

"Of course. I have a master key and I will just take you up there." The guard smiled brightly at her, which she returned with a warmness that aroused the guard. Taking a key from a line of several, he led the young woman to the elevators.

"Here you go." The guard stated as he unlocked the door and it easily swung open. "If you need anything else, my name is Jerry and I will be on the front desk until midnight"

The woman stepped into the apartment then smiled sensuously.

"Thank you Jerry, you have been extremely helpful. Just don't tell Mr. Arnold that I am here, I would like to surprise him."

"I won't." Jerry promised. "And, if I may say so, he should be pleasantly surprised."

The woman smiled and closed the door. As she leaned against the wooden barrier, she allowed herself a self-satisfied smirk.

"I should say that Mr. Arnold will be surprised." Kaya chuckled. "Though I wouldn't make any guarantees about the pleasantly part."

An hour later, at approximately eleven PM, Kaya heard the sound of heavy footsteps approaching the apartment. Kaya hid behind the door and poured ether on a rag. Holding her breath, she listened to the key turning in the lock. Judah Arnold walked in, closed the door but before he could turn on the light, a rag was pushed over his mouth and nose. After a few minutes of useless struggling, Judah sank to the floor.

Kaya dragged the heavy figure over to a waiting chair. Struggling she pulled him into a sitting position then fastened the handcuffs on each wrist connecting the other end to the chair arm. Taking his ankles and placing them against the chair legs, Kaya hooked the unconscious man to the chair. The chair had already been securely tied, the ropes running tightly through the shelves of a heavy bookshelf that was fastened to the wall. The chair was incapable of moving, as was the occupant of it. In the world, there would be very few men strong enough to break the bonds that held Judah captive.

Kaya sat on a sofa a few feet away from the sleeping Judah. Alert, adrenaline flowing from nervous anticipation, the real possibility of personal danger and the general thrill of her actions, Kaya waited for her enemy to wake up.

Groaning, Judah's eyes opened slowly. He groggily went to move before realizing that he was trapped. Suddenly fully alert, Judah looked down in horror at the contraception before tentatively pulling on his arms and legs to break free.

"I wouldn't waste your energy Mr. Arnold." Judah's eyes focused on the woman sitting on his couch that he had just become aware of. Something about her looked familiar but he would be damned if he could remember what it was. Gazing lustfully at her slender form he allowed his eyes to wander over the well shaped long legs that peered out from the slits in the form fitting skirt; his lecherous eyes strayed to the flat stomach and tiny waist which the tight bodice showed to their best advantage; he gasped at the perfectly formed, not too large, breasts that were barely covered by the strapless gown. The long silver hair flowed seductively around her shoulders, bangs framing the extraordinary eyes. His passion filled eyes met her hate filled ones and he felt the erection that had sprung up, wilt immediately. Whoever this woman was she wasn't here for sexual games. The gun she held pointed at him told him that even if her eyes hadn't.

"Who are you?" He croaked. "What do you want?"

Kaya rose gracefully from the sofa, her two-inch heels extending her height to just less than six feet.

"To talk. That's all want, I have no desire to harm you in any way."

"Then why don't you release me? It is very uncomfortable for me sitting here like this."

Kaya gave a sarcastic laugh.

"Oh no, Mr. Arnold. That would be very foolish of me don't you agree?" Without waiting for an answer Kaya continued, "We are going to have a discussion then I am going to leave. In the morning, an anonymous telephone call will be made to the PARR headquarters and they will come and release you."

Judah vainly struggled against his bonds.

"I don't know who you are Miss but you are going to pay for this. No one treats me like this!"

"I think I had better introduce myself." Kaya ignored the threat; she knew the dangers of this escapade before she had even started it. This is why she had not told Gleven or anyone else what her plans were.

"My name is Kaya More and I am here to tell you that PARR might as well give up now. There is no way you are going to stop us." Judah's eyes widened at the mention of her name. He had heard rumors that Kansall More's daughter was now involved with LUPO and was responsible for many of the disastrous PARR activities during the last two years, but he hadn't paid much attention to the stories of others. Now he believed.

"Well, Miss More." Judah said. "I certainly never expected anyone so beautiful to be involved with such a degenerate movement as LUPO."

"If I were in your position," Kaya said, her voice smooth and deadly. "I would be careful of the insults I threw around. You really are not in a position of power right now."

Judah's mouth gaped at the implied threat behind the softly spoken words. Not in years had anyone dared to even consider threatening him. It was at this point that Judah realized just how formidable an opponent Kaya was going to be.

"Ten years ago," Kaya began, her voice turning soft and melodic "you shot a man who was organizing those who disagreed with you. Like the coward you are, you shot the man in the back when he was unarmed and unaware. I was there that night, I saw you so don't try to deny it."

"Why would I deny shooting a criminal?" Judah's arrogance returned. "I was just doing my job."

Kaya raised her eyebrows.

"So your job is, or at least was then, to murder innocent citizens who have the courage to speak their minds? Hmm." Kaya smiled grimly, sending a chill through Judah. "Remember that one day, and you won't know when, I am going to help destroy you and everything you stand for. I may not be able to punish you using the legal system but I will punish you. From this day on, I will make your life a living hell. You will never know what I am going to do, when I am going to do it or how I am going to destroy the policies that PARR stands for." Kaya, tired of this interrogation turned to leave but Judah stopped her.

"The people don't want to have the responsibility of making their own decisions!" He protested. "They like having us do it for them."

Kaya paused at the door and turned to face Judah will a self-satisfied expression on her face.

"We will see who is right about this, Mr. Arnold." She calmly responded. "And I would be willing to bet anything that it will be LUPO and I who are victorious in the end."

"Over my dead body!" Judah yelled, totally enraged as the door was closing behind Kaya. Kaya, who had heard his words before the sound proofed door clicked shut, smiled.

"Just remember you said that, Mr. Arnold."

At a girl's only boarding school on the outskirts of Boston, eighteen-year-old Krista Andrews closed her suitcase. Since the horrifying ordeal two years ago she had been here. Away from LUPO, PARR and New York, her body had healed from the atrocities she had suffered. Unfortunately her mind hadn't.

A deep anger constantly burned within her. She felt her life had been ruined. All because of her father's illegal activities. Illogically Krista refused to place the blame of her ordeal on PARR. Rather, she focused her anger and hatred on LUPO. If her father had never been involved then she would never have gone through what she did.

As she made ready to return to New York, Krista vowed silently to herself that someday, somehow she was going to destroy LUPO and everyone involved with it.

CHAPTER Seven

Three Years Later
New York City

Kaya and Gleven walked along the street in silence. In the five years since Krista's rape and Paul's suicide, Kaya had thrown her heart and soul into LUPO and was now one of the leaders. She had never gone back to school since her argument with the band teacher so she had been able to devote most of her time to LUPO. With her determination to repay PARR for what they had done to Krista, Paul and her father, her efforts with LUPO earned her the reputation of being daring. Some of her exploits were legendary among the members of both LUPO and PARR. In former years LUPO had remained in the shadows, unknown to the majority of the public.

However Kaya's exploits had a flair for the dramatic and LUPO was now becoming known to many. Right now though her thoughts were far away from her earlier achievements. Now they were on the fact that a PARR informer was either within LUPO or was getting information somehow.

"I don't know what to do, Gleven. We haven't had any new members lately and I hate to suspect any of the ones we have of turning on us."

Gleven looked grim. He too hated the thought of having to put suspicion on any of what he considered to be his family. But he knew that it would have to be done in order to save the organization. And perhaps all their lives.

"Maybe we should just sleep on it for tonight. Something may come to us and perhaps PARR is just lucky."

"You know as well as I do that PARR can't be that lucky! I mean, they have found out about every, or almost every, meeting place we have had in the last three months. How have they known when their lectures were going to be sabotaged? Come on! You can't be that naive!"

"No, I'm not. I guess I was just hoping. After all, no one likes to suspect their friends of doing something as rotten as informing on people when it could mean their lives."

"I agree with you but we have to face facts and if we don't, someone could get hurt."

"Let's change the subject. We are just going in circles. I think that you should go visit Krista soon. She has been asking if you are upset with her for any reason and I have just tried to tell her that you have been very busy."

"I have been." Kaya tried to defend herself and ease her guilty conscience. It was true that she hadn't been visiting Krista often but she found that trying to deal with Krista's problems and her own were just getting to be too much. Krista had never been the same since she was raped. Whenever Kaya went over there, Krista was lecturing her on the way Kaya ran her life. Telling her that she shouldn't get close to any men and, worst of all, insinuating that Kaya was partly to blame for what had happened to her. Kaya had never told Gleven this because she still felt guilty about the incident. Her logical mind knew that she was in no way responsible but her emotions kept telling her that she should have found some way to prevent Krista from walking home that day.

"Kaya? Are you all right?" Gleven was concerned about the look of guilt on Kaya's face. "I know that you have been busy and I also know that Krista can be difficult to deal with. Maybe that is why I was sort of relieved when she moved out on her own. Don't get me wrong. I love Krista dearly and I wish that there were something I could have done to prevent her rape but there isn't." He was silent a moment before continuing. "Did you know that she has acquired a new interest in LUPO? She asks me constantly about the history of the organization, the exploits carried out by different members and even when and where we meet! She says that she wants to come to a meeting someday." Gleven laughed ruefully. "But then again, she also tells me that I should quit before something happens. Of course, the thought has crossed my mind a few times but I could never do that. I would rather die than leave LUPO."

Kaya put her arm affectionately around the man that she considered to be her surrogate father.

"Let's hope that you don't leave LUPO that way!" Kaya sighed. "And I promise that I will go visit Krista tonight. After all she is my oldest friend and, problems or not, she still means a lot to me."

"Thanks Kaya. I knew that you were just busy. By the way, she has something extraordinary to tell you."

"Oh really? What would that be?"

“I promised not to tell you but I am sure that you will find it very exciting." At this point they were near Krista's apartment building so Kaya bid farewell to Gleven and they parted ways.

As Gleven walked along he was lost in thought. His mind was in turmoil and, as usually occurred when he needed guidance, his thoughts turned to Kansall More.

"What would you do? Kansall, I need your help this time. I’m worried about Kaya and the future of LUPO. But I just don't know how to find the person who is informing to PARR." Gleven paused, as if expecting an answer from his deceased friend. But none came and Gleven pondered his situation a little more.

“Judah really wants to get Kaya, she has messed him up too much. I promised you Kansall that I would take care of her for you and I’m afraid that I won't be able to fulfill that promise." Gleven was silent, knowing that there was no simple answer to his problem. Feet dragging, he proceeded home to where, hopefully, his wife would be able to help him.

Krista was indeed happy to see Kaya. Kaya was surprised that Krista didn't complain once throughout the whole hour she was first there, though she kept glancing at the clock.

"What is going Krista? You keep looking at the clock every five minutes. Are you trying to get rid of me?"

Krista looked shocked.

"No! I really want you to stay because I have a surprise for you in about an hour. Please say you'll stay! "

Kaya shrugged. She had nothing better to do that evening except go back to her lonely one room apartment so she was happy to stay.

"Only if I can have another glass of that wine. This is really good." Krista hurried to go get it for her and also to bring out some snacks to eat. Once she was back, Krista looked Kaya over closely.

"You are looking tired. Maybe you should get some more rest."

Kaya laughed. Krista didn't know that Kaya was involved with LUPO and, quite frankly, Kaya didn't want her to know just yet. Kaya didn't tell Krista why she was tired; she just said that she had been busy lately.

"Doing what? You are never home when I call and I know that you are off work at four, is it a man? Though you don't look as if romance is what has you so tired. If you were in love, you would positively glow."

Kaya took a closer look at Krista. She seemed to be extremely happy, happier than Kaya had seen her in years. Gone was that haunted look that had worried Kaya so much, gone was the nervous habit of always twisting her hands together. In fact, she was glowing.

"Why Krista Andrews! I do believe that you are in love."

Krista blushed a deep red.

"I have been trying not to tell you because I wanted to surprise you but since you guessed, I am going to tell you everything about him."

Kaya smiled and sat down to listen to what seemed to be the old Krista.

"His name is Gary and he is tall with short red hair. He works in a little government agency as a clerk so he isn't rich or anything like that. I met him at a grocery store. Can you believe that? It sounds like it's out of a romance novel! Anyway, he was looking for a special brand of cleaning fluid for his floor and since I was the only person near him, he asked me. I helped him find it then he asked me out to dinner. He is really kind and caring. He is good looking, sensitive and he has a great sense of humour."

"Sounds perfect."

"Yes. And Kaya, he is even concerned about you!"

Kaya had been leaning back, relaxing, but at these words she tensed.

"Krista, I really wish you wouldn't talk about me with other people. Especially strangers. You know how I value my privacy. "

"I just told him how busy you are and how you never seem to have a real life. Nothing exciting ever seems to happen in your life." The buzzer interrupted Krista's words, announcing a visitor. "Oh! That must be Gary now."

The man who entered the apartment was indeed very good looking. His hair was more auburn than a red and his grey eyes shined with intelligence. Yet Kaya still didn't feel comfortable with him. Perhaps it was because she knew that he had asked many questions about her, which always made her nervous, or perhaps it was she sensed insincerity in his manner. The way he seemed to be so loving towards Krista didn't seem real, almost as if he was acting a part. Whatever it was, she didn't trust him.

"Kaya, I would like to you to meet Gary Shane. Gary, this is my best friend, Kaya More." Kaya stood to shake Gary's hand and, when she did, she felt a chill of apprehension course through her. The man's eyes were cold and calculating.

"How can this man love anyone?" Kaya mused to herself. "Something is not right here."

"So this is the elusive Miss Kaya More." Gary's rich baritone echoed through the silent apartment. "I have been waiting to meet you."

Kaya smiled weakly, her thoughts in turmoil. Premonitions of danger threatened to overwhelm her, she felt as if her security and secrets were at risk around this man. However, Kaya also felt that she must maintain a mask of friendliness towards this stranger or all could be doomed.

"How about another glass of wine, Krista? I haven't got long and I should leave you two alone." Kaya winked at Gary. "After all, three is a crowd."

"Never with Krista's best friend! " Gary replied gallantly." And besides I love being with two beautiful women. I shall be the envy of all the guys at work tomorrow when I tell them."

This was the opening that Kaya had hoped for.

"What kind of work do you do? Any danger involved?" Once more, Gary laughed.

"Not unless you count paper cuts. I am just a paper shuffler, nothing dramatic at all."

"Oh. And where do you work?" Krista was returning from the kitchen with the bottle of wine and overheard Kaya's last question.

"Kaya! I told you that Gary works in a small government office. Don't you remember?"

Kaya smiled at her friend, hiding the fact that she was gritting her teeth in annoyance at the intrusion.

"Yes, I remember. But do you realize how many government offices there are? I'm curious to know exactly which one." Gary looked a little uneasy but he quickly smiled.

"A very thorough person, I see." He said as he put his arm around Krista who had come to sit beside him. "I work for a division that has nothing to do but decide whether or not people are going to get money from the government. I don't even have the power to decide. All I do is mark on the forms whether someone has decided yes or no. Boring, don't you think?"

Kaya shrugged.

"It could be worse. I waitress at a daytime restaurant. Now I feel that is really boring most of the time."

"What do you do at nights? Krista says you are never home so you must do something."

Kaya again felt the warning signals of impending danger so she answered very carefully.

"I do this and that. Sometimes I volunteer my help to different charities or else I take night courses."

"Kaya! I never knew that you were going to school at night! Why didn't you tell me?" Krista was ecstatic to find out this new information about her friend.

Kaya silently cursed her friend for making this even more difficult than it already was. The biggest problem Kaya found with being involved with LUPO was the necessary lying. She had never felt that she was any good at it.

"I just started and I didn't want you to know until I had gotten my diploma. I wanted to surprise you."

Krista turned to Gary to explain to him that Kaya had never finished school and, even though she herself had told Kaya that she should, Kaya had never done anything about it.

"You quit just after Krista's rape, didn't you?" Gary commented casually.

Kaya's eyes imperceptibly narrowed. This man knew more than he should.

"Yes I did. But that wasn't the reason. I found that I wasn't learning anything I thought I needed so I left."

"Krista also told me about your argument that you had with your music teacher. Did that have anything to do with it?"

Kaya was now certain that Gary wasn't who he said he was. Krista had never been told about that argument and the only way Gary could know about it was if he was in a high position in the government. Like a PARR agent.

"No. In fact, I don't even remember that disagreement. But you have to remember that that was five years ago and, when we're teens, we are always disagreeing with someone in authority." Kaya paused to finish her glass of wine. "I hate to do this to you, but I'm going to have to go now."

"So soon?" Krista was disappointed. "Can't you stay a little longer?"

Kaya shook her head.

"Sorry Krista but I have some things I have to do. Gary, it was really nice meeting you and I hope I see you again." The last words felt as if they were being forced out of Kaya's mouth but they sounded sincere.

Krista walked Kaya to the door and showed her out. Once out of the building, Kaya immediately turned in the direction of Gleven's house.

Far below the city, Wind awoke from a deep sleep with a start. Something was going wrong. She sensed that Kaya was in danger but she didn't know how. Rising from her warm bed, she threw on a robe and began to pace in the small enclosure. There had to be something she could do.

Having made sure that she wasn't followed, Kaya arrived at Gleven's in about an hour. Although she knew that it was a bit late to be calling on Gleven and Margaret, Kaya felt that she had to let him know about this evening's events. Ringing the doorbell, she waited impatiently for someone to answer.

After what seemed to be hours but in reality were only a few minutes, Gleven came to the door.

"Kaya! What is the matter? Why are you here so late? Come in, come in."

Kaya thankfully entered the warm, inviting atmosphere of the small house.

"Gleven, I don't want to worry you but we may have problems. Have you ever told Krista about the argument I had with my music teacher in school? The one where I told him that the censoring of music was wrong."

"No, of course not. I felt that that was something that shouldn't be passed on. Why?" Kaya took a deep breath.

"Because, when I was over at her apartment tonight, her new boyfriend mentioned it. He said that Krista was the one who had told him."

"Krista couldn't have. Unless she found out about it from someone else that was in your class at the time."

"It's possible but not very likely. She went out of state to school as soon as she was released from hospital and she doesn't associate with anyone we went to school with. Even if she happened to meet up with someone we knew since she has been back, why would they mention it? More exciting things have happened since then."

"It is possible though. What do you want me to do?"

Kaya thought for a moment.

"I'm sorry Gleven. I hate to be suspicious especially when Krista seems to be so happy. But something about Gary Shane just doesn't feel right He asked a lot of questions about my activities and about me and he knew too much. I'm afraid that he may be a PARR agent. Could you check him out?"

"You might be being a little overly suspicious but that doesn't hurt. Come to think of it, with all the questions that Krista has been asking lately, she has known about the majority of LUPO's activities."

Kaya paled.

"Does she know about all our activities?"

Gleven cursed.

"Not directly. But I have mentioned a few things that may have given her more information than I meant to. Sorry Kaya. It's just that I was actually thinking that Krista might have been interested in joining LUPO. It's hard to suspect your own daughter of being a traitor." Gleven paused. "I will definitely check this guy out. Just give me whatever information you have."

Kaya agreed and told Gleven what she knew then left.

CHAPTER Eight

The next day

California

Boyce stood in the secret meeting place of the Western Chapter of LUPO watching the people make signs for an upcoming rally. His mischievous blue eyes watched everyone, especially the women, intently.

"Hey Boyce! Why aren't you over here helping?" Sara, a petite blond woman, called.

Boyce flashed a charming grin. "I'm supervising."

"Yeah right. We really need a supervisor for this job." Lisa, another young woman, involved with LUPO, commented sarcastically.

"Grab a paint brush and help." Becky growled. The majority of the women in LUPO were young and pretty, a large number here for the purpose of being near Boyce. Not that they weren't committed to the cause because they were. Being near the tall, blond, good-looking Boyce Mitchell was just an added bonus. And Boyce tended to subconsciously take advantage of this.

"OK, OK." He grumbled good-naturedly. "I guess that I can endanger my artistic hands by helping to do a manual job. Picking up a spare brush that happened to be nearby, he proceeded to help the women.

"So what are you doing after the rally?" Sara asked. Sara was particularly interested in Boyce and would do anything for him. Sometimes she felt as if she would even die for him if that were necessary.

"I don't know." Boyce shrugged. "I think, if the rally is successful, I might go dancing. Would you like to go with me?"

Sara's heart fluttered. This was the moment that she had been waiting for.

“Sure. I’d love to." She was so nervous. The other two women working on the sign flashed her looks of envy.

Boyce, however, didn't notice but his father, who had just come into the room, did.

"Boyce. Can I talk with you a moment?" Brent called.

Boyce grinned at the three women.

"I suppose he knows how valuable my artistic hands are." Flicking a spot of paint onto Sara's nose, he went over to see his father.

"Yes Dad?"

Brent motioned him outside.

"Boyce, I have told you this before but I think I am going to have to tell you again. You are going to have problems with those ladies."

"Why?"

"There is so much jealousy and competition among them to get you interested in them that I’m afraid that there is going to be trouble. If one of them gets too vindictive, someone could get hurt."

"Oh Dad. They are more mature than that! They wouldn't let a simple thing like me asking one of them out get the best of them. "

"Boyce, I have already seen it happen. Now I know that all women are not like that but I just have a funny feeling about this and I wish you would be more careful."

"Why don't I invite all of them to go dancing with me? Would that make things better?" Brent thought a moment.

"It might. It is worth a try."

Boyce sighed. "This is getting to be a hassle. I never asked them all to be interested in me. The only one that have ever really been interested in is Sara."

Brent chuckled.

"That is the way it goes. It might have been worse though."

"How?"

"Sara might not have been interested in you at all."

Boyce rolled his eyes and Brent bid his son farewell with one final warning.

"Just watch it. You are playing with emotions and that can be dangerous."

Boyce nodded his understanding then returned to work on the signs.

The rally was set for late afternoon. It was a rally being held by PARR and LUPO planned to disrupt it. The signs that had been painted earlier were hidden in the trees so that all the LUPO members would have to do was pull a string and they would come out of the leaves to hang there for the whole rally to see. A few compact disc players filled with copies of the Mystique CD were also hidden among the bushes and they were remote controlled so that, when a button was pushed, they would start playing rock music. Everything seemed to be set. The members of LUPO were disguised so that, if anything went wrong, the PARR agents would not be able to later identify them. Now they just waited for the right moment to begin.

The rally started with the PARR agents showing people the films of young kids turning to crime, prostitution and other sins. It was told that these kids had done this because of the music they had listened to. Sex was free and loose back then, causing many diseases. Any other difficulties were blamed on the influence of rock and roll music. The people at the rally yawned. They were told these things every time they were forced to come to a rally. It was getting really tiring. Then there was a change in format.

Someone said that they had a very special guest here today - all the way front New York City. Would everyone please welcome the head of PARR, Mr. Judah Arnold? Judah took the stage, a very imposing figure.

"Ladies and gentlemen," he began. "I'm sure that you all know of the Let Us Play Organization or LUPO as it is more commonly called. The people in this organization are traitors and are determined on destroying the way of life that we have taken such care to perfect. They must be stopped at all costs before they ruin our society totally.

"The New York Chapter of this evil society is led by a young woman by the name of Miss Kaya More. In the very near future we will be arresting Miss More and making an example of her and others so that those who desire to oppose PARR will know what happens to traitors."

Boyce stood in the crowd, listening. His blood was boiling with anger and running cold with fear at the words of Judah Arnold The thought of PARR picking up one of the leaders of LUPO and, most certainly, torturing them was a horror that no LUPO member wanted to consider. He turned to another member of LUPO and gave the signal for everything to begin. PARR may have thought that they would shut LUPO down but he was going to prove to them just how hard that was going to be.

Instant chaos erupted along with the rock and roll music. People turned to see where the noise was coming from and saw brightly painted signs stating that PARR was wrong and that the music was not harmful. Members of LUPO started to hand out leaflets stating their opinions and begging others to put a stop to the censorship. The PARR agents seemed confused at first but then they started to move among the crowd, trying to get to the LUPO members. One agent was approaching Boyce's back with his gun drawn. As Sara glanced over to where Boyce was, she saw the agent but knew that, if she yelled, Boyce wouldn't hear her. So she did the only thing she could think of. She started running through the crowd, pushing her away past those in her way. Almost out of breath, she managed to reach the PARR agent before he reached Boyce. She took a stick that was near and struck the agent across the back. Unfortunately, Sara did not hit him hard enough to do any damage and, in horror, she saw him turn to point the weapon at her.

Boyce was still oblivious to the danger he had been in and the PARR agent until he heard a gun shot. He turned in time to see Sara crumbling to the ground.

"No!" He yelled as he raced toward her. It could have been a catastrophe if a person in the crowd hadn't fallen against the PARR agent, allowing enough time for Boyce to pick up Sara then race out of the crowd and the park.

The sea birds wailed mournfully at the lone figure on the beach. Boyce was walking along the sand trying to understand the tragic afternoon. Sara had died not long after they had left the park. She had told him before she died that she loved him and that, if she had to die, she was glad to die for him. Boyce kicked futilely at the sand as he remembered this. He didn't want that type of devotion from anyone. He just wanted to love and be loved and to lead a simple life. Boyce's entire life had been filled with the ease that only a treasured child experienced. Even when his mother had mysteriously died when he was fourteen, Boyce's father had been there to support him through the hard times. Being good looking and athletic, Boyce had never had difficulties finding a female to spend time with yet had never truly risked his heart with anyone. The anger and frustration he felt boiled up inside him and he turned to the sky for answers to his questions.

"Why did you let this happen?" He demanded of the gods above. "Why did it have to happen?" Boyce waited, as if expecting the answer but he received none. He walked a little further in the sand musing aloud as he went.

"Is there a woman for me? I need someone who is her own person and will be committed to something because she believes in it. I want a strong, independent woman who will live for herself but include me in her life. I need someone who shares my thoughts and ideals. Where is that someone?" Boyce stopped walking and gazed out over the water, as if the perfect woman was right there. His vision started to blur a few minutes later and the scene before him changed.

Instead of the blue water of the ocean, he saw a darkened city street. A young woman with silver hair was walking, appearing to be in somewhat of a hurry. She went into a building that was in bad need of repair. She walked down a flight of stairs to an almost completely hidden room. At that moment, Boyce knew who she must be. This was Kaya More. Here was the woman he was looking for. He concentrated all of his attention on her as he tried to get a message to her. He had to warn her that PARR was on to her and the she had to be careful. With all his might, he concentrated on sending her the message. It was with great satisfaction that he saw her stop and turn toward him. She seemed to be sort of lost at that moment, as if she didn't understand what was going on. Boyce closed his eyes and put all of his will power into the one thought that PARR now knew where she was. He was so lost in his concentration that he was startled when a tap came on his shoulder. He opened his eyes to see that the vision had vanished and his father was standing behind him. He hoped that Kaya had gotten the message.

CHAPTER Nine

Same time
New York City

Kaya stood in front of the door to the meeting room of LUPO lost in a trance. Her vision had gone cloudy a few minutes ago and she had been on a beach. Standing there was a young man with long blond hair trying; it seemed, to communicate with her. He looked strangely familiar. Sadly the vision had vanished too soon for her to remember where she had seen him before. One thing remained of the vision though: PARR knew where to find her. Kaya did not know how she knew this, she just did. A part of her wondered if that was what the young man had been trying to tell her. Gleven came out of the meeting room, saw Kaya just standing there, and wondered what was wrong. He tapped her on the shoulder and, startled, she turned to face him.

"Gleven. I have this feeling that PARR knows where to find me."

Gleven was surprised. He had bad news to tell Kaya that had to do with the possibility of Krista seeing a PARR agent.

"Kaya, I have to talk with you. I think that it is a very good possibility that Gary Shane is a PARR agent. I couldn't find anything on him in the computers and he definitely does not work where he said he did I hate jumping to conclusions though."

"What we could do is feed Krista false information and see what happens. If PARR agents show up, then we know that Krista is the leak. That way we wouldn't be hurting her unnecessarily."

"Good idea. Now what makes you think that PARR is onto you?"

Kaya hesitated. The only valid reason she had was that she had seen this guy on the beach and he had apparently told her. How could she explain that to anyone? It didn't sound logical. But she had to try.

"Don't think I'm crazy but I was sort of told."

Gleven raised his eyebrows.

"Sort of? How are you sort of told and who sort of told you?"

"I don't know who he was. I just had this feeling I was being watched and then suddenly I saw him."

"Where did you see this man?"

Once again Kaya hesitated. The vision she had didn't seem possible to her and she was certain that it would seem impossible to Gleven.

"I had this vision. I saw a young man on the beach who looked really familiar. I felt a great sadness emanating from him as if something terrible had recently happened. He seemed to be confused. "

Gleven was immediately suspicious. He had just received a phone call from Brent Mitchell in California telling him what had happened at the rally. However Brent had not been there and all he knew was that one of his supporters was dead.

"What did this young man look like?" Gleven asked slowly, not for a moment doubting Kaya's story.

"Tall with long blond hair. He was slim, had a very strong face and seemed to be in good shape physically."

Gleven thought for a moment. This could describe any number of young men but he had an idea.

"Come into my office with me. I have something to show you."

"Then you actually believe me?" Kaya asked, somewhat relieved. Gleven chuckled.

"Kaya, I learned a long time ago that there are things on this earth that can be seen, heard or touched by most people but they are still to be believed. And with you, I never doubt anything. There are times that if you told me that the sky was polka dot, I would believe you."

Kaya laughed.

"I'll have to remember that!" They both then went into his tiny office that was still full of boxes, to look at a photograph album. Gleven searched for a moment through the album then stopped. Studying a picture for a moment, he then handed it to Kaya.

"Does this look anything like the man you saw?"

Kaya took the album and studied the man for a moment

"Yes, that does look a lot like him."

Gleven paled. Taking the album away from Kaya, he said,

"I think that you had better go underground for a while. Go see your mother." Kaya seemed puzzled.

"Why? Who was that?"

Gleven paused a moment. He didn't want to frighten Kaya but he knew that this had to be told.

"That is an old picture of Brent Mitchell, the leader of the Western Chapter of LUPO and the man who was with your father when he was killed. I think the man you saw today was his son, Boyce. Boyce was at a PARR rally today and there was a bit of trouble. One of the girls was killed."

Kaya gave a little cry of alarm.

"I'm going. But don't you think that you should change the meeting room? I'm afraid that I might have been followed. In fact if I go to the Underground, won't I be followed?"

Gleven smiled weakly.

"I was thinking of that and you do not have to worry. We have enough props and costumes here to disguise you and as for this place being found, we were already thinking of moving. We were actually going to talk about that at today's meeting. So come with me and we will get you out of here."

The woman who emerged from the building a while later bore no resemblance to the tall, slim beauty who had walked in before. She seemed to be shorter and heavier with black hair and glasses. Her eyes were brown and a disfiguring scar ran the length of her face. She hobbled out of the building and stopped, as if uncertain where she was going. Actually she had stopped to see if there was anyone who was watching the door of the building. There didn't seem to be. Slowly Kaya started walking in the direction of the park. She ambled along, stopping sometimes to pet a dog or talk to someone, not appearing to be in a hurry. She had to make sure that no one was following her.

Kaya walked by a park and stopped to sit on a bench. It was almost obvious now that no one had followed her so she continued on her way. Deeper into the park she went until she came to a tunnel that led into the ground. Casually making sure that no one was around, she entered the tunnel.

A little ways into the tunnel there was a dimly lit passageway. Kaya walked assuredly down the dark halls, going deeper into the tunnels and into the bowels of the earth. As she walked along the layers of earth surrounding her muffled the sounds of the city above her. Soon she could not hear any sounds except those of the creatures that lived in the tunnel. Hidden in a wall was an old brass door. The ornate detail on the door was darkened by time and lack of care and, if someone didn't know it was there, it would be missed. But Kaya walked straight to it with the ease of someone who had traveled this path many times. Once more Kaya checked the long expanse behind her to be certain she hadn't been noticed and followed. When she was positive that no one had seen her she pulled a large key from her pocket. The key was fashioned out of brass: with the same ornate detailing on it that was on the door. Sliding the key into the lock Kaya turned it softly and the heavy door slid open noiselessly on oiled hinges. Inside lay the entry to another world.

Once Kaya had closed the door and started to walk along the now paved path, she breathed a little easier. The costume started to come off, as she became herself again. This was the one place in the world where she felt totally safe. Rich, Oriental tapestries hung from the walls, incense burned inconspicuously behind the brocade chairs and, very softly, rock and roll music played in the background. Here was the place that Kaya had set up for the refugees from PARR, the people whose faces were now too well known for them to exist on the street. Presiding over this band of social outcasts was Kaya's mother, Wind. When Kaya had become old enough to take care of herself, Wind had wanted to get away from the world. So Kaya had thought of this.

Kaya, in one of her flights from PARR, had found this hidden chamber and had gone to work installing a haven from the world above.

Only Gleven, Kaya and the people down here knew that it existed. Complete secrecy was the only way to keep these people safe and alive. Kaya wandered through the immense passageways and smaller caves hidden at every turn. These caves served as each refugee's private sanctuary. It was a little world beneath the larger one.

Kaya worked her way towards the large area that had been designated as a gathering area for the residents of the underground city. There she found her mother and the majority of the LUPO supporters sitting comfortably. Her mother looked more calm and rested that she had in years.

"This place is good for her." Kaya thought to herself. She stood silently for a moment, watching the serene scene in front of her. Deep inside her heart she sometimes wished that she could experience this kind of peace but she also knew that until she got was she was fighting for, that was impossible.

"Kaya!" Wind exclaimed happily, having spotted her daughter standing there. "Come sit down and join us."

Kaya moved gracefully across the room and bent to kiss her mother. She straightened and looked around the room at the people gathered there.

"You would never know that these people fear for their lives." Kaya wondered to herself. Taking a seat near her mother, she continued to marvel at the peace and serenity that existed in this place.

Wind watched her daughter shrewdly; having a feeling that she knew what was going on in her daughter's mind.

"Are things going well above?" She asked.

Kaya paused a moment before answering her mother.

"Not really," she admitted. "Somehow, PARR is finding out about a lot of our activities and I think I may know how."

“How?”

Kaya hesitated. She hated thinking that - instead of finding someone who loved her - Krista was being used. And putting the thought into words just seemed to strengthen it.

“I think, actually Gleven and I both think, that Krista's new boyfriend may be a PARR agent. And another thing, I have this feeling that PARR know too much about me. That is why I am here.”

“Do you need sanctuary for a little while? Or is it something more permanent?”

Kaya shook her head.

"If you have the room, I need a place to stay temporarily. Gleven thinks it is too dangerous up above for me at this time.”

“There wasn't even a need to ask. You should know that you are welcome here for as long as you want.”

Kaya hugged her mother.

"Thank you Mom. You don't know how good that makes me feel." Kaya sat back and relaxed. For the first time in a long time she felt secure and protected.

Wind looked at Kaya closely, her thoughts on her daughter's safety.

"Kaya?" She began. Kaya looked at her mother patiently waiting for the still beautiful woman to continue.

"Have you found anyone yet?"

Kaya sighed and restrained the remarks that came to mind. Instead, she gently smiled at her mother.

"No, Mom. I am not really looking for anyone either." Unbidden, the image of the young man she had seen on the beach flashed before her eyes.

"I know." Wind was quick to admit. "It's just that I don't like to see you alone."

"Perhaps if I could find someone who was as dedicated to LUPO as I am and wouldn't be threatened by me, and if the electricity was there, I would consider being romantically involved but that hasn't happened yet." Although Kaya had explained this to her mother numerous times since she was sixteen, her voice was patient as she reiterated her reasons.

"I was always more interested in a man's looks and his build." Wind chuckled. "But you. You have LUPO on your mind so much that it doesn't leave room for anything else. Perhaps it is time that you re-evaluated the priorities in your life."

Kaya felt herself losing control of the temper she kept such a tight rein on. Eyes flashing, voice soft and deadly, Kaya answered her mother.

"I have told you numerous times that LUPO and bringing back rock and roll are the most important things in my life right now. I would rather die than give it up."

Wind went to say something then changed her mind. Kaya was just like her father had been. Stubborn and opinionated. There would be no way that Wind could change Kaya's mind about the matter, not that there ever had been. Instead Wind filled Kaya in on the events that had recently occurred within the Underground City.

"All is well here." She assured Kaya. "We had a little scare a couple of days ago when Thoren went above to get more supplies. One of the PARR agents that he had been fighting against was in the store and Thoren was afraid that he had been recognized. However, the agent was more interested in the pastries than he was in a missing LUPO member."

Kaya smiled at the story though its implications reminded her how much danger they were all in.

"Is there anything you need?" Kaya asked her mother.

Wind shook her head then asked the same question of Kaya. Kaya looked thoughtful for a moment before answering.

"Could you bring back rock and roll so that there will be freedom and peace once again?" Wind reached over to pat her daughter's hand, confident that her earlier remarks had been forgiven.

"If I could, I would. But that is something that I think you are going to do."

Gleven was worried. He didn't like having to hurt his daughter but he knew that this time he had to. He had given Krista the false information and sure enough the PARR agents had shown at the supposed meeting place. Now he had to tell Krista that she was being used. His feet dragged the closer he got to her apartment and his heart grew heavier at the prospect of breaking his only child's heart. It was something that he did not want to do but he thought it might be easier coming from him rather than someone else. With a saddened heart he rang her apartment buzzer.

"Dad! It is so good to see you!" Krista was extremely happy, so different than she had been three months before. Gleven felt even guiltier at the thought of telling her what he had to.

"Krista. I came today because I have something to tell you that you are not going to want to hear. Please sit down and don't interrupt me. Just let me tell you."

Krista sat down, her eyes shining. Whatever her father had to tell her couldn't be that bad.

Gleven looked at the daughter that meant so much to him and who had already gone through so much and prayed a silent prayer for forgiveness for what he was about to do.

"Krista. Gary Shane is not who you think he is. He doesn't work for a small department in the government He is a PARR agent that is using you to get information on LUPO."

"No Dad. You are totally wrong. Why ever would he do that?"

Gleven sighed. This was going to be harder than he originally thought.

"My dear. I have proof of this. You have been giving him information and a few days ago I gave you some false information. PARR agents showed up at the phony meeting place. The only one who knew about it was you."

Krista's mouth set in a determined line.

"That still doesn't prove anything."

"What about him knowing about Kaya's disagreement with Mr. Chay all those years ago? He said that you told him but I know that you never knew about it."

"Kaya! She's behind this isn't she? I just knew it. That bitch doesn't want me to be happy at all!" Krista stood up and started pacing the living room. "All my life she has stood in the way of my happiness, taking you away when I needed you, not stopping my rape when she knew it was going to happen and now this! And I was stupid enough to consider her a friend!"

Gleven was shocked.

"What do you mean she knew about your rape and could have stopped it? How?"

"She knew something was going to happen to me that day but she never told me. She started acting really strange at lunch then insisted that I walk home with someone."

Gleven closed his eyes for a moment. He remembered how upset Kaya had been at the hospital. And now he understood why. However he did not believe for a moment that Kaya was in any way responsible for Krista being raped.

"Krista, you wouldn't have believed her if she had told you. And if she had told you, you and your friends would have ridiculed Kaya at school. No, I'm sorry Krista, but Kaya was not responsible for your rape and she is not responsible for Gary being a PARR agent. Now I knew that this was going to hurt you but I don't want you blaming Kaya or me or anyone else that is not responsible for your problems. The people to blame are the ones involved with PARR. They are the ones who have arranged all this."

"Or you. If you hadn't been involved with LUPO, none of this would have happened to me."

"Krista I am sorry that you feel like that but you have to understand that I believe strongly in what I am doing. I have never meant to hurt any member of my family and I am so sorry that you have been."

"Never meant to hurt any of us? That is a laugh! That is all you've done." Gleven tried to interrupt his daughter but Krista was too involved in her tirade to hear or notice him.

"The only thing you ever cared about was that stupid organization! How many nights did you leave Mom and me alone so you could go out and do something ridiculously dangerous? How many times were you not there for me when I needed you? Quite frankly I wish you would grow up! Actually I wish you would go away! I am tired of your lies about Gary and I don't want to look at your disgusting face any more."

"Krista," Gleven began.

"Get out!" Krista screeched hysterically. "I don't want or need you and as far as I am concerned, you are no longer my father, Not that you were much of one to begin with."

Seeing that there was nothing left to say, Gleven left. His heart shattering, he walked home.

CHAPTER Ten

A month later

The Underground city

The underground dwelling was silent as Kaya strolled along. For a month now Kaya had been living here and it was beginning to drive her insane. She missed the noise, the hustle and bustle of life above her. Perhaps, most of all, she missed the excitement of being a leader of LUPO. She felt so useless living here! Another concern on her mind was the fate of LUPO. Since she had not been able to go above ground and Gleven hadn't visited her, she wondered what was happening. Were they all dead? Had LUPO been discovered and disbanded? What was going on? Her mind was full of numerous possibilities, none of them good. Sitting on a brocade chair, Kaya pondered her options. She could stay down here until Gleven came to tell her all was well or she could go find him herself. Although staying here was the safest alternative, Kaya wouldn't have joined LUPO if she were interested in safe alternatives. In a few minutes Kaya knew what she was going to do, and with a new air of excitement, she went to tell her mother.

Kaya emerged into the cool night air and took a deep breath, feeling the adrenaline race through her veins. The air, though filled with smog, was a relief after the canned air that she had been breathing. After taking a few moments to savor being out in the city once more, Kaya started walking purposefully in the direction of Gleven's house.

The closer Kaya came to her destination the more apprehensive she became. Something was definitely wrong. The hairs on the back of her neck were rising rapidly and she suddenly felt very cold. Kaya walked along casually resisting the urge to run.

Gleven's house was dark and empty. It had that isolated feeling of a place that hadn't been lived in for a while. Kaya was going to approach it but she caught a movement out of the corner of her eye. The house was being watched. Quickly, but without appearing to hurry, she left the vicinity.

Wandering about the streets Kaya felt lost and confused. She would go to Krista's apartment but, if Gleven's house was being watched, there was a definite possibility that there would be PARR agents near Krista's apartment as well.

"Damn! " Kaya swore under her breath. It was apparent that all hell had broken loose while she had been away and there was no way to find out what had gone wrong. As she walked by a newspaper stand, Kaya's blood ran cold as she saw the answer to her unspoken question.

“LUPO Founder to Be Executed!" was the headline that blared out at her. Quickly Kaya bought a paper and proceeded to read the article.

"A week ago one of the founders and leaders of LUPO, Mr. Gleven Andrews, was taken into custody after a twenty five year search.” Mr. Judah Arnold, leader of the government agency PARR, stated that the raid on the unlawful meeting place of LUPO was a successful one.

“Though we haven't managed to capture Kaya More as of yet, we did succeed in capturing many of the LUPO members. They shall face long jail terms and Mr. Andrews will be executed on the twelfth at noon.

“LUPO stands for the Let Us Play Organization which was founded twenty five years ago by malcontents, Gleven Andrews, Kansall More and Brent Mitchell. Kansall More was killed as he resisted arrest fifteen years ago and Brent Mitchell has disappeared. The search for Kaya More, daughter of Kansall More, is still on. Miss More is approximately 5'9" with waist length platinum blond hair, silver eyes and a build that is slim and athletic. If seen please do not approach since she may be armed and dangerous. Please contact the nearest PARR agency."

Kaya's heart sank. Gleven to be executed in three days! She had to do something to stop it. Frantically her mind searched its recesses. Some time ago Gleven had given her a telephone number and code name to use if she ever needed help from the LUPO members in California. However she had been required to memorize the number so that it could never be found. Now the numbers refused to come to the forefront of her memory.

"Calm down.” Kaya silently ordered herself. Closing her eyes and taking a deep breath Kaya tried to visualize the numbers she had seen only once. At first they were cloudy but gradually the numbers took shape. A smile curved Kaya's lips as the numbers took on a clarity that was startling. Opening her eyes, she sought a pay phone.

"Collect from Starlight in New York." Kaya told the operator. Kaya held her breath as the phone rang once, twice, three times. On the fourth ring, a strong male voice answered.

"Yes, I'll accept the charges.” He answered the operator quickly. Once he was certain that the operator was off the line, the man spoke rapidly. “We'll meet you at the usual place. How many?"

Kaya was also quick to answer.

"As many as possible."

"Fine. Give us twenty four hours." The line went dead.

Kaya hung up; satisfied that help was on the way.

"We've got trouble." Kaya stated as she raced into the common room of the underground dwelling.

Wind and the others turned in surprise. Kaya passed her mother the newspaper and Wind read it in horror.

"What can we do?"

"`I have already placed a call to California and they will be here within twenty four hours. I think the safest place for us to meet is here and we are going to have to come up with a plan to get that many people down here without attracting attention."

"How are you planning to free Gleven and the others?" One of the dwellers asked.

Kaya was silent for a moment.

"I haven't really had time to formulate a plan but we are going to have to strike quickly and simultaneously. Or else PARR is going to be forewarned. That's why I need all the people I can get." Here Kaya paused before continuing.

"Now I know that it is dangerous for all of you to be in the city above and this plan is going to destroy your sanctuary but I have to ask if any of you will volunteer to help free Gleven and the others." There was silence among the people in the room for such a long time that Kaya thought no one was going to offer to help.

Then Wind stepped forward.

"Of course I'll help you. Gleven was one of your father's closest and dearest friends." Slowly, one by one, the others all came forward until all the dwellers had volunteered. Kaya looked upon them with tears in her eyes, touched by the love and devotion she saw here.

At about the same time the next evening, the caverns were fuller than they had ever been before. Through the aid of disguises and separating people they managed to get the entire visiting Western chapter of LUPO into the dwelling without being noticed. Now the dwellers vanished into other regions of the caverns to remove their disguises and to fix refreshments.

Brent and Boyce marvelled at the layout before them.

"We should have something like this in California. It seems so safe. A haven from the world." Boyce told his father. "I wonder how they created it."

"Kaya found it." A musical voice came from behind them. Boyce and his father turned to be greeted by Wind carrying a tray of coffee. Brent's face wreathed in smiles as he recognized her.

"Wind!" Turning to Boyce, he continued. "This gorgeous lady once saved Kansall and mine's ass! It was at the first rally we ever tried to crash."

Boyce's eyes lit up with interest.

"Sounds like this is going to be an interesting story." Brent started to laugh.

"We were very disorganized and I got caught in a tree with these PARR agents coming towards Kansall and I. Well Wind was watching closely and, just at the right moment, she dumped her soda on this big guy in front of her. The guy got angry and when he turned to hit someone, Wind ducked. So he hit the man behind her. That started a brawl that the PARR agents couldn't get through.

"Once I was able to untangle myself from the branches, I told Kansall what I had seen this girl do and that we had to get her out of there.

“We started looking for her and Kansall was the first to see her. She was crawling out from between the legs of the people fighting."

Wind blushed at this memory and Brent continued.

"Kansall reached down, picked Wind up then started running. I don't think I had ever seen a funnier sight than that of this tall young man, with his long hair blowing in the wind, running down the street with a young woman flopping on his shoulder."

"So Mom. That is the story you never finished telling me." Kaya had come up behind the group and had listened intently to Brent's narration.

Boyce turned and saw the woman of his vision. However he never got to properly introduce himself since, without further chitchat, Kaya called everyone to gather around to discuss how they were going to free the imprisoned LUPO members.

CHAPTER Eleven

Same Day

New York City/PARR headquarters

Judah sat behind his large desk, scowling at his assistant, Dirk Rogers. "What do you mean, you can't find her?" Judah bellowed. "She can't have vanished into thin air!"

Dirk shrugged.

"Maybe that's what happened. " He commented sarcastically." But there is something I thought you should know. A large number of people have come into the city from California. We don't know where any of them are. They have all disappeared. None of the hotels have had a great number of reservations." This perked Judah's interest.

"How many people?"

"Close to a hundred. Something is going on."

Judah dismissed Dirk with a wave of his hand. Once the young man had gone, Judah went to stand by the window. He gazed out over the city as if searching for a needle in a haystack.

"Where are you Miss More?" Judah pondered aloud. He had to admit that Kaya More was proving to be a formidable opponent. She was clever and Judah admired that in a person. His thoughts turned to what Dirk Rogers had told him.

"What do you have planned?" Judah stared intently at the city below him; giving the impression that he was willing the sparkling lights to give him the answers he frantically sought.

In a jail cell far below Judah, Gleven sat staring at the walls. Tomorrow was going to be the last complete day that he would be alive yet he didn't regret his life. Perhaps the only thing he wished that he had accomplished was to be able to see the rebirth of rock and roll.

Gleven thought back over the last month and shuddered. Events had turned hazardous ever since he had had that talk with Krista. A little while after that, PARR agents had raided the latest meeting place of LUPO. Gleven had been separated from the others and put into this cold, dark room. Little did he know that it was the same room where Krista had been raped.

Pondering over his past, Gleven recalled the major events that had happened. He remembered the first time that Kansall and Brent had approached him about setting up LUPO. They were three hotheaded eighteen year olds that were going to right the wrongs of this society and it had been so exciting. In many ways, it still was. Visions of Margaret whose whereabouts were a mystery to him, floated through his mind. She had been so beautiful. In fact she still was. So many memories raced through his mind that he selected the choice ones to examine minutely. If he was going to die soon, he was going to spend his last hours with pleasant thoughts.

As a child, Gleven had led a fairly innocent life surrounded by friends as well as his numerous brothers and sisters whose whereabouts he no longer knew of. Like many other people of his generation, events and time frames were hazy. Many memories seemed to be just a dream; any rebellious nature that most teenagers experienced just didn't appear to have happened. Deep within himself, Gleven felt that PARR had somehow destroyed those recollections in order to gain further control of anyone who might oppose them.

As usual, Gleven's thoughts turned to LUPO and their struggle. He knew that if they could accurately determine just how PARR managed to keep their thoughts and ideas under the government's control, LUPO would have a better chance of succeeding. If only the public was allowed free thoughts and opinions, the censorship of books, music and the arts would have to end. Gleven sighed, partly in regret and partly in resignation, and thought,

"If only we could find out how!"

Krista brushed the fur of her new coat with pleasure. When her father had told her the truth about Gary, she had been shattered. As soon as Gary had visited her, she confronted him with what she knew. After a moment's hesitation he had told her that it was true. He further explained that, though he was using her at the beginning, he had come to care for her deeply. That night, while in bed, she had vowed to help him stop LUPO in any way she could.

By following people Krista suspected of being LUPO members, she managed to ascertain where the current meeting place was.

The night of the raid Krista had sat in her new luxury apartment that she shared with Gary, doing her nails. She kept glancing at the clock with concern. She was not worried about her father or the other people that may be there who she had betrayed; her concern was only for Gary. She looked around the apartment and nearly purred with enjoyment at the sight of the expensive items around her.

Once Gary had revealed that he was a PARR agent he had also revealed the fact that he was quite wealthy. Gary had led a life that some can only dream about. Private schools in Europe, mixing with influential people from the moment he was old enough to talk and substantial investments made from his various trust funds, all allowed Gary to lead the life he wished to. But the excitement and glamor of being a PARR agent had attracted him early on in life and, once he had reached the age where he could make his own decisions, Gary Shane had enlisted with PARR. It was no wonder that Krista felt that she had latched on to a real prize.

Krista rose and stretched lazily. She moved across the room, and as she passed one of the many mirrors, she paused to gaze at herself. At first she was intent on admiring her image but her mind soon turned to more serious concerns.

"What have I done?" was the first unbidden thought that crossed her mind. Visions of her father and her spending special moments together, of her father attending all of her school functions, of her father always caring about her and what was happening with her brought a tear to her eye. Setting her chin with determination, she forced the other memories to mind: the many lonely nights when she and her mother had spent, the long hours alone, not knowing whether her father was alive or dead. Then she brought back the night he had told her about Gary.

"Feeling guilty?" Gary had slipped quietly into the apartment and had observed Krista looking in the mirror with such intensity and with tears in her eyes.

Krista shook her head.

"No." She answered softly. "Just thinking." In truth Krista did feel pangs of guilt at the havoc she had created but she pushed those feelings aside as she went into Gary's arms.

Now on the night that Gleven sat reliving his life and the LUPO members were hidden away plotting his rescue, Krista was arguing with Gary.

"But I can't do that Gary," She shrieked. "My dad will never believe me!"

"Of course he will." Gary spoke soothingly. "He doesn't know that you are living with me. Besides, we have to find Kaya More before she does something."

Krista bit her lip as she thought Gary's idea out. Gary wanted her to play the loving daughter one last time but Krista wasn't positive that she could act that well. The purpose of the act was to find out where Kaya was hiding. Gary watched Krista intently as she mentally shrugged, knowing that she would agree with him.

"OK. What do you want me to do?"

A few hours later, Gleven was startled to see the door to his cell open. Outside two guards stood at attention and one of the guards growled roughly.

"On your feet. There is someone here to see you. "

Gleven struggled to his feet, wincing at every movement, and followed the guards to the visitor's lounge. He was surprised to see Krista waiting to see him. He was shocked at her appearance. At first glance her hair looked dirty and dishevelled, her plump form shrunken and her spirit broken. But on further examination, Gleven noticed that Krista was looking healthier than she had in years.

"Oh Daddy!" Krista sobbed as she threw herself into his arms causing Gleven to wince with pain as she did so. "I am so sorry that this has happened! What am I going to do?"

Gleven gently untangled her arms from around his neck.

"Why should you be sorry? You didn't have anything to do with it, did you?"

Krista was flustered for a moment. Did her father know about her part in the destruction of LUPO? He couldn't possibly know.

"Of course not!" Krista put all of her limited acting ability into looking forlorn.

Gleven, had seen the look before and wasn't fooled.

"Why are you here Krista? A month ago you disowned me as your father." He said somewhat more harshly than he had intended.

Krista knew then that before she could ask about Kaya, she had to convince her father of her sincerity.

"I'm sorry about that. Daddy. I was upset and I didn't mean the things I said. Please forgive me?" Krista adopted the look she had used so often as a misbehaved child and prayed that it would work.

Gleven softened slightly and asked again,

"Why are you here Krista?"

Krista inwardly breathed a sigh of relief as she heard the gentler tone to Gleven's voice.

"I have to find Kaya!" She blurted. "I was kicked out of my apartment when you were arrested, I can't find Mom and Kaya is the only one that can help me!"

Warning bells sounded in Gleven's head.

"How can Kaya help you?"

"Daddy! I've been on the streets for the last week, my whole family is in jail and Kaya is my oldest friend. Surely she will help me."

"What do you mean that your whole family is in jail?"

Krista knew that she had made a serious error here and stammered as she tried to correct it.

"Well, um, you're here and I don't know where Mom is so I just figured that she must be in jail." Krista's voice was rising hysterically as she tried to convince her father of her sincerity. This was more difficult than she had thought it would be.

Gleven was not appeased. He felt, now more than ever, that Krista was working with PARR to ensure the destruction of LUPO. He felt the sorrow only a parent can feel when their child severely disappoints them as his daughter had.

"I don't know where Kaya is." He said harshly. "And if the only reason you came to see me was to see if you could trap Kaya then you may as well leave now." Gleven turned to signal the guard that he was ready to go back to his cell. Before he left he had a few parting words to say.

"You can also tell that boyfriend of yours, Judah Arnold and whoever else you are working with, that killing me is not going to stop LUPO. There is no way that PARR can halt the rebirth of rock and roll." With a final look of disgust and disappointment Gleven went back to his cell. Gleven seated himself on the cot once more and listened to the sounds of the guards talking outside his door.

"I wonder why they're executing him." One said. The other answered simply.

"Probably to make an example out of him so that others will think twice before disobeying PARR's laws."

"But why not just send him to the Rockies like they did with the others? That would make it simpler."

"I don't know. It's what Judah wants."

Gleven didn't listen to the rest of the conversation. His mind was focused on the idea of the Rockies. Were they hiding someone within those mountain peaks? And who could it be? Gleven wished that he wasn't scheduled to die. Somehow he felt that, if they could find where in the Rockies whatever or whoever was hidden, then LUPO would be able to make a substantial blow against PARR and the unjust censorship they were enforcing.

CHAPTER Twelve

Two days later
New York City

The rain poured down in blinding sheets and a northern wind blew harsh and cold. It was the morning of Gleven's scheduled execution.

Far below the city's noise a final briefing was being conducted. Actually due to the number of people, four individual briefings were being held. They were going over the steps each group of people were to take to free Gleven and the unfortunate LUPO supporters who were in the clutches of PARR. After each phase of the plan was reviewed, that group would leave to go above ground. Within a few hours, the only people left were Brent, Wind, Boyce and Kaya. Quietly, the foursome reviewed their plan. They had, perhaps, the most difficult task of all. They were to release Gleven. Once the plan had been discussed once more and they were all certain of the part each had to play, they left.

Gleven sat in his cell, pondering the events of his life with LUPO. He almost laughed aloud when he thought of the valuable information that Krista had inadvertently given him: One, Margaret was alive. Two, Kaya was still free. He felt like doing a jig and cheering Kaya on. With Kaya and the Western chapter of LUPO, the fight would go on.

Out of the comer of his eye, Gleven saw the cell door opening. He was shocked and enraged. He still had a few more hours to live. Gleven's eyes blazed with anger. If they were coming to take him now they were in for a fight.

The door opened wide and four PARR agents walked in; two of them looking quite smaller than the other two. It took a moment for Gleven to realize that the smaller two were women.

"Christ!" He muttered inwardly. "They must think that I am so weak and that LUPO is so beaten that they don't have to place their four strongest men to guard me." Gleven started to tense, ready to strike when one of the guards spoke.

"So this is the Gleven Andrews I've heard so much about Dad. The way you talked about him, I imagined him to be a lot taller. Like ten feet tall."

Gleven paused to take a closer look at the 'agents'.

"Brent! What are you doing here?"

"Getting myself killed if you don't lower your voice!" Brent hissed in response. "What do you think I'm doing here? I couldn't let you have all the fun and excitement."

Moisture formed around Gleven's eyes as he recognized the two women as being Wind and Kaya. The fourth person had to be Brent's son. Gleven opened his mouth to scold Kaya for taking such a risk when an explosion sounded that shook the cell. Boyce and Kaya exchanged excited grins - the rescue was under way.

"Let's get moving." Kaya suggested, withdrawing her revolver. The others nodded and Brent took out a set of handcuffs.

"Sorry about this Gleven. I won't fasten them completely but, if we get stopped, we want it to look genuine."

Gleven shrugged.

"That's all right. At least I know I'm on my way to freedom and not death."

"We hope," Kaya muttered in an undertone that no one else heard. Once the handcuffs were in place, loosely around Gleven's wrists, he was surrounded by the four and led out of the cell.

Utter chaos reigned in the hallways outside. Prisoners and guards ran to and fro; the prisoners seeking an avenue of escape while the guards sought to maintain a semblance of order without having to use their firearms in such close quarters. Except for a number of LUPO supporters, no one was accomplishing much.

Through this disorder, walked a very important prisoner with his four guards, totally unnoticed. Kaya glanced at the mass of people, furtively checking on the LUPO supporters. All seemed to be following the plan exactly as it was outlined. Relieved that their services weren't needed there, she concentrated on getting Gleven to safety. Everything was going according to plan until they turned down the last corridor before freedom. Standing there, waiting to observe the final walk of Gleven, was Krista.

Kaya hesitated when she saw Krista's eyes widen in recognition. Krista's mouth opened, as if to shout to the PARR agents close by, then abruptly closed. Silently she let them pass undisturbed.

In a matter of moments, they were outside and all breathed a sigh of relief. The first step, and maybe the most dangerous, was over. Still walking purposefully and quickly, Boyce and Kaya led the way to the outside gates where an unmarked van was waiting. Wordlessly, Brent shoved Gleven into the vehicle before the person at the wheel drove away. The four guards exchanged glances of triumph.

"We did it! " Kaya cheered as she started to tear off the uniform she hated so much.

"What about the others?" Gleven asked, concerned and still not able to believe his good fortune.

"They have already been taken care of." Wind explained. "That was what the commotion was all about."

"We are going to meet them in an old warehouse." Boyce further clarified.

"Looks like everything has been taken care of." Gleven smiled. "But how did you know?"

"I got impatient waiting for you and I felt sure that something had gone wrong." Kaya began. "So I came into the city.

"When I went to your house there were agents all over the place. I got scared. I was wandering around town when I saw the article in a newspaper announcing your execution in three days. I remembered what you had told me to do in case of an emergency and I phoned California."

"When I heard the operator saying it was a collect call from Starlight in New York, I really panicked." Boyce laughed. "But Dad had warned me about that call so I was prepared."

"After I found out that Starlight had called, I went into action and got as many people as I could to come out here." Brent added.

"We arranged everything, right down to the final detail, in the underground city." Wind concluded.

Once more Gleven was moved. It touched him deeply to realize that all these people, some who didn't know him, were willing to drop everything and, more than likely, risk their lives for him and the cause. He sat at the back of the van watching the other occupants. As he gazed at Kaya, he felt Kansall's presence enveloping him.

"I hope you're paying attention Kansall." Gleven mused silently. "Kaya is turning into quite the woman and LUPO is gathering more strength than we could ever have imagined. Perhaps the rebirth of rock and roll is soon." He smiled inwardly as he watched Boyce and Kaya bickering quietly over some minor point. Though they didn't know it Gleven could see the beginnings of a romance between the young couple. He turned his gaze to Brent and Wind, sitting close together, discussing something in low tones. It seemed as if both of Kansall's women were on the road to romance. Gleven sighed. He had faced this day with the certain knowledge that he would die and now he was free, he would soon be reunited with Margaret and it seemed as if all the LUPO supporters were safe. Who would have thought, all those years ago in a small college dorm, that three young men would start something that would become so big with members so loyal to one another? LUPO had come a long way.

CHAPTER Thirteen

Two days later

Judah Arnold's office/PARR headquarters

"All those people have to be somewhere in this city but you don't know where? What do I have working for me? A bunch of incompetents!" Judah's roar resounded through the office. It had been two days since the daring rescue of Gleven Andrews and the LUPO members and, though PARR had all the exits out of the city under surveillance, the rebels still hadn't been found.

Gary stood at attention, silently absorbing Judah's harassment, his hatred for the other man carefully concealed. Secretly he admired Kaya for actually pulling the escape. He found that images of the silver haired woman haunted his dreams at night. When he made love to Krista he always seemed to see Kaya. It was driving him crazy. Needless to say, he was losing interest in Krista. The lady with the silver hair was the one he wanted.

Judah's thoughts were also on Kaya More but for different reasons. With grudging respect, he thought about the escape that had been accomplished. If only Kaya More was on the side of PARR. However, she wasn't and therefore she was the enemy. Kaya had bested Judah, made him look like an incompetent fool and that did not make him very happy. He envisioned the torture he would inflict when he had Kaya in his grasp.

"Find them." Judah ordered in a low voice.

"What do you want done?" Judah's answer was immediate.

"Kill them. We will end this rebellion once and for all. All except Kaya More. I have special plans for her."

Gary felt a shiver run along the length of his spine as he saluted and turned to walk away. From the look on Judah's face and his reputation for cruelty, Kaya More was not in an enviable position. Judah's reputation for cruelty was well earned. He had achieved the status he now held in PARR by inflicting horrendous pain on those who dared to violate the laws that Judah had vowed to uphold.

Perhaps Judah's capacity for cruelty could be traced back to his early beginnings. Born to poverty stricken parents, Judah watched his strong, overweight father repeatedly strike his diminutive mother. More often than not, Judah's father would also beat the child and leave scars that lasted a lifetime. It was impossible for Judah not to realize that the world could sometimes be a cruel, hard environment in which to live. And Judah did his best to keep it that way.

Ever since Judah had been a small child, he had possessed the ability to be cruel and harsh. Whereas others seemed to develop an aversion to harming others, Judah had rejoiced in watching other living things suffer. For years, Judah had been responsible for the majority of the physically injured pets in the neighbourhood. Tortures that had been dictated during history as too harsh for humans were what Judah inflicted on the helpless creatures that had the misfortune to cross his path.

His teenage years had seen Judah as a tall, strong, handsome young man that young women were undeniably attracted to. Yet, once a girl had managed to go out on a date with him, they rarely went twice and refused to discuss the evening with their friends. After one outing with Judah Arnold, the young lady neither wanted to associate with Judah or even acknowledge his existence. Judah never wondered why this was so. His inability to love or even care for fellow human beings caused him to see nothing abnormal with the eternal one-night stands. Actually Judah gained little, if any, pleasure from spending time in the company of women, preferring his twisted endeavours of cruelty more. At the age of seventeen, Judah discovered that women did have a use for him after all.

At the insistence of his father, Judah visited a prostitute who was known for her perverse acts. There Judah was able to explore his sadistic tendencies with a willing partner. It was a night that he would never forget.

Now as Judah gazed out over the city, he smiled grimly.

"Well done, Miss More but remember this: You may have won this battle but I assure you, I will win the war!"

CHAPTER Fourteen

Same time

New York City/an abandoned warehouse

For two days the LUPO supporters had been hiding in an abandoned warehouse. The people from both chapters had taken advantage of the time to compare lifestyles and form lasting friendships. If it weren't for the possibility of PARR finding them, the last two days would have been like a holiday.

Kaya felt the tension of the past two days starting to bear down on her. Since she had found out about the PARR invasion, she had had little sleep and her senses always seemed to be on the alert. Kaya was walking an emotional tight rope, the danger of her falling increased by the hour. Perhaps part of the reason for that was caused by the fact that Boyce was in close proximity. Though neither of them realized it as of yet, the sexual electricity between the two sparked almost continuously. Others around them could see it and all were waiting for something to happen.

It was late at night; the evening sky was blanketed with twinkling stars. Just as Judah Arnold was staring at the city so was Kaya More standing at a window, staring at the city but not really seeing it. Instead, her mind was in turmoil. She cursed her ineptitude for not planning what to do with the large number of people she was now responsible for. To further complicate matters, everyone seemed to be looking to her to make the decisions now. With the planning and rescue of Gleven and the other LUPO members she had unwittingly placed herself in the position as the supreme leader of LUPO. Kaya saw that even Gleven and Brent had been asking her advice on certain matters.

Kaya felt that there wasn't anyone she could turn to for advice on what to do. They all seemed to expect her to make the decisions and know the correct path to take. If only Kansall were here. Kaya knew that her father would be able to advise her on which path was the best to take at this time.

"Oh Daddy!" Kaya cried aloud. "I wish you were here, I need your wisdom and guidance so much!" After a few moments, Kaya felt a comforting sensation enveloping her. Almost immediately, a familiar voice, which she had never been able to forget, spoke quietly within her mind.

"What's wrong Starlight? You should know that I am always here whenever you need me."

Kaya choked back a sob.

"Daddy, I'm so confused." She cried inwardly. "I don't know what to do!"

"About what? From what I have seen over the years, you have been doing quite well. I couldn't be prouder of you especially as I watched the rescue of Gleven and the others. That was fantastic. How I wish that I could have been a part of that."

Still communicating silently, Kaya continued seeking her father's advice.

"You were there with us Father. Perhaps not in body but your spirit guides us constantly." Kaya paused. "But what do I do with all these people now? I really didn't plan events out properly and now everyone, even Gleven, Mom and Brent, are looking to me for guidance. I just don't know if I can do it."

"Kaya, you can do it." Her father reassured her. "I see now that you are the one who was destined to lead LUPO and bring back the music. You must never have doubts again that LUPO will succeed. You are the one that will accomplish what I died for."

"But what about all these people? What am I going to do with them all?" Kaya was still having doubts about her ability to lead them all to safety.

"Have you thought of separating them all? With this many people, PARR is bound to get suspicious sooner or later. You can't hide here forever."

"If some of the people would be willing to relocate, we could transfer some of the New York supporters to other parts of the country and the California supporters could stay here. Some could reside in the underground city and others, the less known ones, around the city." Kaya mused. "Of course, Gleven, Brent, Boyce, Mom and I would have to be constantly available to smooth over the transitions but that would be all right with me. Of course that depends of whether Gleven wants to leave LUPO or not."

Kansall's hearty laugh resounded through Kaya's mind, warming her heart as she recalled happier times.

"Not if I know Gleven. He should be fighting mad by now. So don't worry about him, he is as committed to the cause as I am. Now that the immediate problems with LUPO have been settled, what else is upsetting you?"

Here Kaya hesitated. Should, and could she, tell her father about her feelings towards Boyce?

"I don't think that you would really understand, Daddy. I'm not sure that I do."

Kansall was silent for a moment.

"If it is about Brent's son, I'd advise you to do what you feel is right. Follow your heart Starlight"

"How did you know about that?"

"Kaya, I've been watching over you and your mother for years. You are no longer that little girl I left behind all those years ago; you are now a beautiful woman who is fighting for what she believes in. And doing quite well, I might add. Which reminds me. I was really proud of the way that you told your music teacher off. Though I should apologize for showing you those music scores."

"You did that?"

Kansall chuckled.

"Yes. I saw them and couldn't resist showing them to you so that you would have a better understanding of what LUPO was fighting for and what it is about. Even though you weren't involved at the point "

"Why haven't you ever contacted me or mother before?"

"You have never truly needed me before and your mother's mind has never been receptive enough for me to really communicate with her. I doubt it ever will be now that her mind is on Brent."

"On Brent? What do you mean?"

"For someone with your mental capabilities, you sure can be dense sometimes. If you had bothered to truly observe those two, you would see that they are falling in love."

"Do you mind Daddy?"

"No. I actually think it is good for the both of them. Wind has been alone too long shutting herself away from the world. I know that ever since the death of Brent's wife he has also shut himself off from any romantic connections. I think it was destined. The day we met your mother, it was Brent that was in love with her first.

"I think your mother should follow her heart, as should you. You can tell her that for me too. I know that she is having doubts about starting something with Brent, feeling as if she is being unfaithful to me. But she has to realize that I am no longer with her and she is still a beautiful woman with her own life to lead."

"I will tell her." Kaya solemnly vowed.

"Kaya, I don't know if I will ever be able to speak with you again so there are some things I must say now. You were the light of my life and it makes me feel honored to see you fighting for the cause I believed in so strongly.

"As I said earlier, I believe that you are the one that was destined to lead LUPO to its successful conclusion. But it's not going to be easy. PARR and in particular Judah Arnold, are going to fight you with every ounce of strength they have. You will do things that you never thought you could do and you will have your doubts about whether you are able to accomplish what you aim to. But you are able to do it.

"One day, the entire world will join you in your struggle for justice and, when that day comes, the oppressors of rock and roll music will have to realize that they are beaten. Until that day though, just do what you feel is right. Don't ever look back to regret the past but live in the present and always look forward to welcome the future. Pay attention to your feelings about situations and your visions, more often than not they will be correct." Kansall paused, feeling Kaya absorb all that he had said.

"Since you are calmer now, I am going to have to leave. Just remember that I love you and I have faith in your ability to bring about justice." Kansall's voice and presence started to fade.

"Daddy! Don't go!" Kaya was stricken as she felt the comforting feeling start to fade. But no matter how much she pleaded, the feeling slowly faded away, leaving her all alone once more. With tears in her eyes, she turned and walked into Boyce.

"Hey! What's wrong?" Kaya shook her head, unable to speak for a moment.

At a loss on what to do, Boyce wrapped his arms around her and held Kaya tightly. They stood motionless for a few minutes until both realized that something stronger was coursing through them. Unable to resist the urge, Boyce tilted Kaya's head up to kiss her long and deep. A kiss that left them both breathless. Boyce placed his head on Kaya's shoulder.

"Do you know how long I've wanted to do that? I was just afraid you would punch me or something." Kaya laughed shakily.

"I guess I wanted it to. I just never knew it." Boyce's hands started to caress Kaya's body.

"Kaya, if you want me to stop you are going to have to kick me out now. The decision is yours." Boyce's voice dropped to a hoarse whisper as he began to gently nibble on her neck. "I just want you so badly."

Kaya was speechless. She was torn between the rules of respectability that she had been taught all her life and the thrilling sensations that Boyce was causing to run through her body as his caresses became bolder. As she fought against indecision, her father's words rang clearly through her memory.

"Follow your heart, Starlight."

In that moment, her decision was made. She relaxed, allowing Boyce to slowly undress her then they both slid to the floor.

CHAPTER Fifteen

Boyce gazed down at Kaya, sleeping under a layer of clothes. The lovemaking had been so fantastic that Boyce, who was usually difficult to satisfy, felt somewhat drained. Kaya was everything that he had imagined her to be since he had first had that vision on the beach. He felt as if he could stand and look at her forever but he soon heard someone approaching. Quickly, he knelt down to shake Kaya.

"Starlight. Wake up. Someone is coming."

Disorientated Kaya's eyes popped open. She had been dreaming of her father and the voice using her father's nickname for her had seemed to be part of the dream. Realizing that it had been Boyce calling her, Kaya brought herself back to the present to hurriedly get dressed. She had just finished doing her last button when Wind and Brent walked in.

The sight of Boyce and Kaya's flushed faces and the fact that Kaya was wearing her blouse inside out, told the older couple all they needed to know. Brent frowned slightly while Wind hid a smile.

"Just wondering where you two were." Wind commented lightly. “I just wanted to make sure that nothing had happened.”

Kaya blushed and quickly exchanged guilty glances with Boyce. It seemed wrong to her that, in such a time of trouble, they had stolen a few hours of enjoyment.

"Boyce, may I talk with you?" Brent asked sternly, though he was also having difficulty hiding a grin. Boyce, feeling like a guilty teenager, nodded. Then, in an act of defiance, gave Kaya a long deep kiss. Leaving the two women alone, Boyce followed Brent out of the room.

Wind started to laugh as soon as the door closed.

“You should have seen the look on your faces! Anyone would have thought that we had caught you in the act of doing something illegal instead of something as natural as making love!" Kaya blushed even harder, which sent Wind into fresh gales of laughter.

"There is no reason to be embarrassed. You are an adult and what you and Boyce did was as natural as breathing. In fact, everyone was wondering when it was going to happen."

"How did everyone know?" Kaya wondered aloud.

"For someone with your mental capabilities, you sure can be dense sometimes..." Wind stopped at the look on Kaya's face. The color had drained, leaving her looking ghostly and her eyes were glazed over.

"Daddy said the same thing to me."

Wind was puzzled.

"Your father told you that? When?"

"Earlier this evening." Seeing the look of doubt on her mother's face, Kaya hurried to explain.

“I'm not crazy Mom. I was standing at this window watching the stars and wishing I could speak with Dad. It was really weird because I felt so comforted suddenly, as if a blanket of security was thrown around me, blocking out all my problems and protecting me from the world.

"Then I heard Daddy's voice, as clearly as if he was standing beside me. Yet I know it was in my mind. "

"What did you talk about?" Wind was enthralled with Kaya's tale. And she didn't doubt for a moment that it was true.

"Well, we talked about the problems and accomplishments of LUPO then he mentioned you and Brent."

Here Wind was wary.

"What did he say?" Wind asked hesitantly. Kaya closed her eyes for a moment to recall her father's exact words.

"He said that, if I had bothered to watch you two, I would realize that you were falling in love."

Wind smiled gently as she pictured what Kansall’s face would have been like as he said that. She imagined that, though there would have been some pain showing across his features, she liked to think that he was happy for her.

"Then Daddy told me to pass a message on to you."

"And what was that?"

Kaya took her mother's hands in hers.

"The same advice he gave me. He said for you to follow your heart." A single tear ran down Wind's face. It was true that she and Brent were falling in love and she had mixed emotions about it. She was lonely, she knew that she had been alone too long but, though it was irrational, she felt as if she was being untrue to Kansall. Knowing that her previous husband approved and blessed this relationship eased her worries. She held out her arms to draw her daughter close, still too choked to speak.

Outside the room, Brent and Boyce sat on two crates talking.

"So do you think that you and Kaya are serious? Or are you just playing another one of your games and you’re stringing her along?"

Anger flashed momentarily in Boyce's eyes.

"I would never do that!” He hissed then remembered all the times he had done exactly that in the past. Boyce grinned sheepishly." At least not to Kaya. "

Brent laughed, the rich, deep musical tones echoing through the building.

"I'm glad to hear that. If Wind and I do get involved, it would cause additional tension if you had used Kaya."

Boyce's attention was caught with that statement.

"You and Wind? When did this happen?"

"It's been happening all along. We just don't live as fast as you and Kaya."

Boyce flushed. "Could we change the topic please? I am really uncomfortable discussing my relationship with Kaya."

"You shouldn't be that uncomfortable. You and Kaya having sex was a natural occurrence, especially in these times. "

"What do you mean in these times?"

"Look at it this way Boyce. You and Kaya have just been through an extremely exciting, dangerous escapade with rescuing Gleven. Then there is the constant danger that everyone here is in with the thought of PARR finding us at any moment. Your adrenaline has been on a constant high for the last two days and there has been no way for it to be released. Add to that, the sexual tension that has been interacting between you and Kaya and it was obvious that something was going to happen at any time. I wouldn't be surprised if both you and Kaya are feeling much better now that this strain you have been under has disappeared."

"Well, I do feel better now." Boyce admitted. "But I want you to understand that I really do care for Kaya. This isn't just a casual thing for me."

Brent smiled.

"You know the memory of Kaya that stands out in my mind? It's of this little girl crying over the dead body of her father. Somehow, since I was there and also ignored her warnings, it made me feel responsible for her. Over the years I've kept in touch with Gleven, not only because of LUPO but also so I could keep tabs on how Kaya and Wind were doing. They've been like my second family though they don't know it"

"I never knew that. How did Mom feel about it?"

"Your mother was one of the most understanding women I've ever met and she understood completely. The night that Kansall died, I wept in her arms. I can remember telling her how Kaya had looked; it was almost as if she felt it was all her fault."

Boyce leaned closer to his father.

"I remember that night. I must have been about ten years old and, even though that was fifteen years ago, that was the first and only time I had ever heard you cry. You didn't even cry when Mom died."

"Oh yes I did. I cried at her bedside for hours. I just made sure that you weren't around." Brent paused. "I loved that woman so much and I couldn't understand how the gods could take away my best friend and my wife. I was so certain that what we were fighting for was so right that I felt that it was unfair that I had to suffer so much pain when I was trying to do so much good. The only thing that helped me get through the days was you."

"And if it wasn't for you Dad, I would have been a total wreck," Boyce assured his father, "you were always there for me."

Brent shook off the painful memories of the past and smiled softly at his son. "But now you know why I am so protective of Wind and Kaya." Brent stated. “And talking of those two lovely ladies, I think we should join them."

Boyce nodded his agreement, father and son walked back into the room,

Later Kaya met with Gleven privately.

"Gleven, how do you feel about staying with LUPO?"

Gleven looked surprised.

"Hell, Kaya, I started this thing and I am going to finish it. Why?" Kaya shrugged.

"I was just wondering, what with everything that has happened to you with PARR, if you had had enough and was ready to retire,"

"Retire? Hell no! I want to get those bastards for putting me through all this."

Kaya chuckled and hugged Gleven warmly. Looking upwards, she silently sent her father a message, "As usual, Dad, you were right.”

CHAPTER Sixteen

Next morning

The abandoned warehouse

First thing in the morning a general meeting of all LUPO members was held. The senior members had met the evening before and coordinated how they were to arrange the division of all the people. Now Kaya started the meeting.

"We all know that we can't stay here much longer. Not only do we run a greater risk of PARR finding us but we will also start to develop cabin fever soon." Her eyes met Boyce's, who was sitting nearby, and she smiled.

"So unfortunately we are all going to have to leave in small groups. My main concern is that, once we leave here, those members that were picked up are going to be in danger. Before I start talking about any plans, are there any of you who now want to leave LUPO? All of us will understand if you do." This was the moment that Kaya had been dreading. Would anyone stand up to leave?

After a few minutes of silence, Osric, an old time member stood and Kaya's heart fell. If he left, how many others would go follow?

"Kaya. I have followed your father when he began then Gleven and now you. I knew the dangers of being involved from the first day I heard a whisper of LUPO. My dear girl, I live for LUPO. I have never had so much excitement in my life before and neither have most of the others." Here Osric's voice rose. "The only way I'll leave LUPO is in a casket." A shocked silence followed Osric's words then a deafening cheer rose. As when Kaya had asked for support for Gleven's release, one person had spoken up and the others had followed.

"Good! I am glad to see that we remain united because, after all, it is us against them! " Kaya shouted over the roar, "and we will win! "

Gleven listened for a moment then stood to get attention. Almost instantly, the room went quiet again.

"The support is great but if we don't keep it down, people will get suspicious and start investigating this warehouse."

Kaya took over again with a look of gratitude at Gleven.

"Here's the plan. Gleven and Margaret have decided to move to California. " Kaya paused to take a sip of water. "The best thing would be for the people who were captured to go to California or change their identity totally. Boyce will also be returning to California but Brent, Wind and I will be staying here." Kaya paused to look over the crowd of faces, some she knew quite well and others she didn't. "If you would let us know your decision soon, we would really appreciate it since we have to move quickly."

"We are also going to need some volunteers to go with me to the Underground city. We need to make up a lot of phony ID cards so anyone that knows what they are doing in that end would be a great help." Kaya looked over at the other senior members to see if they had anything to say but, when they all shook their heads; she turned back to the crowd.

"I guess that is all except I'm going to be going to the underground city as soon as darkness falls. If there is anyone who wishes to go with me, please see me before noon." With that, Kaya went to talk with Gleven and the other leaders.

"Kaya, I want to go with you." Kaya shook her head.

"I don't think so Boyce. It would be too dangerous for two leaders to leave at a time like this. I could understand it if it were an emergency and someone was in danger but this is a simple mission that I am certain I can handle alone. You would be more helpful here."

"But..." Boyce began.

Here Gleven, who had been listening to the exchange, interrupted.

"I'm afraid that Kaya's right. If anything should go wrong, not only would we lose two of our leaders but also the two youngest ones. You two are the lifeblood and future of LUPO. Brent and I are getting too old for dangerous escapades; in fact I'm surprised that we managed to get through the escape so well. If anything should happen to either of us LUPO is going to need both of you." Seeing that Boyce was going to protest, Gleven hurried to placate him.

"Besides, we are going to need your help here. After all, all these people do have to be organized."

Boyce grudgingly acceded but only with a warning to Kaya.

"Please be careful. Disguise yourself well and don't try to play the hero. I'd feel more comfortable if I knew that you weren't taking any unnecessary chances."

Kaya grinned.

"Don't worry.You have my solemn vow on all the above points."

Boyce watched Kaya leave, feeling apprehensive about the entire mission.

The dusk had deepened into night when Kaya and four others slipped cautiously out of the warehouse. Moving silently, they proceeded into the heart of the city. Neon lights flashed intermittently across the night inhabitants of the street. Kaya tensed as she gazed around at the people lounging in the doorways.

"Damn!" She swore softly. "All these PARR agents!"

Andric, a member of the Western Chapter, was walking beside her. At her words, he turned to Kaya, startled.

"Really? Where? How do you know?"

"Most of these people standing around are too clean cut for the usual night crawlers that hang out here." Kaya smiled grimly.

"Not only that, "she continued in an undertone "but there aren't any regulars down here. They all seem to be in hiding. This is a sure sign that some form of the law is down here undercover."

"Oh." was all that Andric could say. He had only heard of the heroic tales of Kaya's exploits and was slightly in awe of her. He knew could learn a lot from her. Silently, the five moved out of the lighted areas.

Andric Loren was a typical young man who thought he knew everything. His parents, who had idolized their golden boy from birth, had done nothing to discourage that notion. Though Andric's parents weren't wealthy, they had never denied Andric anything. And he had come to expect that from life. In his teens he had never had a problem getting any woman he wanted or any trophy. The day that a good friend had beaten Andric in a race, Andric had thrown a temper tantrum and refused to speak with his friend for a long time after that. But then Andric had joined LUPO. At first it had been a lark, something to do in his spare time. But it didn't take him too long to realize that the cause they were fighting for was just and that the fight was dangerous. At one point, Brent Mitchell had taken him aside and told him that he had better seriously think about his place in LUPO and whether he wanted to be here or not. It hadn't taken Andric long to realize that, for once, he was doing something worthwhile in his life. Without hesitation, Andric had stayed on.

Kaya breathed a little easier as they gradually moved towards the park where the entrance to their hideaway existed. But she still felt nervous. Something ominous was in the air. The closer they got to the tunnel, the more the nervousness increased. Subconsciously Kaya slowed the closer she got. She would be glad when all this was over.

Out of the corner of her eye Kaya caught a movement in the trees. Immediately she stopped in her tracks. Andric, who was following closely, nearly ran into her.

"What's wrong?"

Kaya took a moment before answering. "Something's not right." She whispered. "I thought I saw something in the trees."

"It's probably just a bum." Andric commented derisively. "You are just letting your imagination run away with you." Dismissing what he considered to be foolishness on Kaya's part, Andric stepped forward. Within a few moments, chaos had broken loose.

The figure that Kaya had glimpsed in the trees had been a PARR agent. They were, unfortunately, haunting the parks and deserted areas in search of the rebels. Even the clever disguises worn by Kaya and her group were not enough to deter the agents from investigating the group of supposed street bums. Belligerently one of the agents came up to Kaya. Looking over her grimy black hair, her scarred face and her generally slovenly appearance, he leered disgustedly.

"Hey Shane. Can you imagine sleeping with this one?"

Gary turned to face his colleague and, upon seeing Kaya, recognition flashed in his eyes but he didn't acknowledge her.

"Not really." Gary commented dryly. "We might as well let these degenerates go. They aren't who we are looking for."

His colleagues shrugged. They didn't really care one way or another. They just wanted their shift to be over so that they could go home. With a final menacing glare, the PARR agents let their captives go.

The five LUPO supporters started on their way, each holding their breath in case something else should go wrong. Unfortunately something did. Andric was rushing ahead of the others; anxious to get away when he tripped on a partially covered log. As he was falling to the ground, his head hit a low hanging branch, knocking his dark wig off. For one suspense filled moment, all was silent. Then the PARR agents started to move. Kaya went into action quickly. Since Gary was the closest agent to her, she darted over and grabbed his gun. Before anyone could react, Kaya had Gary's arm twisted behind his back and the gun pointed at his head.

"Don't anyone move or PARR is going to lose one of their top agents." Kaya warned.

"Gentlemen," Gary drawled, "I would like you to meet the infamous Kaya More."

Three pairs of eyes turned to Kaya with interest. Kaya, ignoring their inspection, backed away slowly.

"You guys get out of her!" She ordered the LUPO members behind her.

"What about you?" Andric asked.

"Don't worry about me. Just move it!" Kaya snapped.

"You'll never get away with shooting a top PARR agent like me." Gary warned. "PARR will be out for blood with my murder. They'll hang you for it. "

"Not if they can't find me." Kaya retorted. "And especially not if they can't find the body." This comment succeeded in quietening Gary for the moment.

He wasn't too sure whether Kaya was serious or not. '*Would she really kill him?*' Unconsciously, he shivered at the thought. Kaya continued to back away, holding her captive closely.

One of the agents apparently decided that Kaya was bluffing and slowly started edging his way closer.

Watching him out of the corner of her eye, Kaya let him take a few more steps then fired the gun at his feet. The man was stopped in his tracks.

"Jesus Christ. You almost hit me! "Kaya looked toward him with disgust.

"Wasn't even close and I told you to stay away."

"Well now, there is only one of you and three of us and we are all armed, so I don't think that you are calling the shots any more."

Kaya grinned wickedly, still backing away.

"There may only be one of me, but I got him. And if any of you rush me, not only will he die but also so will at least one of you. Which of you is willing to die?" Silence fell over the group. None of them were too anxious to die.

"I'd believe her if I were you." Gary said. "This lady is quite capable of doing whatever she says so just back off."

The PARR agents halted, uncertain of what to do. One of the men decided that Kaya wasn't as dangerous as she seemed.

'After all she was a skinny woman, wasn't she?' Determined to save Gary and earn himself extra points with PARR, he rushed toward the two.

Kaya, without thinking of her actions, pointed the gun at the oncoming man and fired. With a small cry of pain and surprise, the would-be attacker went down, blood welling from his chest. The other agents were all too surprised to do anything.

"Oh my God!" Andric breathed in the trees where he and the other four men were hidden. "She really shot him!" Andric had decided that they couldn't leave Kaya alone so had stayed to lend a hand wherever they could. Now, with these new developments, they knew that they had to go back to the warehouse and get help.

Andric Loren's heart was pounding furiously as he ran, partially from the exertion he was placing on his body and partly from the panic he felt over the turn of events.

"And don't try to follow me!" Kaya ordered the other agents. "Or this time, he definitely dies!" Kaya jammed the gun into Gary's side roughly, causing him to moan audibly with pain. Then, with a sharp twist on his arm, Kaya convinced Gary to start moving. Kaya More was on the run.

Andric and the others were also running. They were going back to the warehouse to notify everyone of what had happened. Back along the route they had previously taken, the four ran. Without question, people parted ways to let them pass as soon as possible. All seemed to be going well, no obstacles in their way, until a burly man stepped in their path.

"What's going on?" He demanded gruffly. Andric gulped for air. Was this man a PARR agent or not? Somehow, Andric didn't think so but how could he be sure? Andric decided to take a chance.

"A friend of ours is in trouble and we have to get help."

The man's eyes widened.

“Something has happened to Starlight? What have those bastards from PARR done now?”

Andric was taken aback for a moment. He still wasn't sure if he could trust this man and the stranger smiled in understanding.

“Don’t worry. I'm a friend, my name is Calo.” The man held out a giant hand to be shaken, which Andric took warily. As if reassuring Andric, Calo recited, in an undertone, the first stanza of the fighting song for LUPO.

”Do they know what they're doin?

With all their lies.

Will life be worth livin?

If the music dies?” Together, Andric and Calo completed the verse then Andric shook the large man's hand vigorously.

“We have to go to the others for help.” Andric stated after he had explained the situation.

"Tell Gleven to stop in at the Underground Cafe and we will try to round up some help for Kaya. He knows where it is.” Andric thanked Calo then was on his way again.

Calo Jonas was a massive man who was six foot three of solid muscle. And though his physical appearance was threatening, he had the heart of a teddy bear. He had known early on in life that he didn't fit in with normal society so he had left his middle class beginnings and opened a restaurant on skid row. To the street dwellers, he represented security since he was always willing to help those less fortunate. And, in turn, they were more than willing to help him.

Bursting into the warehouse, the four men stopped to catch their breath. After a brief moment, they ran up a flight of stairs to where, they hoped, Brent, Gleven, Boyce and Wind would be.

"Where's Kaya?" Boyce demanded as he jumped to his feet, the earlier apprehension he had felt now overwhelming him. Striding over to Andric, he towered over the younger man and demanded,

“What happened? Where is she?" Andric, still gasping for air, was unable to answer. Frustrated, Boyce started shaking the younger man violently as if he could shake the answer out of him.

"Boyce! Stop it!" Wind yelled as she ran up to them with Brent and Gleven directly behind her. When Boyce kept shaking Andric, she pounded on his back.

"How can you expect him to answer when you are shaking his teeth out?"

Infuriated by the blows to his back, Boyce turned to hit his attacker but fortunately regained his senses in time and his hands dropped to his sides. Gleven then proceeded to ask the shaken Andric once more.

"What happened? Where's Kaya?"

Andric shot a fearful glance at Boyce and stepped back.

"We were almost to the tunnel of the underground city when these four PARR agents were on us. They realized that we were in disguise and Kaya managed to grab one guy's gun before they could do anything. "She was standing there, with this Shane guy's arm twisted behind his back and the gun pointed at his head, telling the others to back off."

"Did you say Shane?" Gleven interrupted.

"Yeah. Why? Do you know him?"

"That's the guy that was romancing my daughter to get to us." Gleven explained in disgust "and he has met Kaya before."

"Anyway," Andric continued "then one agent apparently decided that Kaya was joking and rushed her. Kaya shot him."

"Why didn't you stay with her?" Boyce demanded.

"Because she had already told us earlier to leave and instead we hid. I thought the best thing to do was to get help!" Andric was again backing away from Boyce in case his temper flew out of control.

"It was better that way." Brent commented softly, hoping to calm his son. "Kaya has more of a chance to get away if she doesn't have to worry about anyone else."

"But what do we do now?" Boyce asked. He was sick with worry that something terrible might have already happened to Kaya. Unwanted thoughts of Kaya in the hands of PARR or, perhaps worse, lying dead somewhere, crossed his mind. They had to do something.

Andric continued hesitantly.

"We ran into a man named Calo in the neon district. He said to tell Gleven to meet him at the Underground Cafe and he would try to get help."

"Good old Calo." Gleven commented. "It was outside his cafe that Kansan was shot and, since that day, he has been a loyal supporter. He's the one that has been supplying us with all this food for the last three days though where he got it I don't know. "

"But we have to be careful." Andric added. "There are PARR agents all over the place down there." Gleven nodded his understanding and turned back to Boyce, Brent and Wind.

"I am definitely going to look for Kaya. I think I might know where she would have gone."

"I'm going too." Boyce stated firmly.

"Then we'll stay here." Brent suggested. "We can't leave all these people without some form of leadership."

Andric hesitantly cleared his throat.

"May I go too? I feel kind of responsible. "

Boyce and Gleven exchanged glances then Boyce walked up to Andric and held out his hand.

"Of course. And I'm sorry for giving you such a rough time earlier. You only did what you thought was right."

Gratefully Andric took Boyce's hand and shook it. The escapade to find Kaya was underway.

CHAPTER Seventeen

Kaya gave Gary a hard shove that sent him sprawling. "We'll rest now." She ordered.

Gary pulled himself up to a sitting position and rubbed his arm gingerly. They had been running for what seemed like hours and, although he was in good shape, it was obvious that Kaya was in better.

"What are you going to do with me now? Kill me?" He asked. Kaya didn't answer, just fixed him with an impassive stare.

"You sure haven't thought this one out. Killing a PARR agent means your life. But I do know a way around it."

Kaya was suspicious but curious.

"How?" Gary thought that she was generally interested and leaned forward to outline his plan.

"Marry me."

Kaya laughed.

"What? Do you actually think I would marry you?"

Gary was enraged that Kaya was not only adamant about not even considering marrying him but was also laughing at the suggestion. However he covered it well.

"If you married me," he began "we could arrange something with Judah. Especially since you wouldn't be with LUPO any longer and, therefore, you would no longer be a threat to PARR."

Kaya was surprised. This man was actually serious about her marrying him and leaving LUPO.

"Why would I leave LUPO?" She asked.

Gary sneered.

"Once I was in your bed, all those crazy thoughts about bringing back the music would be crowded out. All you would want is me."

Kaya was speechless with Gary's arrogance. The conceit of this man overpowered anything she had ever faced before. Shaking her head with amusement, she motioned Gary back on his feet.

"Let's go. We have a lot of ground to cover before dawn."

Gary got to his feet, confident that Kaya was giving serious consideration to his proposal. In actuality, Kaya's thoughts were on surviving this night.

Gleven knocked softly on the back door to the Underground Cafe. Within a few moments, the door opened and Calo motioned them inside. Without preamble, he told them what was going on.

"I've got fifty people ready to help look for Kaya. They are ready to go as soon as you say."

"Thanks." Gleven said quickly then turned to introduce Boyce. "This is Brent Mitchell's son, Boyce and you have already met Andric."

Calo's face broke into a wreath of smiles. "The next generation of LUPO fighters! I thought that Boyce looked familiar. Can sure see the family resemblance there. Glad to meet you Boyce." The two men shook hands then Calo greeted Andric before going into another room where the volunteers were waiting.

"So we'll meet back here at dawn to let everyone know what progress has been made. All right?" Gleven stated. A murmur of agreement went through the crowd and all got to their feet and exited the room. Gleven turned to Calo.

"Thanks for the help. You don't know how much we appreciate all you have done for us."

"Just bring Kaya back safely. That is all I'm interested in."

Gleven shook the man's hand silently and then he, Boyce and Andric were on their way.

Kaya was out of breath and had to take another rest. Once again she told Gary to sit down, far enough away from her so as not to be threatening yet close enough that she could still keep an eye on him.

"So have you thought about my proposal?" Gary asked certain that Kaya was now willing to accept his offer of marriage.

Kaya though just stared blankly at him for a moment. After a few seconds, she realized what he was talking about.

“I'm not going to marry you." Kaya stated flatly.

"You don't know what you are missing. Just ask Krista."

At the mention of the woman who had once been a close friend, Kaya's eyes hardened and her mouth set into a thin line.

"I told you, I'm not interested." The change in expression in Kaya's face did not go unnoticed by Gary.

Since she wouldn't marry him he had to think of another way out of this predicament. It appealed to Gary that any mention of his and Krista's relationship seemed to infuriate Kaya. If he could perhaps get her angry enough, then Gary knew he would have the upper hand.

"Yeah, you should really talk to Krista. That little slut was made in my bed." Gary stopped to look at Kaya but she just stared back at him, her face impassive and her emotions hidden.

"The things that chick can do in the sack. That is the only reason I am keeping her around. I wonder who taught her some of the things she knows." Here Gary turned sly.

"Did you two have the same teacher? Did you all have an enjoyable threesome? I could just see you and Krista in the sack together."

Kaya remained silent though she was raging inside. None of this however showed on her face. Gary edged a little closer thinking he was unnoticed.

"Did you teach her how to lick me in certain places so that I always have a hard on? Did you two practice on each other? Come on, you can tell me." All the while Gary was edging closer to Kaya, getting ready to attack.

"Why don't you show me some of your talents? We could make this an evening you will remember."

Kaya lifted the gun she was holding and pointed it at Gary's genitals.

"Come any closer and I will make sure that this will be an evening you will remember."

Gary hesitated, uncertain of his next move. Before he could decide, a gun was pointed at his head from behind.

"Good night, Prince Charming." Boyce said sarcastically as he hit Gary across the side of the head with his gun. Gary fell unconscious to the ground.

Kaya stared at Gary's limp form for a moment then up at Boyce.

"Would you really have shot him in the groin?" Boyce asked.

Kaya grinned.

"I don't know. I think I would have done the world a favor if I had though."

Boyce laughed as he came forward to take Kaya in his arms.

"Glad you're safe." Calo told Kaya. "We were all worried about you." They were all in the back room to the Underground Café; dawn was just breaking over the horizon.

"The next thing to do, Kaya, is to get you out of the city," Gleven remarked.

"How are we going to do that?" Kaya queried. "All the exits are blocked and PARR is definitely going to be looking for me now."

"Then we are just going to have to think of something else then aren't we?" Calo smiled and led them down to the basement.

CHAPTER Eighteen

Same time
Judah Arnold's apartment

The dawn cast a misty haze over the large, solitary figure lying in the bed. A sudden shrilling of the telephone broke the silence, causing the figure to stir restlessly. A large arm emerged from the bedcovers to pick up the receiver.

“This had better be important." Judah growled in way of a greeting.

"Kaya More has been sighted." The voice on the other end related. Instantly, Judah came awake.

"What? Where?"

"In a park last night. She shot one of our agents then ran away with Gary Shane as a hostage."

“Anything else?"

"Just that the search is on for Kaya More and we won't stop until we find her."

"I will be in the office within the hour." Judah hung up without further conversation and hauled his ever-growing body out of the bed. His bare feet padded heavily on the carpeted floor on the way to the bathroom.

In the shower, Judah allowed himself the luxury of laughing.

“Miss More, you've fixed yourself this time." He crowed gleefully. "Shooting a PARR agent really puts you in my hands! I’ve got you now!”

Judah walked into his office to face utter chaos. Agents were running around everywhere, the ones that had been on the patrol when Kaya had been sighted were waiting in his office. The others were trying to find out all they could. Someone had actually seen the legendary Miss Kaya More! A scowl from Judah though brought everything back to order. Without saying a word he walked into his office to interview the agents waiting there.

“So Gary Shane introduced her as Kaya More after she had him prisoner?” Judah asked once more.

“Yes.” One of the agents gulped. “It was as if he knew her.”

Judah's brow furrowed in concentration. He knew that Gary had met Kaya More before but was it possible that he was going to let her go last night? Judah knew that she was beautiful but he refused to believe the possibility that one of his top agents would turn on him and PARR.

“Mr. Arnold.” One of his minions cried as he burst in the door. “Gary Shane has been found! He is currently in the General Hospital if you want to go to talk with him.”

“The General Hospital?” Judah repeated. “What happened to him?”

“Just a bump on the head. A big one by the sounds of it. The doctors think he may have a concussion.”

Judah nodded then stood.

“Our interview is over gentlemen. I am sorry about your comrade's condition but I assure you that Kaya More will be brought to justice.” Judah then exited the office on his way to the hospital to question Gary Shane further.

Gary's hospital room was bleak and bare of flowers. In one corner Krista sat weeping. Upon entry, Judah merely glanced at her then proceeded to talk with Gary.

“Did you know it was Kaya More before she took you hostage?” Judah growled without a greeting. Gary was prepared for this and his face showed nothing.

"No, I only knew after she grabbed me.”

“What helped you figure it out?”

Gary's mind rapidly sought an answer.

"I just kind of guessed. She was the right height and build for Kaya, even under that disguise and, I mean, who else would it be?"

Judah was still suspicious but didn't say any more on the topic.

"The doctors tell me that you can be released tomorrow. You can take tomorrow off but I want you back at work the following day."

"Excuse me, Mr. Arnold." Krista began hesitantly from the corner.

Judah turned in surprise. He had forgotten that she was there.

"What are you going to do with Kaya when you find her?" Krista asked quietly.

"That is not for public information but I assure you that she is going to have to withstand a lot of pain before she is put to death."

"Good." Krista licked her lips in satisfaction. "Did you know that she propositioned Gary and promised to do all sort of disgusting things to him if he wouldn't mention he had seen her and promised to help LUPO?"

Judah swung back to Gary who was silently cursing Krista for opening her mouth. Though Judah didn't say anything to either Krista or Gary, he felt that it was more than likely Gary that had made the comments and not Kaya. Judah tipped his hat and left.

Once Judah was gone, Gary swore at Krista.

"Jesus Christ. Didn't I tell you to keep your mouth shut on that topic? I only told you so that you would realize what pain and suffering I had to go through! "

"I'm sorry, Gary." Krista's voice was meek. "I just get so angry whenever I think of Kaya doing something like that. She has always tried to take away what I have and ruin my happiness."

"Well, don't worry. Just please don't mention things I tell you to other people. You could get us both killed."

Krista nodded her agreement as she approached the bed. Her hand went under the sheets and started caressing Gary intimately.

Gary's moan of pleasure was music to her ears.

"Lock the door." Gary ordered in a husky voice.

CHAPTER Nineteen

Later that day

An exit out of New York City

The fluorescent van pulled up to the PARR check stop and waited for the guard to pass them through. The PARR agent approached the van warily. He had seen enough weirdoes since his shift had begun and didn't know if he could keep his composure for another. Hiding a smile of amusement, the agent went up to the window on the driver's side.

The window was rolled down to reveal a young man in his twenties with long, dirty blond hair. His clothing consisted of a sack like robe, with a string of beads and a peace sign hanging from his neck. His face wore spectacles, small and round and a few days growth of beard was visible.

"Can I help you brother?" The man asked.

The agent cleared his throat, trying to cover a laugh.

“Yeah. Where are you going?"

"To California. The land of sin and sunshine. We are on our way to preach the ways of peace.”

Once again, the agent fought to control his himself.

"How many of there are you?" He managed to choke out.

"Myself and four others. We are going to save the world from its own destruction."

This time the agent had to turn away to keep from laughing aloud. *‘Where did these people come from?’*

"Have you seen these people?" The agent handed the driver a paper with copies of four photographs on it.

The driver looked carefully at the pictures of Kaya, Brent, Gleven and Boyce then carefully shook his head.

"No, I’m sorry but I haven't." The driver passed the paper back to the four others in the back seat for them to look at.

A girl in a large sun hat passed the paper back to him.

"Sorry Brother John. None of us have seen them." The girl said in a distinct southern drawl.

"Why don't you just keep this and, if you should happen to see any or all of these people, phone a PARR agency near you."

"Oh we will!" The driver solemnly vowed. "There will be no peace in this land as long as we allow people to be on the run. If you men are looking for them, they must be serious criminals."

“Just be on your way." The agent responded gruffly.

With a final salute for peace, the van pulled out of the check stop, leaving the agents laughing.

Once the van was out of sight, it pulled over to the side of the road. The occupants of the van were also laughing uncontrollably.

"I don't believe they fell for that." Kaya laughed as she pulled off the large sun hat. Boyce was lying besides her, also laughing hard.

"We were lucky." Gleven admonished gently. "But Andric you did a fantastic job." The driver turned around and smiled.

"It was easy." Andric commented. "I was born to do this kind of stuff."

"Let's get going before we get checked again." Margaret suggested. Sobering, the rest agreed and Andric once more put the van into motion.

All day they traveled along the highway. California was their destination and, hopefully, some place they could be safe for a while. Boyce sat with his arm around Kaya, listening to the comforting sounds of her breathing.

"Kaya," he began.

"Mmm." Kaya, who was almost asleep, answered.

"Why did you decide to join LUPO?"

Instantly Kaya came awake.

"Because I felt, at first, that I owed it to my father. Then, as time went on, I realized what a crime censorship is. No one in this world should be able to tell adults what they should hear, see or do. As long as they are not hurting anyone else, who has the right to say?" Kaya's voice had risen on each phrase until she was close to yelling at the end. Embarrassed by the stares of the others, she subsided beside Boyce.

"Why did you join?" She asked meekly.

"One day, I had just finished surfing, I saw my Dad on the beach waiting to talk to me. He told me about this girl back in New York that had just been raped by PARR agents."

"Krista Andrews." Kaya interrupted.

"Yeah. Well, he explained LUPO and its cause. Then he took me to hear some music. I'm telling you Kaya, I have never felt the same feelings as I felt that day. It was fantastic! Almost as if I could do anything."

Kaya nodded her understanding.

"I know what you mean. I played keyboards in a school band and one day, at rehearsal saw this music score in my mind. I started to play and, like you, as soon as I heard the music I felt as if I could do anything. I guess that is what rock and roll is all about."

"The power of good feelings. The invincibility of youth." Boyce finished for her. Gleven, who had been listening in the background, added his piece.

"It's us against the world. And, if you are one of the members of the establishment, you are one of them."

Boyce and Kaya thought about that for a moment.

"Us against the world." Kaya repeated thoughtfully. "Kind of like us, don't you think?" Boyce and Gleven laughed.

"Yeah, I guess so." Gleven admitted.

Andric, who had also been eavesdropping, spoke up.

“But we are going to win!" Silence reigned for a moment and then Boyce lifted his right arm.

"To victory! To the success of LUPO!" He cheered.

"Long live rock and roll!" Kaya joined in.

Amid the noise of everyone cheering, Gleven offered a silent prayer to the heavens.

"Let us live to see that day."

CHAPTER Twenty

Five days later
A California highway

As dawn was breaking on the fifth day, the fluorescent van rolled along the California highway. The ocean rolled and pitched as it had done for all time, welcoming the rebels to a haven from harm.

Kaya looked out over the ocean in wonder. Being the first time she had left New York, she was astounded at the beauty of it all. She had seen the ocean before, of course, but this was somehow different. Grabbing Boyce's arm, she tugged urgently on it.

"Boyce! Is this what you have always grown up with?"

Boyce smiled at her excitement.

"Of course. The ocean doesn't really change, no matter how hard we try to make it."

Kaya let go of his arm to go to the window and once more watch the scenery before her.

The van pulled up in front of a restaurant near the pier. This was the same restaurant where Boyce had first joined LUPO and the owner was the same. Donning their costumes, the five went into the restaurant.

The dining room was almost empty which fit Boyce's plans. As he motioned the others to take a seat, he went to find Steven. In the kitchen he found the man preparing a meal for the restaurant's few customers.

"Peace be with you my brother." Boyce's voice was low.

Surprised, Steven turned to see a crazy looking man standing there with his arms in the air. Scowling, he moved closer, intent on kicking the man out. However, when he drew close enough to get a clearer look at the face of the stranger, he drew back in astonishment.

"Boyce! What are you doing in that get up?"

Boyce just grinned.

"I have some people for you to meet outside. How long before the restaurant is clear?" Steven glanced at his wristwatch.

"Shouldn't be long now. I think those people are just waiting to hit the beach so they will probably eat quickly then leave."

Boyce nodded.

"We will be right outside in the dining room. And I must confess that we are hungry." Steven chuckled.

"And how many are there?"

Boyce looked sheepish. "Five."

"Five! You LUPO guys are going to eat me out of business." Steven joked.

"Trust me; it will be well worth your while. You just wait until you see whom I've brought back for you to meet!"

Steven looked curious and urged Boyce to go back out to the dining room. With a final wish for peace, Boyce went out to join his friends.

Steven locked the restaurant door, drew the curtains then came to sit beside Boyce and his companions.

"So what's my surprise?"

Boyce grinned and pointed to one of the men.

"This is Gleven Andrews."

Steven looked impressed.

"The Gleven Andrews? Very pleased to meet you." Steven shook hands with the older gentleman happily as Gleven introduced Margaret.

Boyce just kept grinning. Steven had often admired the exploits of Kaya More and expressed the desire to meet her someday.

"Excuse me, Steven. Before you get overwhelmed with meeting royalty." Boyce paused to wink at Gleven who winked back. "There is someone else here that I am sure you would like to meet."

Steven turned to Boyce expectantly.

"Wipe that stupid grin off your face and tell me who it is." Steven snapped good-naturedly.

Boyce took a deep breath, trying to be dramatic and removed Kaya's hat and wig with a flourish.

"This is Kaya More!"

Steven was speechless for a moment. For the last five years, he had been hearing stories about Kaya More and all she had done for LUPO. Now he finally had the chance to meet her.

"Very happy to meet you. I can't believe this. I have two of the most famous members of LUPO right here in my own restaurant. One day, this is going to be a landmark."

Kaya's laugh was honest and natural.

"I don't think we're that great! If anything, it will be a landmark because you, as owner, supported the fight to bring back rock and roll, not because we are here."

Steven looked thoughtful for a moment then shrugged.

"Whatever. It is still an honor to have you two here." Turning to Boyce, he continued, "By the way, what are they doing here? And where are all the others?"

"Dad had decided to stay in New York and I'm not sure about the other members. Some are going to stay there and some are going to come back here. Some of the New York members are also going to come here."

Kaya interrupted.

"It is too dangerous for some of them to stay in New York. PARR knows their faces too well and anything they tried to do would only be complicated by PARR knowing how to stop it."

Steven nodded.

"And what about you two?" He asked." Are you two also in immediate danger?"

"Kaya, Boyce and the others rescued me from jail." Gleven explained. "And they waited until the last possible moment. I was scheduled for execution two hours later when they rescued me."

"Was it ever exciting, Steven. You should have been there." Andric threw in. "Dressed as PARR agents and sneaking into PARR headquarters. Then we had explosions going off all over the place and it was like a madhouse. Though I missed most of it because I was driving."

"Was anyone hurt?" Steven asked, concerned.

Gleven smiled.

"Miraculously, no."

"Except for that PARR agent that Kaya shot." Andric said.

"But that wasn't part of Gleven's rescue," Boyce argued. "That came later."

Steven looked at Gleven and Margaret with his eyebrows raised.

"Sounds like it was quite the trip!"

Margaret laughed softly.

"It is a time that I will never forget. Later, Gleven and I will tell you everything. All right?"

"That sounds great." Steven agreed. Looking out the window, he noticed that the shadows of people walking past.

"I think you guys had better go downstairs so you're out of sight. Boyce, you know the way. I think there are some things that Kaya and Gleven would be very interested in. After it gets dark, we'll move whatever vehicle you came in."

"Sure thing. Let's go people." Boyce stood and motioned for the others to follow him.

Down in the secret room, Kaya shivered. This place looked like a replica of days gone by. On the walls hung posters of rock bands that had long been abolished, the primary one being Mytique.

Boyce went to the safe, took out the CD, and turned the music on. It was like a dream come true.

"I feel so close to these musicians." Kaya commented.

Boyce shrugged.

"So you should. This place is a monument to them and all their kind."

"It's like everything we've been fighting for." Gleven marvelled.

"True." Boyce answered. "But, for the moment, it is just for one person and the select few that he invites down here."

"And he has to live in fear of being caught and imprisoned by PARR if they find out." Kaya added. "This is what we have been fighting for. What good is it if the entire population is not allowed to listen to the music? If those who have been fortunate enough to find the music are made to shut themselves up so that they can enjoy it and always have to worry about being caught? It isn't right!"

The entire room started to laugh.

"That's my Kaya! " Gleven remarked proudly. "Always the righter of wrongs."

Kaya blushed, realizing that she had perhaps gone off the handle again.

"Sorry guys. I guess I just get a little upset and vocal about what we are fighting for."

No need to apologize Kaya." Andric said quickly. "That fire is what makes you a good leader of LUPO and what makes PARR so afraid of you."

"PARR? Afraid of me?" Kaya said.

"Yes." Andric added. "Why do you think that they want to shut you up so badly? They are afraid that, if you get a real chance to talk with the public, you could start a revolution like this country has never seen before. At least not since the first civil war."

The occupants of the downstairs room were silent for a moment while they thought this out.

Then Kaya smiled, remembering the words spoken to her that night in the warehouse.

"But we won't win until the entire world joins us in our struggle for justice." She said quietly. "Then the opposition to rock and roll will know that they are beaten."

Once again, the room was silent, ruminating on Kaya's words. Then Boyce shook the introspection off and turned to Kaya.

"Did you know that this restaurant was built on the site of the last rock concert that was ever played? And the band playing was..."

"Mystique." Kaya interrupted. "I know the history. The place was levelled by an earthquake that night and no one knows what ever became of the equipment that was used at that concert."

"Top of the line stuff." Boyce mused. "Maybe Mystique made it vanish into thin air at the right moment?" He jokingly added.

Kaya threw him a look of disgust.

"They were rock musicians not demons. No matter what PARR said at the time."

Boyce pretended to sulk.

"I was only kidding! Can't you take a joke?"

Kaya blew him a kiss then proceeded to look around the small enclosure.

"I would really like to know what happened that night." Seeing that Boyce was about to speak, she held up her hand to stop him. "I mean really. Not what we learned in school or what PARR has told us but really happened. What the fans that were there, against all laws of course, the musicians and the bystanders thought."

"I heard it was a real massacre." Andric timidly submitted.

"I can well guess it was." Kaya said thoughtfully. "I mean they were breaking the law. And we know what PARR can be like now, what were they like then?"

Gleven started to laugh.

"I wonder if a relative of Judah Arnold was leading PARR at that time. If they were, I can bet you that it was just as nasty as it is now."

Kaya chuckled then stopped as she felt the ground below her start to shake. Confused, she looked at Boyce.

The color had drained from his face and he was looking quite apprehensive.

"Earthquake." He moaned. "We haven't had one of these in years." Without thinking, all sank to the ground to sit and wait things out. Violently the building and ground shook, almost as if the ghosts of days gone by were angry with the LUPO members for invading their solitude.

"Oh my God!" Kaya said.

Gleven, Boyce and the other two turned to stare at her.

"What?" Boyce asked, frightened.

Kaya was unable to speak. Instead she pointed to the one wall, which was crumbling before their eyes.

"I don't believe it!" Boyce gasped.

Gleven, Margaret and Andric just sat there speechless and watched the scene unfold before them.

The earthquake stopped and the wall ceased crumbling as if on order. Before the astonished five lay a room that had been hidden for years. Concert equipment lay in perfect order waiting; it seemed, for the musicians to pick up the equipment and start playing once again.

Kaya, having gotten to her feet first, wandered over to the previously hidden room. Picking up a sheet of music she gave a cry of surprise.

"This is the same music score that I saw that day in high school! And it is one of Mystique's."

Boyce hurried to look over her shoulder while Andric was in search of other treasures. Gleven and Margaret just sat in the same position they had been before. They were too stunned to move.

"Look at this!" Andric yelled." Come look at what I've found. "

Placing the music score down carefully, Boyce and Kaya went over to see what Andric had discovered. In his hands, he held an old VHS video.

"Do we have anything that will play this?" Kaya asked.

Boyce shook his head.

“I don't know but I will go upstairs and check with Steven." He raced up the stairs to inform Steven of their discovery, leaving Andric and Kaya to search a little more.

Upstairs, Boyce stopped in amazement. Nothing up here was disturbed.

Steven, who was doing some book work at one of the tables, looked up at Boyce.

"What's the matter Boyce? Is everything all right down there?"

Boyce just shook his head.

"Didn't you feel that earthquake? It was a massive one!"

"Earthquake? You must be joking because I never felt a thing up here."

"Well it knocked down one of your walls downstairs and really shook us up!"

"Come on Boyce! Enough of your jokes." Steven chuckled and went to go back to his books but Boyce stopped him.

"Didn't you hear what I said? The earthquake we felt knocked down one of the walls and that revealed a secret room."

Here Steven's attention was captured.

"A secret room?"

"Yeah. With music scores and equipment. God, it looks like it was set up for a rock concert that never happened."

"You're kidding, aren't you?"

"I'm not! We also found this old video. It looks like it was used on a VCR. Do you have anything that will play it?"

Steven thought for a moment then nodded.

"Yes, I do. I will just bring it downstairs. By the way do you realize that, if that tape has on it what I think it does, you people might be seeing your first rock concert?"

CHAPTER Twenty-One

The evening of the same day
New York City

The sun was setting on New York City as Brent and Wind relaxed on a couch near the window. The inhabitants of the warehouse had all been successfully disbanded to safety throughout the city and, finally, Brent and Wind could take a breather.

"I hope that Kaya, Boyce and the others got out of the city safely." Wind said with concern.

Brent hugged her close.

"Don't worry." He reassured her. "The road blocks are still up and nothing has been announced. I think that if PARR had captured them it would have been all over the news by now."

Wind silently agreed though she was still worried about them.

"I guess I should stop worrying. After all, there isn't anything I can do about it" Wind admitted.

"That's my girl." Brent said cheerfully. He too was concerned though and, even if he didn't want to tell Wind, he was afraid something had happened to the kids. Shaking the thought from his mind, he cuddled closer to Wind.

The midnight moon was turning everything silvery as Brent pulled himself out of bed quietly. He moved rapidly around the room, trying not to disturb Wind but as soon as he reached the door he heard her voice.

"Are you going to call California?" Wind asked softly.

In the darkness Brent smiled.

"Yes. Do you mind?"

"No. Just give them my love."

Brent went back to the bed to give Wind a kiss.

"Be back as soon as I can." He whispered. Then, without further conversation, Brent left.

At a pay phone near their apartment, Brent placed the call to California. Shivering with the cold and nerves, he waited for someone to answer the phone. Relieved he heard Boyce's voice.

"Are all the lambs safely tucked away?"

Immediately, Boyce knew who was calling.

“The sheep have all come home."

"Good. The ewe sends her love."

"I'll pass the message along."

The line went dead then and Brent went back to the apartment to tell Wind the good news.

"That was Dad." Boyce said as he came into the room.

Kaya looked up from the music score she was studying.

“Are they all right?”

"Yes and your mother sends her love."

"I got it!" Steven exclaimed from the machine he was working on.

Gleven, Margaret, Boyce, Andric and Kaya all gathered around to see what was on the video that had been found. With anticipation, they waited for the picture to come on the screen.

At first it was fuzzy, the scene hard to distinguish. Then it came together with alarming clarity. There, right in front of them, was a video of a rock concert. Steven turned up the volume before he came to sit beside them.

The concert opened with an unknown band to the spectators playing. Everyone was unconsciously holding their breaths as they watched the antics of the lead singer.

Kaya, curious to know whom this band was, picked up the video case to see if there might be any clue to their identity.

“Raser and Mystique.” She read aloud.

With pelvic thrusts and amazingly high jumps, the lead singer of Raser visually entertained the audience. Kaya smiled as she saw the screaming young girls trying to get closer to the band. Then, all too soon, Raser finished their show and went off the stage. The main act was about to begin. Kaya shivered with excitement. She could just imagine how the people that had actually attended the concert had felt. The rush of adrenaline was incredible! Impatient for the show to continue, she fidgeted in her seat.

Bradley Mitchell was the first on stage. Doing a lick on his guitar that had the fans, both live and watching the video, spellbound, Bradley signified the beginning of the main act. Once Bradley was finished, the other band members came on stage.

Boyce and Kaya felt a twinge of excitement when Daniel More stepped up to the keyboards, Cal Jensen to the bass, Rick Young to the drum kit and, last but certainly not least, Ron Stopford to the mike at the front of the stage.

"Hello rock fans!" Ron yelled over the crowd's cheers. "I'm sure glad to see that you are still supporting us even though PARR is making it very difficult."

"Are they ever." Gleven muttered.

"We won't let rock and roll die, will we?" Ron waited only seconds for the enthusiastic response from the crowd. "And if PARR does manage to take it away, we won't stop until we bring it back!" The video camera moved in for a close up of Ron's face and Kaya felt a chill run along her spine. It was if the man was staring straight at her.

"We will bring it back." She solemnly and silently vowed to the figure on the screen.

“Now that all that bullshit is out of the way,” Ron continued. “Let's rock!” With that, the concert was under way.

However, after the third song, the now all too familiar uniform of PARR was seen on several men. The horror that had occurred that night became apparent as the PARR agents swung their clubs without regard to who was in their path. Through it all though, Mystique kept playing. Then the picture went out as the camera was obviously destroyed.

The occupants of the room were silent as they watched the blank screen where, just a few moments before, they had been watching the exhilarating event of a rock concert. If any of them had possessed doubts concerning PARR’s violence earlier, they had all vanished with the scene they had just witnessed. Each thought about the horrors that had progressed after the video had been switched off. To everyone came a thought simultaneously,

"No matter what it takes, PARR must be stopped and never again be allowed to submit others to the horrors that occurred that night.”

CHAPTER Twenty-Two

The next day
New York City

Judah Arnold sat at a meeting with his PARR superiors. And they weren't pleased with his recent performance.

"Finding a young girl that looks as distinctive as Kaya More shouldn't be so difficult." One of the men argued.

"After all, she is only human. She can't just vanish into thin air." Another added.

Judah gritted his teeth.

"We have all the men we can afford looking for her." He explained. "She must have a good hiding place."

"What about that woman that Gary Shane is involved with? Thought that she was a close friend of Miss More."

"She was. But when she turned her father in, somehow, Miss More found out about it."

One of the superiors opened a file. Inside it contained photographs of some of the members of LUPO. Handing the file to Judah, he proceeded to explain.

"I want those pictures to be copied and distributed all over the city. Again. You are going to catch those criminals and stop this rebellion before it gains control if it is the last thing you do."

Judah looked up from the pictures of Wind, Brent, Boyce, Kaya, Gleven and Margaret with horror. The tone of his superior's voice told him that, if he didn't catch the rebels, he would be in danger of losing his life. With a quick salute, Judah left the room.

CHAPTER Twenty-three
Late that night
California

Kaya lay awake in the narrow bed that she and Boyce were sharing. Her thoughts were on the room downstairs and what it contained. She felt as if something, or someone, was calling her down there. For close to an hour she had been experiencing this feeling and had logically tried to figure out why she was feeling it. Giving up on trying to affix a logical reason for the feeling, Kaya quietly slipped out of the bed. Throwing on a robe, she silently slipped out of the room.

Downstairs, the secret room was hidden by a large wall unit that had been placed in front of it. This was done by the men in case someone happened to find their way down here. At this point in time, it could mean the lives of any LUPO members on the premises if the room was found. So, for the moment, the room remained hidden.

As it had happened when she was a child, Kaya felt an unknown force drawing her towards another part of the room. Here, hidden by the dirt and grime of years, was a door. Kaya tried the knob and it opened easily. She walked through it to find herself once more in the secret room. Slowly she walked up to the wall rack. Admiringly her hands ran carefully over the set of Korg keyboards.

"All these years and you are still a legend." She murmured lovingly to the musical instrument. Looking around the set up, she mentally noted the acoustic guitar that lay against the wall, the speakers and the amps. Her breath caught as she caught sight of the lead guitar that had been used by Bradley Mitchell, the bass that had felt the fingers of Cal Jensen and, at the back of the stage, the drum kit that had belonged to Rick Young. The history these pieces had known. The mixing board had once performed its duties for one of the greatest bands in history. By the looks of it, the mixing board seemed, as all the pieces did, to be in perfect working order.

"Whom are you waiting for?" Kaya silently asked the enclosure she was in. Expecting no answer, she continued to look at everything… closely. Spying a music score on top of the keyboards, she reached up to take it.

Turning the pages over, a letter fell to the ground. Curious Kaya bent to pick it up and read it.

"To the person who finds this:

> I really hope that you are a supporter of rock and roll or I shall feel that all our work has gone to waste. The other band members and I feel that the end was near so we built this room for someone to find one day. Here we can tell our story.
>
> PARR was started because a few people decided that the music, rock and roll, was leading the young astray. They felt that it

was up to the industry and government to control and censor the music. Unfortunately, none of the supporters of rock and roll took PARR that seriously so they got what they wanted. The end of rock and roll.

We, the band Mystique, feel that the end of our lives is near. PARR has been executing any and all members of rock bands for the past year. We don't feel that, since we have vocally denounced PARR numerous times, we will be an exception.

What I am asking you, dear reader, is that you never give up hope that rock and roll music will live again. I don't know when you will be reading this or who you are but I have to have faith that you are a person who believes in freedom of choice and is set on stopping PARR.

You will find many videos, music scores and instruction books in this hideaway. Please use them to help others discover what rock and roll was. Rock and roll wasn't bad.

Towards the end the music industry became too damn corporate. Making money became the only thing that was important and the music itself became lost in the confusion. No one knew what they were doing anymore, with artists signing billion dollar deals and losing their integrity. But please don't ever believe that rock and roll was something to be done away with.

It wasn't harmful to people and it wasn't a form of devil worship. All rock and roll music was the form of expression for those who are young. It gave much more than it could ever take beginning it has always faced criticism and the threat of censorship. It looks as if now, someone has succeeded in taking it away.

Please bring the music back.

The letter was signed by all the members of Mystique.

Kaya felt a lump growing in her throat as she fought back the tears. This was meant to be. She was destined to come out to California and find this room and read this letter. Suddenly, all fell into place. For years, the restaurant had existed and no one had found this room. Yet, within hours of her arrival, the room had revealed itself. Kaya knew what direction LUPO should take to defeat PARR. Excited, she ran upstairs to wake Boyce and tell him.

Gleven, Boyce, Steven and Kaya sat in their nightclothes around a table in the restaurant.

"What was so important that you had to wake us up at this ungodly hour?" Gleven yawned.

“Look at what I found." Kaya was almost jumping with excitement as she handed Gleven the letter. Steven read over Gleven's shoulder and when they had finished, both looked at Kaya with amazement.

"Where did you get this?" Steven asked.

“In the room downstairs. I just had a feeling that I should go down there so I did and this is what I found. I also have an idea of what direction LUPO should follow now."

Gleven and the others looked questionably at Kaya patiently waiting for her to continue.

"I think that we have been in the shadows too long. What we are fighting for, so many people haven't even heard! They don't care because they don't know what is being taken away from them."

"What do you propose to do? Put rock and roll music on the airwaves?" Boyce asked somewhat sarcastically.

"That's a thought. The point I am trying to make is that it has been fine for us to be hidden all these years but I feel that the time for secrecy is over. It is time to come out into the light and let the public know what they are missing."

Steven grinned.

"Boyce, I like this lady! You guys have to admit that she does have a point and I have been wondering about exposing ourselves more for years."

Gleven nodded to himself before answering.

"I think that it is a good idea though it will increase the danger. And we will have to contact Brent and Wind so that they can decide on what is to be done with the chapter in New York."

"That is another thing." Kaya stated. "Why have two chapters? We would be more united and powerful if most of the people were in one place. Then we would know immediately if something happened to someone or if a disaster occurred. Gleven, when you were in jail, there is a good chance that you could have been executed because I may not have come up into the city. I may have decided to take your advice for once and stay in the underground dwelling.

“Or if I hadn't been able to get in touch with Boyce and the others or if they hadn't been able to make it out to New York. So many things could have gone wrong and then what would have happened to LUPO and the revival of rock and roll music?"

"Thank God that Kaya is so stubborn and doesn't listen to what she's told!" Gleven chuckled. The attempt at humor relaxed the group and sent chuckles through the four.

"But you see what I mean!" Kaya persisted. "The two chapters may have worked at the beginning but now I think that it is time for us to become one. And what better place than here?"

”But we aren't in the city where it is all happening." Boyce pointed out.

"But we are in the city where PARR finally put a stop to rock and roll." Kaya pointed out. "And make them come to us. PARR knows that we are still around and still active. In New York I think that we are too close to everything. Every move we make is watched and that hampers us.

Though PARR is active here, they aren't as strong as they are in New York. "If we could start the revolution here, and I mean really start it, it would soon spread."

All thought about that for a moment before Steven spoke up.

"I happen to think that that is a very good idea. We have all the equipment here. It would cause too much suspicion if we tried to move it to New York."

"Agreed." Boyce commented. "We could change this part of the country around and watch the wave ride its way across the land."

"I guess I might as well agree too." Gleven said. "After all, it does seem like a good idea. How will we get a hold of everyone in New York though?"

Here Kaya smiled.

"Fly there. I could go in disguise because I don't think that Judah and the rest of PARR would expect me to just walk back into the city as if I had done nothing wrong."

"As long as you're disguised well, I don't see any harm in that." Gleven commented. "But I don't want you to go alone."

"I'll go with her." Steven offered. "It would probably be better than either of you going." Kaya nodded.

"I totally agree. We should leave tomorrow though."

"And come back as soon as possible." Boyce added. Though he would have liked to have gone with Kaya, he felt it would be too dangerous for him to leave with her then return to New York with her. So he didn't argue with the idea of her going with Steven.

"There's another mystery to solve that I feel would truly help LUPO in its objective." Gleven mused aloud.

"And what's that?" Kaya asked.

"Well, we have managed to learn that PARR has used mind altering drugs in their control of the people. When I was locked up, it occurred to me that many of my early memories don't exist, sometimes it seems as if I can't remember what happened before I turned eighteen."

"Same here." Steven exclaimed. "There are even times when I have difficulty remembering things that happened a short time ago."

"Right." Gleven was getting excited as his thoughts began to form with more clarity. "Now some of that can be attributed to passage of time but not all of it. So PARR must be using something to affect our memories. The question is what and how are they making us take it without our knowledge."

"Have you ever really watched some of the people leaving a PARR rally?" Boyce questioned. "Some of them appear to be extremely nervous and fearful of anyone and everyone around them. I never really thought about that being strange before, but it does seem to happen quite regularly. Could that be a side effect of these drugs?"

"When I was young," Gleven remarked thoughtfully. "I can remember those same symptoms as well as a few people having seizures at these events. Now that I really think about it, all of these could be attributed to the drugs since they are definitely not, as PARR claims, the effects of the exposure to rock and roll music."

"Absurd and something to delve into more." Kaya commented firmly. "We have to find out what they are using and how they are using it As well, if we can find a drug that will counteract theirs, then we can eliminate PARR's control without them even knowing about it"

"Correct. But how? We first have to discover what they are using before we can find an antidote or something that will eliminate the effects and then we have to discover a way to administer it to all the people." Steven was quick to point out.

"And without them knowing about it" Boyce said.

"OK, OK." Kaya said. "It's not going to be an easy task and it is not one that we can solve tonight. But if we write down what information we need to find out as well as what we need to do to counteract PARR's control, we are at least organized."

Boyce moved as if to rise from the table to find some paper and pens but Gleven stopped him.

"But we had better get some sleep now." Gleven's voice was firm. "Then, in the morning, we will book a flight to New York for Mr. and Mrs. Steven Went. The problem with the drugs can wait for now."

All heads nodded their agreement then, after the proper goodnights were said, everyone headed for their separate bedrooms.

Boyce ran his hands lovingly down Kaya's body.

"You'll be careful, won't you?" He sought reassurance to try to ease the worry he felt over Kaya walking back into the city where they had only recently left and where her life was in the utmost danger.

"Of course I will." Kaya's mouth sought his. "I want to come back to you in one piece." Knowing Kaya too well, Boyce still wasn't comforted but he didn't say anything else on the matter. Instead his mouth closed on Kaya's in a long, passionate kiss. Sighing Kaya gave herself up to the feelings that Boyce was arousing.

CHAPTER Twenty-four

The next day
California

Early the next afternoon, Mr. and Mrs. Steven Went were getting ready to leave for the airport. Mrs. Went was a heavyset woman of about forty with long black hair pulled into a bun. The horned rim glasses she wore didn't improve the appearance of her nondescript face. She wore a shapeless dress of an iron-grey color and sensible flat shoes. There was nothing about the woman that would attract the attention of even the most observant passer-by.

In the car, little was said. All had their own thoughts. Steven was excited about the changes being brought to LUPO; Gleven was considering the positive and negative aspects of these changes; Boyce, who was driving, was filled with concern for Kaya and Kaya was filled with concern for Brent and Wind. Though they had attempted to telephone the two this morning, it seemed as if the pair had dropped out of sight. Could something have happened to them? Were they alive or dead? What was happening in New York? Shaking her head, Kaya forced these worries from her mind. Whatever the case, she would know soon enough.

Gleven and Boyce stood at the window of the airport lobby watching the plane taxi to the end of the runway then lift to the air. Each breathed a sigh of relief that Kaya and Steven were on their way but both experienced an overgrowing concern about what would await them when they reached New York. Burying the concern for the moment, the two men just reveled in the fact that Kaya and Steven had managed to leave without incident.

Kaya sat back and breathed a little easier. Getting out of the Los Angeles airport had been scary, especially with all the PARR agents standing guard. But they had done it. Now it was on to New York.

Wind and Brent sat in the basement of the Underground Cafe, talking with Calo.

"I don't know what we should do." Brent commented. "It has been so long since I have lived in New York that I doubt if all the hiding places I knew still exist. And Wind has been in hiding for a few years so I doubt that she would know either."

Wind nodded her agreement.

"How I wish that we could fight PARR in the open." Wind mused aloud. "Somehow I think that would be so much easier."

"Let's just get you through this part then we can worry about the future of LUPO." Calo advised.

Night was falling as two strangers approached the Underground Cafe. The man looked around him, as if seeing this area for the first time but the woman moved with the confidence of someone who had been here many times. Purposefully they went into the cafe.

Calo was cleaning the tables when the strangers walked in.

"Sorry but we're closed." He said without looking up.

"Even for me?" A familiar voice asked.

Startled, Calo looked closely at the woman with the schoolteacher's appearance. She sounded familiar but he knew that he had never seen this woman before.

"Kaya?" He asked hesitantly.

Kaya laughed.

"Yes. How do you like the costume?"

Calo walked around her in wonder. What had happened to the slim, beautiful girl that had left New York? Shaking his head, he spoke,

"What in the hell are you doing here? You are supposed to be far away from New York." Kaya smiled as she turned to Steven.

"Calo, I would like you to meet someone from California. This is Steven Went."

Calo greeted Steven and shook his hand then turned back to Kaya.

"Well? What are you doing here?"

"I'm looking for my Mom and Brent. We have decided to make some changes in LUPO, if they agree."

"You have come to the right place. They are downstairs right now."

"Why are they there? I thought that everything was fine."

"They are in hiding. PARR has circulated more pictures of all the major leaders of LUPO so I thought it would be better for them to lay low for awhile."

Kaya nodded then went to the door that led downstairs. The single light that Brent and Wind had lit broke the darkness of the cellar. Kaya felt her heart tug as she watched the couple sitting alone in the cold, dark basement.

"Never again will we have to hide." She vowed to herself. Making her presence known, she came into the feeble light. Wind and Brent just started at her for a long moment, not recognizing the woman who stood before them.

"Mom, it's me." Kaya spoke quietly.

"Kaya! What are you doing back in the city? I thought that you were safe and sound in California."

"Mom, we have an idea for changes in LUPO and we wanted to discuss them with you and, if you agree, convince you to move to California." She threw an apologetic glance at Brent.

"Sorry Brent. I didn't mean to ignore you. Of course we want your opinion too."

"Anything that means moving back to California is OK with me." Brent joked.

Kaya's eyes lit up and she sat down to explain the plan to Wind and Brent. Once she was finished, Kaya smiled at the older couple.

"If you will be all right, I have something to do."

Wind regarded Kaya warily. Something told her that Kaya was planning something dangerous and, more than likely, highly illegal.

"You aren't going to do something stupid, are you?" Wind asked concerned.

Kaya breezily brushed off her mother's worries.

"Of course not. I have just got some minor things to do. I will be back in a little while." Kaya waved calmly at Brent and Wind then walked up the stairs.

The headquarters of PARR were dark and deserted when Kaya's black clad figure approached the extensive buildings. Years ago she had studied the layout of the building just in case she ever needed to enter it. Now that time had come.

Taking a deep breath Kaya crept along the side of the building to the back door, which she knew was always unlocked. Turning the knob carefully she held her breath in anticipation of the protesting squeal from the hinges. Fortunately the door had been oiled recently and was silent.

Inside the building, Kaya took a moment to allow her eyes to adjust to the difference in light and to get her bearings. As well, she tuned her ears for the slightest movement that would signal the approach of the PARR sentries.

Cautiously Kaya moved towards the staircase and, flattening herself against the dark wall, she proceeded upwards. At the door to Judah's office, she saw a large, dark shape at the desk and knew that Judah was working late. Silently she went over to the fuse box that controlled the circuit in Judah's office and removed the necessary fuse. In half a second she heard Judah's grunt of frustration and anger. Ducking behind the secretary's desk, Kaya watched Judah leave his office to repair the fuse.

Within a moment after Judah had left, Kaya had entered his office and switched off the now powerless light on his desk. Then she stood on the other side of the door and waited patiently for Judah to return.

Upon entering his office Judah swore and walked over to his desk to see what the problem was with his lamp. With a switch he turned it on, confused since he was certain that he hadn't turned it off when he left. Shrugging, he sat down in the immense chair and that was when a movement beside the closed door caught his eye.

Judah stopped and stared at the figure standing motionless against the door. Quickly he came to his senses and reached for the gun he kept in a drawer.

"Are you looking for this?" Kaya asked as she held up the man's weapon. "I took the liberty of removing it before you got here."

Judah sat back and calmly regarded Kaya as his fingers sought the alarm button that would bring the PARR agents to his office. Ever since that day, three years ago, when Kaya had broken into his apartment, Judah had installed security measures every where he was likely to be found.

"You are in a lot of trouble, Miss More." He commented as he vainly sought the button. His fingers found a mess of torn wires and he stared at Kaya angrily.

"You bitch!" He hissed.

Kaya sat in a chair and smiled serenely.

"I told you the last time we met that I wasn't stupid but you wouldn't believe me." Kaya held up the other hand. In it was a small button with several mangled wires dangling from it. "I wasn't sure which wire to destroy so I destroyed all of them."

"What do you want?" Judah asked coldly, now realizing that he was trapped, again.

"What I want, you won't give me." Kaya stated simply. "But I did warn you before even though I kind of knew you wouldn't listen. But I must ask, are we making life for you and PARR difficult yet?"

"Nothing we can't handle." Judah assured her.

Kaya's eyebrows rose and a knowing smirk on her face.

"Really? Well, then I should tell you that we are just getting started. We have lots of fun in store for you."

"Why don't you give it up, Miss More? Your organization has tried for years to bring back rock and roll music but to little avail. When are you going to realize that you are fighting a lost cause?"

"I will fight for the justice that you have denied us until the day I die. And maybe after." Kaya answered vehemently.

Judah smiled, confident that he was enticing the young woman to anger.

"Oh really? You do realize, I hope, that that may be sooner than you think."

Kaya shook her head merrily.

"You haven't changed Judah. Still happy to exchange threats instead of listening to reason. So, I will have to tell you what I came here to tell you." Kaya paused. "You really shouldn't have done that to Gleven. You're lucky that he didn't die or else I would hate to consider what would have happened to you. But, since he didn't die, you are allowed to get off with another warning. Harm anyone close to me or any LUPO members again and I will make sure that you will live to regret it."

Judah shivered at the coldness of her words. His eyes were locked with hers and he didn't notice that Kaya had crept closer to the desk. Suddenly, she switched the lamp off and knocked it to the floor. By the time Judah had regained his wits, struggled to his feet and raced to the door, Kaya was nowhere to be seen.

The next day, there were four people leaving New York for California by plane. The Underground Cafe was up for sale and numerous of people were leaving the city, going to such places as Canada. Within a month they would all meet in one city.

The City of Angels.

CHAPTER Twenty-Five

That evening
A prison camp in the Canadian Rocky Mountains

An undernourished, physically abused middle-aged man dressed in grey prison garb and wearing the expression of someone who had lost all hope, stood looking out at the window at the magnificent sight before him. Daniel More was not seeing the peaks that rose majestically to the sky or the trees that had stood firm for thousands of years. His thoughts were turned inward, speculating on what the world had become and all the freedom it had lost.

When PARR had invaded the auditorium thirty years ago, Daniel had been twenty-five years old and at the top of success in his career. That night Daniel and the others had honestly believed that their death were imminent but, instead, PARR had shipped them to this place in Canada's mountainous region where escape was beyond hope and it seemed as if no one had known that they were here. Surely, Daniel himself hadn't realized that this place existed and was quite shocked, though slightly pleased, when he came upon the multitudes of rock musicians that resided here. Within all of them was the desperate hope that the citizens of the world would rebel and once again revive rock and roll, hopefully freeing them in the process.

But, as the musicians began to die, some from old age, some from disease and some from the abuse that was inflicted on them regularly, hope began to die out until the majority of the residents here were as he was, without hope and waiting for the mercy of death to take them from this world.

Daniel's thoughts turned to the brother and nephew he had left behind. Daniel's brother had been ten years older than he with a son that was fourteen years old when Daniel had disappeared. Daniel had often wondered how Kansall had survived and hoped that he was doing well since Daniel had loved him like his own son.

Daniel sighed. All the original members of Mystique had managed to survive their imprisonment, at least so far, and perhaps there was still hope that someone would be able to rescue them.

In the same cell, Cal Jensen ran a hand through his thinning hair. When he had played bass for Mystique, his hair had been thick and full, the object of many young ladies' attention. He sighed as he thought of what he had lost, beside his luxuriant head of hair, when PARR had ended rock and roll.

Although Cal had always been considered the black sheep of the family, constantly getting into trouble when he was a child and in his teens, he had found his niche in life when he started playing rock music. It had been the happiest day of his life when Mystique had first played on a stage to a crowd of adoring fans. He smiled as he remembered the thrill he had gotten when the stage lights first came on and the cheers from the audience had grown to deafening proportions.

Granted, life hadn't always been perfect as a rock star, but it was sure a hell of a lot better than what he was facing now. Back then he had complained bitterly about the lack of privacy and the inability to do many of the things he wanted to do. Simply shopping for groceries or clothes was out of the question unless they could convince the stores to remain open after everyone else had closed. He wasn't able to go out on a simple date, like to dinner and a movie, without being mobbed by photographers and fans.

Now, whenever that cell door opened, Cal wasn't sure if it was for their poorly cooked meals, to be beaten or if it meant death for one of the occupants. He realized if he could just walk out of those high prison gates, he would never complain about anything again.

Bradley Mitchell lay, staring at the grey stone ceiling, wondering about the future. After all this time, it didn't seem as if they would ever be free again. At times he wondered what was happening on the other side of those gates and down the mountain but they had no contact with the outside world whatsoever. The guards were under strict orders and didn't even speak of occurrences outside these walls. They didn't even speak of what was happening within the prison. The members of Mystique had been, and still were, totally cut off from everyone but each other.

A younger brother and loving parents were what Bradley had left behind when PARR had locked him up. Whenever he found that the imprisonment was wearing down on him, Bradley would retreat into the memories of happier times. However, all too soon, concern for their welfare would flood his mind and Bradley would try to blank his mind and not think of anything.

Rick Young didn't find sharing the cell difficult; having spent his former life with numerous cousins, but what bothered him was the inability to go outside. All his life, Rick had been the one that had enjoyed the outdoors. On tours he would often take his ten-speed bicycle and tour the town they were in. Or else, on breaks, he would go hiking, skiing, and water skiing, whatever the sport happened to get him in the fresh air and appealed to him at the time.

When he had first been locked up, Rick had attempted to keep a physical regime going. But doing exercises in the limited space the cell provided or standing at the bars, desperately hoping for a breath of fresh air had not been enough. Then, as time wore on and his body craved the essential nutrients missing from their inadequate meals, Rick's body had grown too weak for any sort of physical exertion. He was a forty nine year old man who was old before his time.

Realistically, he had no real hope that he and the others would ever leave this place alive. Yet, somewhere deep within him, a tiny flicker that one day events might change kept him going. Kept him longing for the outside and dreaming that one day he may see and feel the wind against his skin once again.

Ron Stopford stood against the wall, as he often did, trying to distance himself from the situation. Although not legally married, Ron had been involved in a common law relationship that had produced one son. Ron's eyes misted over as he recalled his girlfriend, Fiona, or Fi as she was commonly called. Tall and willowy, her dark brown hair had fallen gracefully to her waist. Her delicate features always seemed to fill with laughter and she was the light of his life. Next to his son, John, that is.

John had been a troublesome two-year-old when Ron had disappeared. Though Fi and John came to every performance, that evening they had missed it. Ron thanked the heavens above for that small favor.

Fi had been tired most of the time on that tour so she had returned home to Los Angeles with John halfway through the tour. She had gone to the doctor earlier that day and, when she had telephoned Ron at the auditorium, she had joyously told him that she had a surprise for him. With much wheedling and prompting Ron had gotten her to tell him that she was pregnant again. After the concert, Ron was going to return home and celebrate the impending arrival in style. But he had never made it home again. Now he wondered, as he had many times in the past, what had ever happened to Fi, John and the unknown child. Would PARR have killed them all, out of spite? Would they have left the relatives alone? Did Fi and the others escape PARR's wrath and move on? These were questions that haunted him continuously as he knew they must haunt the numerous other political prisoners that resided inside these godforsaken walls.

The members of Mystique had no way of knowing that the fight to bring back rock and roll was being fought intensely this day. Nor could they know that the letter they had left behind had been found and that, south of them, their illegal music and forbidden faces filled the hearts of certain rock and roll music supporters.

CHAPTER Twenty-Six

Kaya sat at a table in the upstairs of Steven's restaurant. Downstairs she could hear the men working on insulating the area uncovered by the earthquake. It had been decided that, since the members of LUPO were going to use this area as a general meeting room as well as a practice area for learning rock and roll music, the area had to be soundproofed.

Kaya herself was working on a flyer that was going to be distributed by LUPO supporters to as many people as possible. Scratching her head, she looked the piece over one more time to see if she was satisfied with it.

> "This society we live in is not a democracy as the government claims. The people of this great land are being controlled and led to think what others wish them to think. If you don't believe me, think of these facts. How many of you reading this can remember events of their past without being told? How many of you know what year you were born? Unless told, do you honestly know how old you are? How many of you often feel confused and how many of you can say what year this is and prove it? In some way, our minds are being tampered with and our memories destroyed. Somehow, someone is destroying everything in an effort to totally control us. The time for this to end is now! We do not have freedom of choice any longer since we are allowing the government to tell us what we can listen to, what we can read, what we can do with our lives and we are even allowing them to dictate what we should think and feel.
>
> But, if enough people unite to fight this injustice, then we can have our lives back. If this really matters to you then watch for more information on how we are going to defeat those government agencies and take back our freedom."

Kaya smiled in approval. This flyer was a start to making people aware of what was going on and there would assuredly be more items of this nature in the future. Kaya sighed in satisfaction and put the piece of paper aside. She then pulled out a list that was being made. They were currently looking for any and all people related to the original musicians of Mystique. It was a trying job since the files that would have readily placed the information on the computer screen were controlled by PARR, making them nearly inaccessible.

Then, if Kaya was lucky enough to find someone who was related, they had to be checked thoroughly. She had never realized how many Jensens and Youngs there were in the area. There just didn't seem to be any Stopfords that could declare a relation to the vocalist of Mystique. The plan was that, once the relatives of Mystique had been located, Kaya and

Boyce would approach certain people to discover if they were open to the idea of starting up a version of Mystique with all relatives of the original band. There were times, especially like this when dead ends were all they could seem to find, that Kaya truly wondered whether their plan was feasible.

Kaya sat back closed her eyes and attempted to work out just how they were going to find the people they needed. Her mind was racing with the different possibilities but one viable solution seemed to pop into her consciousness. Clearing her mind of any thoughts of rebellion or LUPO, she switched on the mind control factor of the computer that was waiting for her to begin.

Attaching the controls that would link her mind with the technology in front of her, she thought of PARR's files. Within seconds a file appeared in front of her. Keeping her thoughts calm Kaya read the command on the screen that asked for a password. Without hesitation, she thought of most unlikely word to be used in association with PARR.

"LUPO." She commanded silently. After a brief pause the computer screen listed the contents in PARR's numerous files. Quickly scanning Kaya noticed that there was a file labelled, Mystique. Confident that this file would give her the information she needed, Kaya silently said the name. Once again, her actions were rewarded with the information she desired.

In front of her eyes was a list of every living, and deceased, relative of the members of the original Mystique. Included was a record of vital statistics such as height, weight, eye and hair color and marital status as well as their current living arrangements and addresses. It wasn't listed just what the relationship between these people were. The only lists that were incomplete were those on her, Wind and the two Mitchell men. PARR still wasn't aware of where she or the supporters of LUPO were.

Kaya stared at the lists, pondering her next move, when an idea struck her. She excitedly thought of Ron Stopford, visualizing him as she did so. Only one name appeared. Brian Malloy and his current address was here in Los Angeles. Kaya was puzzled. No one else was listed and there was no explanation. Shrugging she copied down the information then switched her thoughts to Cal Jensen.

"Why didn't I think of this before?" Kaya said. "It would have been a lot easier." The file on Cal Jensen appeared quickly and Kaya soon found the person she was looking for. He was a man about the same age as Kaya and Boyce by the name of Jared Jensen. The last known address for Jared was in a little town south of Los Angeles. Unfortunately, the data on his activities contained a special security code that, at the moment, Kaya was unable to break. Leaving his file for the time being, Kaya concentrated on Rick Young.

The computer screen was blank for much longer this time, causing Kaya to become apprehensive about perhaps being discovered. But just when Kaya's cautiousness dictated that she switch off the machine, the information she wanted appeared. Rick had belonged to a large family and there were numerous people that could claim a direct relationship with the musician. Kaya willed the computer to print the information it was now spewing forward then groaned as she studied the information. These people had addresses all over the country and many of them were in the same age group as the other prospective members.

"Oh well!" She sighed inwardly. "No one ever said that this was going to be easy." Kaya rapidly went through the list, crossing off those whom she could immediately see were not what LUPO required and placing asterisks beside those who seemed hopeful. Then she turned her attention back to the computer and breaking the code on the possibilities' histories.

Kaya ran her hands over her eyes with weariness. For two hours she had been trying to break the code that would bring up the information on Jared Jensen and the others. It seemed to be impossible to break, PARR having inserted strict safeguards. Sitting back and detaching herself from the computer, she stared at the screen in front of her, trying to think of fresh ideas. Suddenly it hit her. PARR had used LUPO as a password to get into the majority of their files so it would stand to reason that PARR would also use another word just as obscure when associated with the agency. Once more attaching herself to the computer banks, Kaya struggled to contain her rising excitement.

"Rock and roll." Kaya thought with anticipation. Her intuition paid off as a new list of files appeared on the screen. There were millions of names and Kaya rapidly scanned the alphabetical listing for the people she desired. Quickly the computer drew up the information on Jared Jensen as

Kaya read it with increasing excitement Jared was twenty-five years old and had a long record of rebellion.

When in high school he had been expelled from numerous schools for questioning the rules of establishment Jared had once tried to organize the students to rebel for shorter classes. Kaya looked at his later escapades to make sure that he hadn't settle down over the years. She grinned with satisfaction when she read that he had been jailed for telling off a PARR agent. The only puzzling item on the file was a notation at the end that stated the Jared required a double dose of Regonol. What was Regonol and why did Jared require more of it? Kaya wondered but shrugged it off. She felt as if she had found the man she was looking for and went on to the information on Brian Malloy.

Brian's information showed that, though he was a rebel, he tended to do things in a more secretive way. His record showed that he was a suspect in many illegal activities but he had never been charged. Fortunately none of his potential charges were anything major and, strangely enough, they all had to do with opposing the censorship of music and the arts. Once again Kaya noticed the reference to Regonol but this time it stated that Brian had a reaction to it. At a PARR rally, he had suffered a seizure as well as some twitching episodes before hand Kaya mentally placed this piece of information in the back of her mind as she added his name to her list of people to contact.

Kaya had saved the best for last. Checking on any direct relatives of Rick's was going to take a long time. The first person she checked was a young male by the name of Ansel Young. She wrinkled her nose when the first thing she read was that he was a PARR agent. Quickly changing names, she pulled the name Larret Young. Larret was a casino dealer in Reno, Nevada. At twenty-seven years of age, he was reputed to be a womanizer and very heavily into partying. He was also known for doing things on impulse, including playing a Mystique CD at a party. Definitely this was a man that Kaya wanted to talk to. She circled his name and address on her computer sheets then turned the computer off and sat back. They had found their men. Now if only these guys were open to the idea of joining LUPO and forming a new Mystique.

Kaya's face furrowed in a scowl of concentration. The mention of Regonol so often was confusing. What was it and why did everyone seem to have a mention of it on his or her file? Once more positioning herself at the computer, Kaya brought up files on drugs, both legal and illegal. Even if it was just to satisfy her curiosity, Kaya had to find out about this drug. The information that presented itself to her confused her even more.

The next day, Boyce and Kaya set out early in the morning. First of all they were going to see Brian since he lived the closest. Then they would approach Jared and finally Larret.

Pulling up in front of a nondescript house, Kaya took a deep breath. What was this man going to say about the idea of forming another Mystique? What if he didn't even know that he was closely related to the lead singer of one of the greatest rock bands in history? Too many ifs. The only answer was to go inside and discover out the answers to these what ifs.

A tall blond man answered the ring of the doorbell. Recognition flashed momentarily in his eyes when he looked at Kaya and Boyce but it was quickly replaced by curiosity.

"Yes?" He inquired. "How may I help you?"

Kaya and Boyce exchanged glances of caution. They had both seen the flash of recognition and wondered at its cause.

"We were wondering," Kaya began "If we could use your phone?"

"Our car broke down in front of your house." Boyce further explained. "And we have a meeting to get to. We forgot our cell phones." Brian shrugged. Their explanation did sound plausible enough but something didn't seem right. Yet he couldn't begin to figure out the reason for this unexpected visit so he decided to let it go for now. As soon as he had opened the door, he had recognized Kaya from the PARR notices and Boyce was the mirror image of Bradley Mitchell.

"Sure. Come in." Brian opened the door a little wider to let them enter.

"Nice place." Kaya said as she looked around.

"It'll do." Brian shrugged then, containing his curiosity no longer, he asked,

"So what are two leaders of LUPO and relatives of the band Mystique doing on my doorstep?"

Kaya and Boyce started. Brian, seeing their discomfort, hastened to assure them.

"Hey, I don't mean you any harm. Actually, I am a big fan of Mystique. I have studied what I can of their history and have managed to collect some of their CDs."

Kaya and Boyce breathed a sigh of relief.

"What we are doing here," Boyce started "Is seeing if you would be receptive to the idea of starting a new Mystique."

"Made up of people related to the original band members." Kaya added. Brian thought for a moment. A very short moment.

"Of course. But how would we get it past PARR?"

"We have that all arranged, at least for the moment" Boyce paused. "Since you are open to the idea of starting a new Mystique, why don't you come with us to try to convince the other two men?"

Brian quickly grabbed his coat.

"What are we waiting for?" He asked with a grin.

An hour later, the trio was in front of a beach house.

"Is this it?" Boyce asked.

Kaya looked down at the address once more and nodded. "Last known address of Jared Jensen. And I think that PARR would keep tabs on this guy."

Boyce nodded silently, thinking his own thoughts.

"What if PARR is watching Jared at this moment?" He pondered to himself. "Would contacting Jared mean the capture of me and Kaya?" They had to be careful. Taking a deep breath, Boyce decided to take a chance. Getting out of the car, he motioned for Brian and Kaya to follow.

A very bleary eyed replica of Cal Jensen answered the door.

Kaya experienced a chill as she stared at Jared. This was getting too strange.

"Yeah. What do you want?" Jared demanded.

Kaya took a moment to gather herself together after the shock of seeing him then decided to be straight with Jared.

"May we come in? We have something to discuss with you that we think you will be very interested in."

Jared narrowed his eyes suspiciously. This could prove to be extremely interesting by the looks of his unexpected visitors.

"Sure." Jared stepped away from the door and led the way into a very messy living room. Throwing some clothes off a couch, he motioned his unexpected visitors to sit down.

Kaya decided to get right to the point.

"We know that you oppose the censorship of music and that you are considered quite a rebel."

"So?" Jared lit a cigarette.

Boyce leaned forward, his eyes bright.

"How would you like to do something to stop the injustice that PARR is enforcing?" Now Jared was interested.

"Like what?" He asked.

"Like forming another band named Mystique that plays the same type of music."

Jared started to laugh then choked on the smoke from his cigarette.

"Yeah, then get caught and with my record I would be thrown away forever."

"But we all have to take chances." Kaya stated quietly. And I think you are just the man to do that."

Jared opened his eyes a little wider and stared at Kaya intently. He threw back his head and laughed as he recognized the woman sitting there.

"Taking chances is something you are really good at, Miss More! I can remember when I was in jail. You had just screwed up one of PARR's plans in New York and they were certain that I knew where you were. Sure I will join your band. It will be great to give PARR hell."

Kaya, Boyce and Brian exchanged triumphant glances. One more to go.

On the way to Reno, the car had four passengers. Jared leaned back in the seat and studied Kaya's back a little closer. That was one fine looking lady! Too bad she seemed to be with that Mitchell guy. Jared smiled to himself as he thought of his life. One adventure after another.

Boyce was looking impatiently for the hotel where Kaya had said that Larret lived. It seemed to be nowhere in this city until Brian said from the back seat,

"Isn't that it?"

Boyce breathed a sigh of relief as he followed Brian's finger and saw that he was correct.

Larret Young answered the door with just a towel wrapped around his slim hips. He stared at the people at his door with frank curiosity then his eyes fell on Kaya.

"Whew!" he whistled. "Now that is what I like waking up to! Come on in, little lady." Kaya smiled grimly, hoping that her earlier instincts concerning Larret weren't wrong.

"I am not your 'little lady' and if come in, so do these men."

Larret smiled a charmingly boyish smile.

"Of course, whatever you say."

Boyce, Kaya, Brian and Jared sat in the hotel room while Larret went to the bathroom to get dressed.

"So what can I do for you people?" Larret asked as he came out of the washroom fully dressed.

"Do you know who we are?" Boyce asked.

Larret studied them for a moment.

"You do look familiar but I see so many people in a day that I have difficulty putting names to faces."

"Did you really get drunk one night and start playing a Mystique CD at a party?" Kaya asked.

Larret looked suspicious.

"If you guys are from PARR, though you don't look it, I have already explained that I didn't know it was banned music. So just leave me alone!"

Brian hurried to explain.

"No, no. We are not from PARR. Far from it actually. We are all relatives of the original members of Mystique, as you are."

"This lady is the infamous Kaya More from LUPO." Jared drawled lazily.

"We are interested in starting another Mystique." Boyce further explained.

Larret narrowed his eyes as he thought this new information out.

Now that Kaya More had been identified to him, he recognized her. The others were beginning to take form in his mind too. It was almost as if he had the original members of Mystique sitting in his room. Except for the fact that Kaya More was female of course, but that just made things a little more interesting. His mind turned to the idea of starting another Mystique. That might be fun. Women, after all, loved musicians. Mentally he shrugged.

"Sure. Why not?"

CHAPTER Twenty-Seven

It was getting close to dawn when the vehicle with Kaya, Boyce, Brian, Jared and Larret pulled into the parking lot of the Revolution Restaurant. Silently directing the others around to the back way, Kaya and Boyce led the procession. Once inside, Kaya led everyone downstairs while Boyce went to get some food.

Jared looked around him with interest. Except for the wall on the one side of the basement, this basement looked like any other. It was obvious that some work had been done to repair that one wall and that it wasn't finished yet. Jared wondered what had happened to damage the surface.

Larret sat down with a sigh. Everything was moving so quickly. On the drive out here Boyce and Kaya had explained their plan. First and foremost, they were going to learn the instruments and become the best they could be in as short of time as possible. Then they intended to expose the public to rock and roll music as much as they were able to without being caught. The target market of the new Mystique would be the teenagers and young adults since, as Kaya stated, they had always seemed to be the ones that were willing to support the music.

"What have I gotten myself into?" Larret said to himself.

Brian was relaxed and happy. For some reason, he had trusted Kaya and Boyce immediately and immensely. He knew what they were fighting for was a just cause and he was more than pleased to have an active part in the struggle. Everything about this plan seemed to feel right.

Boyce stopped Kaya in the hall.

"So what do you think?"

"I think we have a real mixture down there. Each one of them is so different yet, in so many ways, so alike. I mean, they are all rebels, they have all fought the rules in some way or another and they are all committed to their ideas. Yet, they all have very distinct personalities, which I hope will compliment each other perfectly. I think we have the makings of a true rock and roll band here."

Boyce laughed.

"I guess we do!"

After everyone had eaten the hamburgers that Steven had prepared, Jared was the first to speak.

"OK. Where is everything? And where are we to sleep?" Kaya smiled as she stood and led the way to the hidden doorway. The others followed. Gasps of surprise greeted the scene when Kaya turned on the lights in the secret room, revealing the equipment that had been cleaned and polished. The colored lights that had been recently installed cast a mysterious and inviting persona to the stage.

"Are these for real?" Larret asked. "They can't be."

"That isn't all." Boyce added. Leaving through one of the stage doors, he led the way to another area that preceded further underground. He opened a door to reveal an old hotel that had been long since forgotten.

"This would have been the hotel that housed all the rock stars that came to town. " Boyce explained. "At least that is what our research tells us."

Kaya further explained.

"It was called the Rocker's Paradise. This was where all the musicians stayed when they came to play here. You see this hotel had a connecting door to the concert hall. That way, if the musicians wanted, they never had to leave the hotel.

"On the night of the final rock concert, PARR stormed the concert hall. A violent earthquake shook the hotel and the concert hall, sinking the majority of the buildings into the ground. Some say that the gods were angry about what was happening to their music so they vented their anger by destroying everything and burying it from sight.

"It would remain that way until the person, or people, who were worthy enough to bring back the music happened to come across it."

"I guess that means that we are the chosen ones." Brian whispered, half to himself. The others were silent, each thinking of the responsibility that this placed on everyone. No longer could this be considered a high-risk game, and if anyone had thought that before, they no longer could.

"Would you guys like to see your rooms now?" Boyce asked. "It has been a long day and I think that it is time for all of us to hit the sack."

The others nodded, still too shaken to say anything.

CHAPTER Twenty-Eight

The next day dawned sunny and clear. Kaya was up early and in the kitchen, fixing breakfast for everyone. She could barely contain her excitement at having found the people they were looking for. Now, at last, Kaya felt as if LUPO was actually going to make a stand for rock and roll. For quite some time Kaya had felt that LUPO wasn't really accomplishing much. Sure, they were a nuisance to PARR but for how long? And how long was it going to take for the public to get sick of hearing LUPO's name? It was past time for them to do something drastic. Now that the majority of the population knew who they were and what they were fighting for, LUPO was going to make an explosion.

Boyce, Kaya, Larret, Brian and Jared gathered in the old concert hall for a meeting. Boyce wheeled out a video recorder while Kaya got the videos down from a shelf.

"Have any of you ever seen Mystique play?" She asked.

The three men shook their heads, signifying that they hadn't.

"OK. I thought it might be a good idea for everyone to see some rock concerts so that we know what the total rock and roll experience was."

"But how are we going to learn to play those instruments?" Jared asked.

"With the help of videos. Of course, since we are short of time, everyone is going to have to work night and day practicing. Kaya has the advantage of already knowing how to play her keyboards and I have learned classical guitar. Do any of you have any musical experience at all?"

"I once went out with a singer. Does that count?" Larret asked with a boyish grin. "

"How about a drummer? That would make things a little easier."

"Sorry. Never got the chance. Which brings us to another question. How long are we going to have to stay down here away from everyone?"

Kaya and Boyce exchanged glances of concern. This was the question that they had been dreading and the others reaction to it would give them an impression of how serious they were about LUPO and Mystique II.

"We don't know. " Kaya admitted. "That all depends on how long it takes to get everything together."

"Like what?" Jared asked.

"Like the band." Boyce offered. "And the new chapter of LUPO."

"It is all going to take some time." Kaya further explained "But, if you want to go out, we can always disguise you and it wouldn't be that dangerous unless anyone of you started to make a scene. Of course, you can never let anyone know about this place."

"And it won't be forever." Brian mused, "I think that I can handle it. By the way, what exactly is the plan?"

Kaya, feeling more at ease with Brian than any of the others, explained.

"The first step is to learn everything as well and as quickly as we can. Then we are, going to hold a rock concert."

Jared gulped as he almost choked on his coffee.

"A rock concert?! Lady, are you crazy? PARR will have us in jail so fast that it will make our heads spin!"

"Not if everything is done the way we have it planned." Kaya remarked calmly. "By that time we should have so much public support that there is no way that PARR will be able to do anything."

"And how are we going to get this support?" Larret asked.

"By making the people more aware of what they are missing. When rock and roll first started, it had to face a lot of opposition. Granted, it wasn't a crime punishable by death as it is now, but it was difficult for those musicians.

"We start with the younger generation. The teenagers are the ones that are going to make the changes we need."

"But the teenagers don't have the power that is going to over turn the laws already made." Jared argued.

"They have more power than we give them credit for." Boyce pointed out. "If we can get enough of the teenagers to support the music, I think that we will stand a better chance of getting it heard by everyone than we would if they don't realize what is going on."

"How do we approach these teenagers?"

"By going to the local high school. That may sound like something really simple and it is true that we will only be talking to a few at first but it is a start. Also teenagers like to tell their friends and they will be sure to spread the word."

"This is dangerous and it isn't going to be easy. We are also going to have do odd jobs and get paid under the table. There isn't stability here right now. Why would each of you agree to do it?" Kaya spoke quietly and simply yet her words seemed to resound in the enclosure. There was a surprised silence all around. Her words came as a shock and each person was thinking of the consequences of their actions, especially if anything went wrong. Finally, Brian spoke up.

"All my life, I've opposed things quietly, not making too much of a fuss for what I believed in. This is something that I truly believe in and it is a way to finally come out of hiding."

"I've always been in trouble, in some way or another." Jared added. "But you seem to think that you have use for a rebel that couldn't make anything of his life."

Larret cleared his throat.

“As for me. I haven't done anything right since the day I was born. I've spent my life playing cards, raising shit and chasing women. But I do think that I can accomplish something here."

Kaya smiled.

"Good! Now time is a wasting and we have a lot to do, so let's get busy."

Boyce switched on the video and all sat down to begin their training.

"It's a good thing that this room's soundproof!" Kaya yelled in Boyce's ear. Larret was practicing on his drums with much enthusiasm and was making a real racket but he was beginning to sound good. Kaya felt that she had better hurry up and carry out the rest of LUPO’s plan since this band was coming along faster then anyone had expected.

"Yeah! But isn't it sounding great?!"

Kaya nodded in answer. Boyce smiled, an idea suddenly occurring to him. Motioning for Larret to stop playing a moment, he said,

"Now that everyone seems to have the hang of what to do, why don't we have a jam? I feel as if I'm ready for it, what about you guys?"

Jared and Brian exchanged glances then nodded their agreement, Kaya shrugged her answer and Larret vigorously hit his drum set. Everyone got on stage and went to their respective instruments.

Halfway through the first song, Brian and Boyce started laughing.

"Do we ever sound horrible!” Brian gasped. "I don't even think that everyone is playing the same song.”

Kaya giggled.

"Yeah, I guess that we're pretty bad right now, but let's keep at it."

"Practice makes perfect!" Jared said solemnly with a twinkle in his eye. "One more time!"

That evening, the five musicians sat around a table.

“I told you that practice makes perfect." Jared commented to the others. "By the time we finished playing, we were beginning to sound not too bad."

"But a long way from perfect." Larret threw in.

“Maybe we should start practicing together more." Kaya suggested. "That way we can get the feeling of playing together and help each other out."

"And we can start writing some of our own stuff, too." Brian threw in shyly. "I’ve got a couple of ideas that I think would work."

Everyone agreed that they would start playing together more and that they were interested in seeing Brian's songs before Larret threw in a comment,

"I don't know about the rest of you guys here but I am getting really tired of this basement. Why don't we all go out tonight?"

Kaya and Boyce exchanged smiles. They had been waiting for the right opening to suggest something.

"I think that is a good idea too." Boyce added casually. "Kaya and I had planned on going out tonight."

"Where?"

"To a local bar. We had some things we wanted to do there."

"Like what?" Jared was getting suspicious. From what he knew of Kaya and Boyce, when they said they had something to do it usually meant something dangerous.

"Like taking the first step in getting LUPO really known."

"And how are you going to do that?" Larret asked.

"The nightclub that we had planned to go to has got a DJ playing music." Boyce started to explain.

"So this absolutely gorgeous redhead is going to distract the DJ for a few moments so that someone can inject a CD of Mystique." Kaya threw in. "I realize that it won't be teens that are listening but we're feeling restless."

"I'm just feeling as if I have been sitting here too long, not doing anything to continue the movement."

"These people aren't teens but they are people in their young twenties, which is also our target market. So what do you say? Are you guys game for this?"

"Sounds like it might be fun." Jared commented.

"And dangerous." Brian pointed out. "But what the hell. Why not?"

Larret looked at the others and threw up his hands in defeat.

"It looks like I'm outvoted. And it does get me out of the basement for a while. So I guess I'll go along for the ride."

An hour later, four men and a very beautiful redheaded woman entered a nightclub downtown that was packed with people. Getting themselves drinks, everyone started to walk around the place. Jared stuck close to Kaya as Boyce went to the washroom.

"Can I ask you a question?" He asked in an undertone.

Kaya nodded her thoughts on other matters.

"Do you ever think of anything else besides LUPO?" For a moment Kaya was startled. Thinking back she tried to find a time when LUPO wasn't a part of her thoughts and her life and when it hadn't ruled her every action.

"No, I guess not. At least not since I was sixteen years old."

"You should relax more. I mean, rock and roll and battling censorship aren't everything, are they?"

Kaya's head went back and her eyes behind the green colored contacts flared.

"If you think that way," she hissed "why are you here? To me rock and roll and the fight to end censorship is everything. The destruction of PARR is the most important mission that I have."

"Why?"

"Because they killed my father, raped my best friend and totally destroyed my life. So don't tell me that what I'm doing isn't important because it is! As far as I'm concerned, spending your life hanging out and not caring about what we are missing in life because some government agency has decided that it isn't good for us is a waste of time!" Kaya brought herself under control with difficulty.

Jared stood there, stunned over her outburst then laughed good-naturedly.

"Whew! I guess that you told me. Though I think that it sounds more like a mission of vengeance than anything else. "

Kaya shrugged, her good humor now restored.

"Maybe it is. Whatever the reason, the outcome is still the same and I won't stop fighting now."

"Don't worry. I'm here with you until the end."

Kaya flashed a look of gratitude towards Jared. Though he could make her angrier than she had ever been, she was glad of his support. Looking at her wristwatch and at the growing amount of people in the nightclub, she decided it was time. Signalling to the other guys, she made her way towards the DJ booth.

"It must be so exciting to be a DJ." Kaya cooed to the scrawny, dirt encrusted man sitting near her. The DJ swelled with pride. He had been really surprised when this good looking redhead had come up to his booth and even more surprised when she had asked him if she could buy him a drink. He wasn't supposed to leave his booth but, with someone this sexy, how could he resist? Now, he sat across from this woman, who was beautiful but didn't seem so bright, totally forgetting that he was supposed to be watching his booth. Kaya, though, was watching it very closely. She imperceptibly held her breath as she saw that Boyce had entered the booth and let it go when she saw him leave. Within minutes, the music of Mystique flooded the nightclub, causing the people on the dance floor to stop in their tracks. The DJ, who had been sitting there with his eyes on Kaya's temporarily enlarged bust, quickly got to his feet.

"Excuse me." He muttered as he rushed off.

Jared came up behind Kaya and grabbed her arm.

"Time to make our exit." He commented under his breath. "PARR should be here at any moment."

Kaya followed Jared unwillingly, more interested in the peoples' reaction than the dangers PARR presented. Looking over the crowd of dancers on the floor beneath them, she saw that they were enjoying the music and, when it was abruptly stopped, an angry uproar rose.

"Turn it back on!" Someone demanded.

"Yeah! That is easier to dance to than what we usually hear!"
"What type of music was that?"
"Where can we hear more of it?"
Kaya grinned at Jared and from her purse, drew a stack of flyers. Dropping these over the railings, she quickly followed Jared out of the club.
"What in the hell were you doing?" Jared demanded angrily." And what was that you dropped over the railings?"
Kaya smiled and pulled another flyer from her purse. Jared took it and, holding it to the shine of a nearby streetlight, read the words aloud.

> "The music you just heard is by the band Mystique. It is rock music, one of the artistic expressions that PARR has so unjustly outlawed. In order for PARR to keep the people of this great land under their control, they have been slipping us drugs to distort our perception of events around us and of time periods. For your own sake, DON'T take anything that is given you by a government official and neither should you allow the children to do so.
>
> We are the members of LUPO and we are trying to stop PARR so that we can once again enjoy the sounds of bands like you just heard. If you like having your freedom to choose what you wish and feel it has a place in our society, then be prepared to fight for it. We have been fighting to stop this injustice for over twenty years and now we need your help. Keep your eyes and ears open for more information."

Jared grinned.
"You two don't mess around do you? First, the revival of Mystique inside and now this. What did I get myself into?"
Kaya leaned over and gave Jared a kiss on the cheek.
"The evening is not over yet, my friend. There is plenty of more excitement ahead."

Jared followed Kaya to the waiting van, a look of confusion and apprehension on his face. When Kaya said that there was plenty of more excitement ahead, she could only mean danger.
With lights turned off, the dark van sat across the street from the Los Angeles PARR office. Inside Kaya was finishing the final touches to her second costume of the evening. Like the other four occupants of the van, she was dressed all in black with her light colored hair secured beneath a black knit cap. As she put the black grease on her face, she stared at the mirror and laughed softly.
"Don't I look fetching?" She giggled then peered closer at the four men. "We look like a bunch of filthy raccoons!"

Jared leaned closer.

"Would you like to kiss me now, my sweet?" He teased.

"Let's get this thing over with." Boyce commented shortly. He knew that Jared was only kidding around yet he couldn't help but feel the jealousy surge through him. He had finally found the woman of his dreams and he wouldn't let anyone take her away from him.

The five people slipped across the street to the darkened government building. Circling the building, Boyce found a loose window and forced it from its frame, wincing as the pane squealed in protest. All stood motionless for a moment as they listened intently for noise from within the building. Fortunately no one seemed to be disturbed and quickly everyone crept into the building through the now opened window. Small penlights lit the way through the halls and stairwells as the members of Mystique II made their way towards the executive offices at the top of the building.

Kaya gazed around her with interest, mentally recording the layout of the building and taking note of the marked offices. If she ever had to come back here it would be good to know her way around.

"Damn! It's locked." Boyce hissed in frustration as he tried the door that led to the offices of the upper echelon.

Jared's blackened eyebrows rose.

"What did you expect?" He whispered in answer. 'Did you honestly think that they would have left the door opened with a big sign that said 'Welcome LUPO, come on in and destroy what we have taken years to build?' Jared's tone was sarcastic yet contained an element of humor in an attempt to lighten the seriousness of the situation.

Kaya giggled nervously as she studied the scowl on Boyce's face. For some reason, which Kaya was not able to figure out, Boyce had been extremely touchy lately when it came to Jared.

Brian, sensing the tension that was building, smiled weakly.

"Does anyone have any suggestions on how we are going to get in? It would make too much racket if we tried to kick the door in."

Jared grinned mischievously and took out a small, black packet from his jacket pocket. "With these. The finest lock picking instruments in the country." Kneeling by the locked door, Jared studied the lock and the paraphernalia in his hand for a moment.

Curious, Kaya came forward to lean over his shoulder.

"Interesting." She commented. "Where did you get those and why do you have them?" Larret chuckled from behind her.

"I don't think you want to know. I have a feeling that Jared was up to no good with those." Larret paused as Jared swung open the door that led to an inner sanctum. "Am I right?" Larret asked of the now triumphant Jared. No vocal answer was issued though Jared shrugged and his eyes twinkled.

Once inside, everyone got to work quickly. Studying the rows of file cabinets along one side of the first space, the LUPO members were searching for any hard files that weren't on computer that may pertain to rock and roll or Mystique. Brian, searching a section given to the 'Rs', had stumbled upon something equally as important.

"Kaya." He whispered loudly.

Kaya looked up from where she was looking and raised her eyebrows. Brian, still studying the information in front of him walked the few feet that separated them.

"That first night we came to the hotel, what was the name of that drug you asked us if we had taken?"

"Regonol."

Brian smiled victoriously and handed her a sheet of paper. There was an order for Regonol in liquid form as well as instructions on its use. Kaya whistled softly.

"So that's how they do it. Now that we are certain of it, we also have a better chance of fighting it" She leaned up and gave Brian a hug. "Good work!"

"There's a cross reference here." Boyce whispered. "And I think it's one that we should check out." Copying down the information, Boyce proceeded into one of the inner offices. The others, curiosity overwhelming them, followed silently. When they saw what Boyce had found, all were astounded.

Boyce had discovered a panel in an office wall that slid out to reveal rows upon rows of rock and roll CDs. Upon closer observation, they saw that every rock and roll group that had ever existed and managed to make any sort of name for them appeared to be represented. Each person taking a section to cover, all five tried to grab as many of the precious articles of music that they could.

With pockets bulging, Kaya suddenly stood straight and cocked her ear towards the window.

"Do you hear something?" She asked.

The others listened for a moment then went to stand with her when Brian spoke.

"Sirens." He stated simply. Within moments of the realization that the sirens were approaching, the five also heard the sound of the elevator rising. Quickly and silently, Boyce closed the panel and everyone moved towards the stairwell.

Just as they were leaving, Kaya saw a computer sitting on a desk just waiting for someone to use it. With a mischievous glint in her eye she rushed to it and rapidly typed something on the keyboard. Then she hastened to join her comrades waiting by the stairs.

Kaya had showered and was now sitting in what they were using as a lobby of the Rocker's Paradise Hotel with the rest of the band. She mused to herself about how considering the guys sitting around her as the 'band' but somehow it seemed right. And it seemed even more right to be sitting here.

"So what did you type in on the computer?" Boyce asked.

Kaya grinned.

"You really want to know?" Kaya asked with a smile.

"Yes!" The four men chorused.

"Long Live Rock and Roll and then I signed it the members of LUPO."

Jared groaned.

"That is what you risked our lives for?" He demanded. "Now PARR is sure to know who broke into their offices and stole all those CDs."

"So they know." Kaya shrugged. "And I never asked you to wait for me!" She shot back angrily.

"What did you expect us to do? Leave you there to get caught then be executed?"

"Calm down you two." Brian played his part as peacemaker once again. "And let's take a look at the CDs that we obtained."

"Obtained." Boyce reflected. "I like that terminology. It is so much better than stole."

Brian smiled in answer as they bent to look at the collection that was now before them. Although most of the group had managed to only take about twenty or thirty of the outlawed musical items, Jared had somehow managed to get closer to eighty.

Boyce looked at the other musician with wonder in his eyes

"How did you manage that?" He asked. Jared went to answer but Larret, with a mischievous grin, answered for him.

"I have a feeling that this is another one of those things that you would be better off not knowing." Silence for a second then laughter resounded in the room. Even Jared, looking sort of sheepish, laughed along with the others.

"What is our next move?" Brian asked.

"Monday, Andric and Boyce are going to go back to their old high schools to visit the teens now attending." Kaya explained with a loving smile in Boyce's direction. A smile that not only warmed his heart but also assured him that he had nothing to worry about.

Brian caught the exchange and was inwardly relieved that matters seemed to be on track with the couple again.

"What are they going to do there or should I ask?" Jared commented.

"We are going to let the teens know what LUPO, Mystique and rock and roll are all about." Boyce stated. "But we are going to have to get copies of these CDs made up over the weekend so that we can pass them along to the kids."

"And warn them about the Regonol." Kaya advised. "According to the information that Brian found, PARR has been slipping it into the school cafeteria food, refreshments at the rallies and at any other government organized function."

"What in the hell is Regonol anyways?" Larret asked." And are you sure that this is what is controlling people?"

"Regonol and Mestinon are the brand names of a drug called pyridostigmine. I think that PARR is using this drug to control the people because it will cause confusion and they order a damn lot of it. Although the confusion and irritability are supposed infrequent side effects, I think that someone at PARR may be tampering with the drug in order to enhance the mental side effects."

"Is it possible that there are just a lot of people that require this medication?" Brian asked innocently.

"Pyridostigmine is used to treat myasthenia gravis which is a disorder of neuromuscular transmission. Until I did my research, I had never even heard of myasthenia gravis."

Jared was listening to the exchange intently and looked at Kaya with respect.

"Wow! Not only is the lady beautiful and talented but she is also remarkably smart too. How do you know all that stuff?"

Kaya blushed.

"Don't give me too much credit. I don't know a lot about drugs I just looked this one up when I came across it on PARR's computer."

"Well I do know a lot about drugs but they aren't the medicinal kind. Usually they are just the type that gives you a good time." Jared joked in response, revealing more of his character and past.

Everyone chuckled before Larret made his own observation.

"But why hasn't it affected us and others in LUPO? We should be the same as everyone around us if we are also being subjected to this stuff."

"I never ate at the school cafeteria or at any PARR rally." Kaya offered. "I used to have such a sensitive stomach that my mother had to prepare special foods for me. I know that Boyce was also very particular about what he ate so he never ate when he wasn't sure what it was."

"I did a lot of drugs when I was younger so I was stoned most of the time." Jared remarked. "Perhaps they counteracted the Regonol"

"If anyone showed too much of a sensitivity to the drug, it appears that PARR would be certain to serve them something special. And, for some of us, the drug just may not work." Boyce further speculated.

"PARR has never been out to kill the public, just control them." Kaya insisted. "They only want to kill those who they cannot control."

Boyce added an after thought.

"And some of us are feeling the effects of this drug. Gleven, Margaret, Wind and even my Dad have difficulties recalling past events. In fact, the older generation doesn't even seem to be sure how old they are, they can't really remember the members of their own families and don't ever expect to get a true answer to any question on the past. They just aren't sure."

"So," Brian thought aloud. "It would seem that the drug was in higher quantities to the generation before us. For some reason, PARR felt it was necessary to distort their memories to a greater degree than ours. I wonder why that is."

"Perhaps it has something to do with the time lapse between the end of rock and roll and now." Larret commented. "If PARR is playing with our memories so that we won't recall much of the past maybe that is because it wasn't so long ago that the freedom to make our own choices existed."

Kaya looked at Larret, surprised at his observation.

"That's right! As long as they keep telling us that the world has been this way for a long time, the people will have doubts about the wisdom of trying to change things."

"It is something to look into." Boyce added. "But that may mean another trip into the PARR offices."

"Or perhaps a trip to New York. " Kaya mused aloud. "I've always been curious about something Gleven mentioned when we rescued him from jail."

"And what was that?" asked Jared.

"Gleven overheard some guards talking about something hidden in the Rockies and were wondering why Gleven wasn't being sent there. It sounds as if they might have a prison or something there."

Jared was puzzled.

"What good would that do us?"

"If," Kaya speculated "they are hiding former rock stars up there and we freed them, PARR would soon realize that we are going to bring back the music and, with these musicians' help, we can show people what rock and roll is all about."

"But they would be all dead by now." Jared insisted.

Kaya smiled smugly.

"Perhaps not. Some would be I'm sure but if it isn't as late in the future as we are being made to think, there may be a lot alive."

Brian suddenly looked up then disappeared from the room only to return a few moments later with a folder in his hand.

"Did you say the Canadian Rockies?" He asked Kaya.

Kaya nodded, confused as to what was happening.

Brian grinned and showed her the file. At the top was the title. 'Canadian Rocky Mountain Hideaway'.

Kaya took the file and skimmed some of the contents with an incredulous expression.

"Where did you get this?" She asked Brian.

"It was lying on top of the filing cabinet and I meant to show it to you but that was when Boyce found the hidden panel and, in my excitement over the CDs I forgot. I just tucked it away in my jacket."

"Do you realize what this is?" Kaya asked him, her eyes shining with suppressed excitement.

Brian shook his head. The others leaned forward, held speechless in anticipation of what Kaya was about to say.

"This 'hideaway' appears to actually be a prison camp. I'll have to study the list a bit more but it seems to have the names of every rock musician they put in there, the date they were captured and, if applicable, the date of death."

"Excuse me if I seem stupid, but what are you thinking Kaya?" Larret asked hesitantly.

"I'm thinking," Kaya began "that if the members of Mystique are still alive wouldn't it be something to free them? With them on our side the truth would certainly come out and then we would be another step closer to defeating PARR. "

"What about the other musicians there?" Brian inquired. "Would it be fair to just leave them behind?"

Kaya thought for a moment

"By the looks of the area, I think it would be risky enough to rescue Mystique never mind the others. Once rock and roll is once again legal, the first thing we would do is to go up there and free everyone. Until then, we have to choose one band and my vote is on Mystique because that is who we feel the closest to. Besides, what is the name of our band?"

Jared grinned.

"She does have a point. By the way, where is this place?" Kaya consulted the map that lay before her.

"It appears to be outside of Banff, Canada and it is located on a mountain peak."

"Great!" Larret mumbled. "Now how in the hell do we get up there?"

"We fly to Calgary, Canada then rent a car and get as close to the camp as possible. From there on, I'm not sure." Kaya admitted. All were silent as they contemplated this new adventure then Jared spoke again.

"But what do we do now?"

"I think that we, or at least Kaya and I, are going to go to bed. It has been a long, stressful day. Why don't we set up a practice session for first thing in the morning? That is, if everyone agrees."

Jared, Larret and Brian all looked at one another.

"Sounds good to me." Brian offered. Getting no refusal from anyone else, Boyce set the time and then bid everyone goodnight

He and Kaya left the lobby hand in hand. Watching them leave Jared felt a twinge of jealousy.

"Hold it!" he silently commanded himself. "She and Boyce have been together since I first met them and I have no reason to become jealous." Though, logically, Jared knew this to be true he still could not help the way he was feeling. The memory of the kiss on his cheek that Kaya had given him remained in his heart.

The youngest of five boys, Jared had always been a hell raiser, defying authority every opportunity he had. And if an opportunity didn't arise itself, Jared would be sure to create one. Early in his life, his passive parents had given up on trying to raise their son and just prayed for the best. By the time Jared was in his teens, he had managed to calculate the consequences of the majority of his rebellious actions. Shorter than average, Jared found that he could not physically threaten those who opposed him and therefore he used his wits to avoid being beat on. Girls loved his gregarious nature and enjoyed spending time with him since he always made them laugh. Yet when he had reached maturity, Jared had just wandered through life. Constantly seeming to be in trouble with no one to turn to since his family had long since given up on him, Jared drifted through the days and fought to survive. But thanks to Kaya More, Boyce Mitchell and LUPO, it now seemed as if his life had direction. Granted it wasn't the path that many would wish to take but it suited his rebellion-geared tendencies perfectly.

Brian settled himself into his bed that night thinking of the revelations of the evening. The speculations concerning time came to mind.

"Was it possible," Brian wondered silently. "That rock and roll hadn't ended that long ago. Had the previous generation openly enjoyed the music that a person now endangers their lives to hear?

"Life is strange." Brian thought to himself. "Here I am fronting for an illegal rock band that is thought to be destined to change the course of time. When rock and roll may have existed within our life span." It was an interesting thought to be considered and one definitely to be investigated.

Brian Malloy had grown up as the middle child in a very loving family. It was a family that believed in the right to be happy as long as your happiness didn't harm others and Brian had always felt safe and secure. His older brother had been a very vocal person and that had led to some concern among the elder Malloys but they didn't feel that they had the right to discourage him so they never had. Perhaps events would have turned out happier if they had done so.

One night when Brian was fifteen, his entire life collapsed around him. While walking home from a date, Brian noticed that there were a lot of vehicles outside his home. For some reason, Brian hid behind a tree to watch the goings on instead of approaching and investigating.

His heart crept up to his mouth when he saw the men dressed in PARR uniforms escort his older brother out of the house. Moments later his parents and little sister were also herded roughly into the back of the van. Brian had the sinking feeling as he watched the van drive away that he would never see his family again.

Wisely Brian had disappeared the moment the PARR vehicles had left his house. Hitchhiking across the country until he reached California, Brian had formed a wall between himself and others. Though he had still opposed the wrongs in this country, he had done so on the quiet and therefore could never be blamed. He had learned that night that, without power, those in the government would destroy you. Yet it felt good to finally be coming out from behind his walls and fighting injustice publicly.

Larret sat in his room, musing on the events of the last month. He had gone from being a no good gambler and an avid skirt chaser to an important member of an illegal underground movement that was fighting for a just cause. He laughed aloud when he thought of the look on his brother's face if only he knew.

The younger of two boys, Larret had always been in the shadow of his older brother, Ansel. All Larret's life he had been held up to Ansel and his accomplishments and found lacking. Ansel had always gotten whatever he wanted and what he didn't get, he took.

At the age of eighteen Ansel had joined the forces of PARR, which had made his parents extremely proud. With Ansel now out of the house, Larret had assumed that the pressure for him to be like his older brother would diminish a bit. Unfortunately, if anything, the comparisons became worse as Ansel excelled within the strict disciplinary confines of PARR. How ironic that Larret would make his mark working with the other side.

Kaya snuggled closer to Boyce, radiating in the body heat that was emanating from him. It was good to feel protected and secure. For some reason, she sometimes felt the need to be vulnerable and the advances of LUPO were overwhelming at times. But everything seemed to be progressing the way it should be.

Boyce felt Kaya moving closer to him and inwardly smiled. Though the world saw Kaya as a strong, independent individual, which she was, he knew that she had her moments of weakness when she needed someone near. At times her activities worried him. Like with the latest developments with LUPO. Kaya was taking unnecessary risks, as in stopping to type the message on the computer screen. Also she was also working herself too hard. She was not only practicing day and night to get Mystique II ready for performances but she was also still arranging much of LUPO's activities. And with other members coming in from all over the country, there was a lot to do. Yet no matter how much Boyce talked to her about it or what he said, Kaya wouldn't or couldn't slow down. Boyce sighed. That was the way that Kaya was and there nothing he, or anyone else, could do about it. The most he could do was to be there for her when she needed him. Quietly, the young couple drifted off to sleep.

PART THREE

THE WORLD UNITES

CHAPTER Twenty-Nine

In a little coffee shop in Liverpool, England, a young man sat staring at the paper. He was reading a report from the United States that told about the rebels involved with LUPO. He longed for the opportunity to join the fight. With each passing day, Robert Blaine felt the injustice more and more. The injustice of being told what type of music he could listen to, where he could go and the restrictions that was constantly being inflicted on citizens. Having seen some illegal tapes and DVDs of rock bands performing, Robert longed to pick up a guitar and just play whatever he felt. However, that was not allowed in this society.

Robert was a typical young man of his generation. Life was strictly ordered and one was taught never to disrupt the order of things. Rebellion was a word and action that was unthinkable. He had always been told that it was easier to accept the way life was than to try to change it. Now he was desperate to make changes in the societies of the world.

"Damn it!" Robert swore quietly. "If Kaya More can do it, why can't I?"

Another man slid into the booth across from Robert and grinned.

"If Kaya More can do what? And who is Kaya More?"

Wordlessly, Robert handed his friend, a young man from Wales named Cedric, the paper he had been reading and pointed out the article in question. Silently Cedric read the short article and whistled softly.

"That's quite an undertaking. And it's dangerous." Cedric peered over the paper at his friend. "Do you think you can do it?" In a moment's retrospect, Cedric realized how ridiculous that last question was. Shy, retiring Cedric and impetuous, outgoing Robert had grown up together and he knew that Robert could do anything he wished to. At boarding school together, Robert had organized many an outing for the group that were against the harsh regulations. And sometimes the head masters had never discovered that anything had happened. Perhaps that was why Cedric had stayed around Robert. Being on the cautious side himself, Cedric was able to live vicariously through hearing of his friend's activities.

Cedric had been the youngest of five children and had grown up on a poor, Welsh farm. But he was proud and had been hesitant on accepting the scholarship he had earned to the boarding school that could one day change his life, thinking of it as charity. A teacher who had recognized the fact that Cedric was destined for great things, had submitted his name and school records. Then managed to convince Cedric's parents that this was their son's chance for a future. After all his four older brothers were more geared towards the farm work whereas slender Cedric with his intellectual nature was suitable for other pursuits. Somewhat grudgingly his parents had sent the young man to England to pursue his schooling.

The first few days had been difficult for Cedric; he had never felt like he fit in with his awkward manners and peasant breeding. But soon Robert Blaine had taken his Welsh schoolmate under his wing and introduced him to a life that he had never seen before. And although the majority of escapades that Robert enticed Cedric into participating in would be considered wild, the two boys had enjoyed themselves. The wild nature had softened over the years but Robert was still known as the instigator in many activities that never hurt anyone else but were considered a touch illegal.

Now Robert was getting a familiar gleam in his eyes and becoming more and more excited about the idea of starting an organization similar to North America's LUPO.

"Yes, I think I can." Robert declared confidently though there was also a twinge a fear that ran through him. "Would you like to help me?"

Cedric was silent for a moment, thinking of the ramifications of opposing the government agencies.

"You do know that there was a group like this a couple of years ago, don't you? They just disappeared from sight; no one knows what happened to them."

Once again Robert felt the twinge of fear that had risen earlier. However, that didn't discourage him. Instead he also felt a rush of adrenaline that came when he knew that he was right. Facing Cedric with a raised chin, he stubbornly declared his intentions.

"Yes I do realize that but they could still be out there. Even if they aren't, why should I let that stop me from fighting for what I think is right? I'm going ahead with this no matter what you say or do!"

"Hold it a minute!" Cedric laughed at his friend. "I never said that I disagreed with you, I was just warning you of the dangers."

Robert looked at his friend suspiciously.

"So you aren't going to try to talk me out of it?" He asked, still pondering Cedric's earlier words.

"Hell no! I think it is a great idea and I think you need me around to keep you level headed. If we can bring back the music that would be a great feat."

Robert's eyes lit up at the mention of 'we'.

"So you're with me on this one?"

"Why not?" Cedric shrugged fatalistically. "After all, someone needs to take care of you."

In a little pub in Scotland, a similar discussion was being held. Two men, Glen and Angus, also felt strongly about censorship and were determined to find a way to stop it.

Glen was short and stocky with sandy hair and blue eyes. His fair skin was apt to burn easily in the summer sun yet he endured the misery of sunburns since his first love was the open fields where the sun burned hot and steady.

A simple man, Glen had no illusions about the world or its problems. He possessed the strong attributes of frugality and hard work. It was very rare that his even temper got out of control. Not even now, in the face of his friend's hot temper with the discussion of censorship.

A complete opposite, Angus was tall and slender with artistic hands and a creative nature. He abhorred the manual labor required in many of the present day's occupations and longed to be able to put his imaginative mind to use somehow.

Whereas women found Glen's honest face somewhat attractive, they were always attracted to the dark, aristocratic, brooding features of Angus. Midnight black eyes shone fiercely with an unquenchable passion from his angular face, the fullness of his deep red lips enticed young maidens to dream about his kisses. Whenever a cause he felt was just was brought into the discussion, he would feel his emotions rise and his speech would remind listeners of the great orators of long ago. And, with the topic of censorship, Angus was exerting the strength of his speaking powers at full range.

"What the governments of this world are doing is wrong! They do not, nor have they ever had, the right to tell us what we should be doing and what choices we should be making!" Angus held up his work callused hands.

"I am an artist, a creative person. I should be creating beauty in this world, not farming fields! But I am not allowed to since the unjust rulers have decided that I belong as a manual laborer. Where is the justice in our world?" Angus ranted.

"Don' know." Glen replied, enjoying Angus's ravings more than he would ever admit.

"I'll tell you what happened to it. It was taken away, along with rock and roll music, books that the governments felt inflicted thoughts other than what they are going to tell us and our freedom to choose in this life. I say that enough is enough. It is time we stopped it and took back control of our own lives."

Glen took a sip of beer.

"And how do you propose that we do that?"

"By first bringing back rock and roll music. Once we have accomplished that, then the rest will follow in due time."

"Once again, how do you propose we do that?"

Angus leaned forward, his eyes gleaming somewhat maniacally with the passion for his cause that raged through him.

"By going to England and meeting up with Robert Blaine. Knowing his nature, he would love this fight. Remember that he was always involved in these sort of escapades in school."

"But how do you know that he will support this cause?"

"Even if he didn't support us, he would still work with us for the adventure of it all. And I happen to think that he would be supportive."

Glen thought for a moment then shrugged.

"Might as well." He mentioned casually. "After all, what better way to spend my time?" The two men returned to a more normal conversation, the thought of fighting censorship reigning foremost in their minds.

In a ski lodge in Switzerland, the topic of conversation also centered on the injustice of censorship. Damien Bowers sat scowling at his friends.

"What do you mean that censorship isn't that important to you?" He hissed vehemently. "They are taking away one of our most important rights. The freedom of choice."

One of the men in the group looped his arm around the shoulder of the girl sitting next to him.

"Yeah, yeah. Damien, we have heard you say that a million times! When are you going to do something about it?"

One of the guys chuckled.

"You know Damien. All talk, no action."

The entire group laughed and Damien, red in the face, stood up to leave. Immediately one of the guys sobered up.

"Hey Damien! We were only kidding! Where are you going?"

Damien took a moment to calm himself before turning back. Then, in a cool voice, he announced his intentions.

"I'm going to England. I met some people there last year. I'm going to do something about it." The group was speechless as Damien turned and left.

As he was walking towards his parents' chateau, Damien thought about what he had said in the lodge. It was true that he had vocally opposed the loss of their freedom of choice yet never had physically fought it but the comment of his friends had still hurt. Especially since they were right.

Like the majority of the people he had come into contact with, Damien Bowers was rich and spoiled. He never had to even think of working for a living or fighting to stop the injustices of society. Most everything he wanted, he was able to purchase or influence someone to give to him. But freedom of choice was something that Damien realized he had to fight for.

After his statement in the lodge, Damien knew that he had to go to England or be further ridiculed by his associates. Yet the question still remained in Damien's mind of whether he could do it or not. Setting his shoulders, Damien decided that, not only would he do it, but also he wouldn't use his parents' money unless it was deemed to be absolutely necessary.

With a quick stop at home to pack a few items in a knapsack, Damien hit the road, intending to hitchhike his way to Robert Blaine in England and to right the wrongs in society.

Denmark was also having its share of discontent among the young people. Melissa Turner sat over a cup of coffee shaking her head miserably.

"It just isn't right!" The seventeen year old wailed. "How can they be so unjust?"

Her friend Beth Biscoll tried to comfort her.

"It isn't so bad Melissa. You have only been suspended not expelled. In a month you can come back to school as if nothing has happened. In the meantime, I will make sure that I bring copies of every assignment so you won't fall behind."

Melissa, however, was not mollified.

Melissa, an impetuous, spoiled teenager, was used to getting her own way in almost everything and never getting in serious trouble. A pampered child of elderly parents, Melissa had led a charmed life of ease. And even though Melissa could be wilful to the point of annoyance, stubborn to the degree of ignorance, self indulgent to the extent of all else and, very rarely, overly selfish, she was usually a charming and enjoyable person to be around. On the other hand, Beth was the steadying influence that balanced Melissa's highly-strung nature. Beth rarely became overly emotional about anything, preferring instead to act on logic. Her academic parents had always expected Beth to be calm, behaving more like a miniature adult than the child she was. Now she patiently listened to Melissa's emotional speech.

"Can you imagine? Suspending me for playing some music that they don't like. How I wish that there was something that I could do."

Beth wisely didn't say anything. When she and Melissa had first found the illegal tapes in an antique store, they had thought it would be fun to listen to them. Both girls had felt an uplifting feeling as soon as the first notes had started on the tape and they felt they had to share it with their friends. Unfortunately Melissa had been caught with the tapes and that was when all the trouble had started. Now, with a suspension hanging over her head, Melissa feared the consequences of returning home. Morosely Melissa picked up a paper that lay nearby. Her eyes were immediately drawn to a small article on the front page.

> LUPO STRIKES AGAIN
>
> The Los Angeles offices of PARR were recently broken into and several of the outlawed rock and roll CDs were stolen. Members of LUPO reportedly left a message on a computer

reading ‘Long Live Rock and Roll’. Though no one has been apprehended at this time, the local chapter of PARR feels that they have enough leads as to lead to the identity the intruders.

Beth sat across the table and watched her impetuous friend intently. What was going through Melissa's mind was a mystery to her. The only thing she knew for sure was that it probably meant trouble.

"What are you thinking about?" Beth asked Melissa warily.

After a moment, Melissa circled the article and passed the paper to Beth. Beth read it, confused to the reason that Melissa seemed so excited about it. After she had finished, Beth raised her eyes to her friend.

"So, what do you think?" Melissa asked excitedly. Beth was silent for a moment, trying to determine what she was expected to say.

"So? A group of rebels in the States broke into the government offices and stole some CDs. What's the big deal?"

"What's the big deal? I'll tell you! There is a group of people in the States who have the guts to see when something is wrong and try to do something to change it. If they can do it, why can't we?"

"That's illegal, Melissa." Beth calmly reminded her." And if you think you are in trouble now, wait until you start something like this."

Melissa shrugged.

"So I get into trouble. Do you think that any of the rockers in days gone by worried about that? Do you think that they were concerned that their music might scare someone, or that someone might not like it? No! They went ahead and did it no matter what the opposition was." Melissa was working herself into a righteous fever over the injustice of it all.

Beth meanwhile, who had seen this reaction before, sat back and calmly listened to her friend's tirade.

"OK. That was them and it was a long time ago. Not only that, they were adults! We are just kids." Melissa looked at her friend scornfully.

"The age doesn't matter. We are the ones that are going to one day have to run this world."

"What are you going to do?" Beth knew that there was no use arguing with her friend but she was curious to see what she was going to do.

“I’m not sure yet. But I feel that I have to do something."

"Would you like some help?" Beth asked impulsively. She just hoped that she wasn't going to regret the offer.

"Of course I would like some help. When I know what I'm doing, I will let you know. In the meantime, if you have any ideas, don't worry about passing them on."

Beth smiled, still not sure if she was doing the right thing and glanced at her wristwatch.

"We had better get going. Meet you back here tomorrow after school?"

Melissa nodded, her thoughts on the lecture she would get when she got home.

The next day the two girls met in the coffee shop. Today though there was a stranger in the cafe. Seated close to the girls' table was a tall blond haired man with intense blue eyes. Melissa found herself looking that way a little too often but she was comforted to realized that, every time she looked his way, the stranger was looking at her. Trying to concentrate on Beth, she focused her gaze on her friend.

"Were you really serious about fighting the censorship of music?" Beth asked, half heartedly hoping that her friend had forgotten all about the idea.

"Of course." Melissa answered. "I know that the governments of this world are totally wrong and need to be destroyed. I just don't know where to start." The young man at the next table lifted his head suddenly as he overheard Melissa's comment. Quickly he came over to their table and took a seat without asking for permission.

"Lower your voice." He hissed. "You don't know who could be listening!"

Melissa's eyes glared as she fought to control her temper.

"And who the hell are you?"

The young man smiled.

"A friend. My name is Damien Bowers and I'm on my way to England."

“Why England?" Melissa asked her temper overshadowed by curiosity and sexual attraction.

"Because I have friends there that would do something about bringing back rock and roll music. I'm going to join them and see if I can help."

Indecision flashed briefly through Melissa's mind but as always, her decision only took moments to form.

"I want to go with you." She stated flatly.

Beth, who had been listening to this exchange with interest, choked on a swallow of coffee she was taking.

Damien was also startled but covered it well.

"Why?" He asked.

"Because I think that freedom of choice is important and I want to be involved with the fight to stop the governments of this world from telling us what to do. And if you don't take me, I will just follow you anyway."

Damien chuckled.

"OK. You might as well come along. But I’m warning you that this isn't going to be a luxury trip." Suddenly Damien thought of something. "How old are you anyway?"

Melissa thought quickly. If Damien knew how old she was, he would never let her come along. Glancing over at Beth, she prayed that her friend wouldn't tell the truth.

"Twenty one." Melissa replied confidently.

Across the table Beth rolled her eyes but didn't say anything while Damien gave a sigh of relief.

She may look young but at least this girl wasn't underage. Holding out his hand, he reintroduced himself.

"As I said before, I'm Damien Bowers."

Melissa held out her hand.

"Melissa Turner and this is my friend Beth Biscoll."

Damien greeted both ladies then turned to Beth.

"Are you also coming on our quest for justice?" He asked with a twinkle in his blue eyes. Beth thought for a moment. In her whole life she had never done anything rash. She had always followed rules, causing as little trouble as possible. She was sick and tired of being that good little girl who pleased everyone but herself. Setting her shoulders, she looked Damien and Melissa straight in the eye.

Melissa, who was hoping that Beth would agree to come with them, held her breath.

"Yes, I would be delighted to come with you."

Melissa's breath came out in a rush. Knowing how cautious Beth was, it was a bit of a surprise that Beth had agreed to come. She felt a rush of adrenaline as she had the feeling that they were embarking on the adventure of their lives.

Back in Liverpool Robert Blaine was astounded at the response he was receiving to his idea of forming an organization to bring back the music of his ancestors. Though he had been confident a week ago when he first had the idea that it was something that needed to be done, Robert hadn't realized that so many people were also feeling the same way. Both he and Cedric had received numerous phone calls and letters, all lending support. Their little group of rebels had grown measurably within a week. Now Robert and Cedric sat in the same coffee shop marvelling at the response they were getting.

“I guess more people than we thought are against censorship."

"How did they find out though?" Cedric asked, half to himself. "I mean, we didn't advertise the fact."

"Word gets around." Robert said.

"But how? That is what I want to know. If the common person can find out, what's to say that the authorities can't?"

"You worry too much." Robert answered. "Why not go with it and face whatever happens when it comes?"

Cedric nodded, lost in his own thoughts. Concentrating on this dilemma, he didn't notice the arrival of two men until Robert exclaimed.

"Angus! Glen! What are you two doing here?"

Cedric turned to see the two men and smiled gently. He had a strange feeling that they were here for the same reason he was staying.

Glen and Angus came and sat down at the small table. Without preamble, Glen came straight to the point.

"We need your help. We are all sick of this business of the government not letting us listen to the music we want to. Or read the books we want to. It is time that it all stopped and we want to do something to stop it"

Cedric and Robert exchanged glances of amusement. This was exactly what they needed.

"Do we have something to tell you?" Robert started with a chuckle.

On the outskirts of Liverpool, Damien, Melissa and Beth walked. The road from Denmark hadn't been easy but they had made it. The trio had left soon after the decision had been made to go, the only delay being Melissa and Beth going to their separate homes to pack a few clothes into knapsacks and leave notes for their parents that they were going. Both girls knew that, if their parents had been home, they would have stopped the girls from their quest. However, this was something that they both believed in with all their hearts and they weren't going to let anything stop them from their adventure.

"Are we almost there?" Melissa asked Damien.

Damien, who was having second thoughts about bringing the two girls, nodded. On the journey here, he had figured out that Melissa was younger than she had said and that he could be in trouble with the law for crossing borders with her. Suddenly he shrugged. He was already going to be in trouble with the law for what he was about to undertake and Melissa usually seemed to be mature for whatever age she was so what was he worried about? Just take it one day at a time.

"Let's go! We're almost there!" Running along the streets, the trio went in the direction of downtown.

Entering a coffee shop, Damien immediately saw his friend, Robert Blaine. Almost at the same instant, Robert happened to turn and see him. Shocked at the sight of his friend, Robert rose unsteadily to greet him.

"What in the hell are you doing here?" Robert choked out when he managed to find his voice.

Damien grinned that grin that Robert remembered so well.

"I've come to join forces with you and your friends to stop the injustice of the censorship of rock and roll music."

Speechless, Robert turned to the two women that were with

Damien. Melissa smiled and stuck out her hand.

"I'm Melissa Turner and this is my friend Beth Biscoll."

"I met up with them in Denmark and invited them to come along." Damien felt there was no harm in changing the events slightly and, since Melissa didn't correct him, he felt that it was agreeable with her.

Robert cleared his throat in an attempt to find his voice again. It was too much of a coincidence that everyone had gathered for the same reason at the same time. Surely it seemed as if higher forces were at work to bring everyone together with the same purpose in mind.

"Come and sit down. You guys look like you're starving." Gratefully the three travelers sat down at a table with everyone else. Almost immediately the talk turned to what they were going to do to stop censorship.

CHAPTER Thirty

London remained the way it had been for years; time worn but always standing proud. At Scotland Yard, a group of officials were discussing the same article that Melissa had read a little over a week ago.

"I'm sure glad we don't have those problems! " Jake Morley said.

"Yes." Josh Hurt agreed. "I don't think we ever will. Our people are too afraid of us to ever think of doing anything remotely similar."

"Don't count on it." Their captain Lester Aran, warned. "Never underestimate the people."

Josh and Jake scorned the idea. After all they felt they knew the population better than Lester did and they were certain that none of their people would ever think of inciting something that went against the rules. Gone were the memories of days past where the people had revolted against rules they felt were too strict and unjust. Gone were the memories of the famous rock musicians that had come out of England. Josh and Jake had forgotten all of this but Lester hadn't. With a sinking feeling, he realized that the people were only going to take so much before fighting back. The only difference between England and the United States was that the Americans had moved first.

"Not quite true." Lester mentally corrected himself "we were just able to control the rebellion easier." He felt a shiver crawl up his spine. Something was in the air and he knew that trouble wasn't far in the future.

Perhaps he was being overly cautious but Lester made a mental note to keep a very careful watch on any suspicious activities.

CHAPTER Thirty-One

A feeling of unrest and rebellion descended on the world, affecting each and every nation. From Asia to the United States to Great Britain and beyond, people were now questioning the rules of their society. The young people were no longer meek and mild accepting anything they were told. Now they were rebelling against authority, experimenting with the realization that they too had minds of their own. Many of the older generation were beginning to wonder if the world was perfect after all as pieces of their memories began to resurface and they sketchily remembered another time. The world was headed for an explosion that would rock the foundations of different nations and it wouldn't be long before major changes were going to take place.

CHAPTER Thirty-Two

REBELLION IN FRANKFURT Frankfurt Germany

The city of Frankfurt, Germany today saw the actions of a rebel organization trying to stop censorship and bring back the artistic materials that have been taken from the public. A group of demonstrators marched from the center of town to the city hall, chanting along the way. Their opinion is that censorship is wrong and should be stopped. Government officials refused to comment on the demonstration.

THE MUSIC ISN'T DEAD! London, England

A group of people belonging to the rebel organization, CIO, gathered around the government buildings today to vocalize their opinions. CIO, or the CHOICE IS OURS, is an organization founded recently to combat the censorship imposed by the government. Their primary goal is to bring back the outlawed rock and roll music.

ROCK AND ROLL IN JAPAN! Tokyo, Japan

Students marched today on government property to loudly criticize the censorship of music. The banned rock and roll music blared from CD players carried by many demonstrators. Though there were some minor injuries, no one was seriously injured.

AUSTRALIA JOINS THE BATTLE! Sydney, Australia

People of all ages gathered today to oppose government censorship. Carrying placards with slogans such as: ‘The Choice Is Ours, Not Theirs’ ‘Let Us Decide' and 'Ban Censorship, Not Rock and Roll'; the demonstrators impeded noon time traffic and enticed passer-by’s to sign a petition. It was all over when armed police squads appeared on the scene. No injuries incurred.

WHO IS RIGHT?

The issue of censorship has once again raised its ugly head. Worldwide people of all ages are fighting for the right to make their own choices and it all seems to have happened overnight. Granted, years ago a rebel organization called LUPO was founded in New York City but other than that the world has been fairly quiet. Now it seems as if everyone is demonstrating for his or her rights.

The main issue seems to be the censorship of the music rock and roll. It was decided that rock and roll should be banned after a few teenagers turned to devil worship and crime. Some even committed suicide. Though it was never proven that rock and roll music or rock or any other of its off shoots were the direct cause, some people felt that the music was evil. So, lobbying for government support and creating an uproar, these people managed to get the music banned.

The rebels that have been interviewed are not denying the facts of what has happened in the past. What they are saying is that it was never proven that the music was the cause and they feel rock and roll was used as a scapegoat. Some parents feared the music and, as is natural when a person fears something, they did their best to destroy it. All the rebels are asking for is the right to make a choice. If you don't want to listen to it, you don't have to but don't take that choice away from others.

Interviewing government officials proved to be a harder task but Judah Arnold, leader of the agency PARR, finally consented to speak with me. Sitting in his office in a tower overlooking New York, Mr. Arnold spoke his views.

"Rock and roll music is wrong. It is dangerous and it deserved to be banned. Everyone looks to the past as the better times but if you compare our world with that one, you will see that unemployment is almost non existent, there are fewer crimes committed and everyone is happier."

"Are you saying that all this is because of the banning of rock and roll music?"

“Not entirely but that does play a large part in everything."

"But what about a person's freedom of choice? Don't you feel that a person should have the right to make their own choices in life?" Mr. Arnold drew himself up and replied,

"The government knows what is best for the people and we will stand behind anything and everything we have said and done. Now, I think this interview is over."

We have heard both sides of the censorship issue and the decision of which side is right and which side is wrong is yours to make.

LETTER TO THE EDITOR

Dear Editor;

First of all, I would like to compliment you on the article "Who Is Right?” I found it very well written, straight to the point and, most importantly, fair to all concerned. Now I feel that it is time to voice my views on the subject.

All my life I have been fighting censorship. My father was killed in the process of running the Let Us Play organization in New York. Yes, my name is Kaya More and I am one of the leaders of LUPO. For years we have been branded rebels and malcontents but let me tell you something. If it weren’t for the rebels and malcontents, the people that see something wrong in the world and try to fix it, we would still be living in caves.

Rock and roll music isn't wrong, no matter what Judah Arnold says. Censorship is wrong. It restricts the freedom of the common person and stunts the growth of society. Controversial issues expand the mind and exercise the right of free speech. These essential liberties of the people should not have been taken away. We have the right to say and do what we think is right. Give us back that right. That is all we ask.

Kaya More.

CHAPTER Thirty-Three

Heathrow Airport was filled with government officials flying in from every country in the world. They had all gathered here to discuss the recent rash of demonstrations and rebellions. Their main goal was to find a solution so they could end the revolution and once again bring the people under control.

Judah and Gary stepped off the plane and glanced around for someone to meet them. Judah scowled at first since he didn't recognize anyone but then his face cleared when he saw the cardboard sign with his name on it. Going up to the young man holding the sign he announced himself.

"I'm Judah Arnold. Are you here to take me to my hotel?"

The young man gulped nervously. He was new to the force and this was the one job that he hadn't wanted to take but, as things go, he was assigned to it.

"Uh...yes sir." The young man looked down at the three bags that Judah had on the floor beside him and smiled cautiously.

"Would you like me to take those?"

Judah looked at the man as if he were a simpleton.

"Of course." He said then stalked away, going in the direction of the exit.

Gary, meanwhile, had taken pity on the young man and reached down to take one of the bags. Giving the man a wink, Gary followed him out of the airport.

Their room at the hotel was plush and luxurious but Judah wasn't pleased.

"A waste." He muttered to himself. "Imagine spending all this money on hotel rooms when it could have been spent squelching the revolution."

Gary was sitting in a nearby chair reading the paper. At Judah's words he glanced up but, seeing the scowl on his boss's face, he wisely kept his comments to himself. Instead his eyes and mind went back to the article he had been reading. It was, oddly enough, all about censorship and the people's views on it.

"There's going to be trouble." Gary thought to himself as he read along. The article stated that many people felt that censorship was destroying the minds of the population. That without the freedom to think and do what they thought was right, everyone would just stagnate. They would be no better than animals. In fact that was what they were at the moment Gary chuckled to himself as he read a little further. These people really meant business. He breathed a sigh of relief that they were not in the United States then stopped himself. In a way they were.

In the last few months LUPO, under the total direction of Kaya More, had taken more and more daring steps. After the incident at the nightclub and the subsequent break in and robbery at the Los Angeles PARR offices, LUPO had lain low for a while but soon they were going as strong as ever. Perhaps stronger. It seemed as if every meeting of PARR had been disrupted somehow by the people in LUPO. Simple things like the refreshments being tampered with, wrong directions being given and the constant feeling that they were being watched and questioned, served to undermine the unity of PARR. Some officials were now beginning to wonder if, perhaps, they were wrong in censoring the music. Was it that bad after all? Gary himself wondered at times. But he had sworn his allegiance to PARR and until something happened to change his mind, he was honor bound to uphold that vow.

"Are you listening to me?" Judah's voice broke into Gary's thoughts.

Quickly, Gary brought himself back to the present and sat up straight.

"Excuse me, sir. What were you saying?"

Judah scowled his annoyance before answering.

"I'm hungry. We should go find out if this place has a decent restaurant."

"You're always hungry." Gary muttered in an undertone that Judah couldn't hear. Since this trip had begun, Judah had consumed so much food that Gary was discovering how disgusting the other man could be. But he stood ready to follow his boss.

Somewhere in the slums of London a meeting was beginning. The members of CIO were gathering to review their plans for the next day. After talking a while Robert glanced over the crowd of people seated in front of him.

"So is everyone clear on what their assignment is?" In unison heads nodded. Robert smiled slightly then adjourned the meeting. CIO was ready for action.

The next day, the government officials from around the world met in a formerly undisclosed location. Lester looked around the group of people seated around the board table.

"Since everyone appears to be here I think we can call this meeting to order. The main issue of concern here is how to control these rebels."

"These rock and roll rebels." Judah corrected harshly. "They are running wild in my country. Inciting riots, breaking into our offices and stealing from them, convincing the people that the music is all right to listen to and, worst of all, telling people that they have their own minds and that they shouldn't let us tell them what they can do. It is creating chaos. I have never seen the people so worked up."

"It is the same in my country as well." The representative from Japan confessed. "At one time, our young knew how to respect and obey their elders and the government but in the last little while they have been doing their own thing."

"And in my country." The man from Australia agreed. "Nothing is the same, nothing is as it should be."

"I say it is time to stop them in their tracks." A growl came from the ambassador of Germany. "They are being allowed too much freedom."

Lester rubbed his hands over his eyes wearily. This was going to be a long meeting.

"I realize that gentlemen but things have to be done step by step. Now I know that these rebels are difficult to catch. In the United States, Miss Kaya More is still running free..."

"And wanted for murder." Judah put in.

Gary looked sharply at his boss. That agent hadn't died. In fact he had been promoted. Kaya was not guilty of killing anyone.

Lester continued.

"We have our own rebels here in England and we can't seem to catch them. Some of my force has joked that they must be witches or demons since they vanish as soon as they strike. I don't like these sorts of comments, even said in a humorous manner. They are human and as such they can be brought down. Our goal today is to formulate a plan that will bring them down."

Each representative sitting around the table nodded their agreement solemnly. However, before they could start to vocalize the ways to accomplish their objective, the room suddenly became very cold. It was if the heat had instantly been turned off, the dampness of the London weather immediately seeping into the room and through their bones.

"What is going on here?" Lester muttered. Standing up, he went to the door to get a maintenance man to see what the trouble was. With horror he realized that the door was locked from the outside. They were trapped in a small, windowless room with the temperature dropping steadily. Just as the cold was getting too much to bear, they felt the temperature start to rise. Breathing a sigh of relief Lester sat down once more.

"You see we can be merciful unlike some of the people in this room." The deep male voice boomed over the room.

Judah's face went white with compressed rage. It was those rock and roll rebels again. Another male voice echoed over the intercom system.

"Yes, we are willing to let things be. As long as you give us our music and freedom of choice back. Don't you people realize that you can never take away rock and roll?"

"There is no way that you could ever hope to." A female voice added. "We all have our own minds and we demand the right to be able to choose what we wish to."

The first male voice spoke again.

"Perhaps if you just listened to it you might see that it isn't so bad after all." The sound of a machine being switched on was heard and then the voices disappeared to be replaced by the banned music of long ago. The occupants of the room were horrified. All except one.

Gary sat there and listened to the music with an open mind and found, quite surprisingly, that he was enjoying it. To him, it expressed all the pent up feelings of frustration he had been experiencing since he became Judah's right hand man. The music was a form of release, it made him feel free once again and ready to face the world. But he didn't want to face it with PARR anymore. He had found the one thing that was going to cause him to break his vow to PARR. Silently, he mused over his new situation.

"I can't believe that they got away with that. If they were in my country, they would have been caught and put to death." Judah stormed as he packed his clothes in the hotel room.

Gary looked at Judah with disgust.

"Like Gleven Andrews? You were going to put him to death, weren't you?"

Judah whirled on Gary.

"Yes, I was. But the incompetence of my force let him get away."

"Or are you just afraid to admit that Kaya More is smarter than you give her credit for?" Gary was walking a thin line here and he knew it but somehow didn't care. The laws they were upholding were wrong.

Judah' s eyes narrowed.

"If you want to remain a free man you had better keep your mouth shut before I accuse you of being a LUPO supporter."

Gary shut up immediately. There would be a time in the future to see that Judah got what was coming to him, but that time wasn't now. So, for the time being, Gary played the meek and mild servant.

CHAPTER Thirty-Four

Damien and Melissa whirled into the room.

“That was great!" Melissa exclaimed as she danced around the room.

Damien watched her with amusement. He agreed that their latest escapade had been thrilling but he didn't think that Melissa realized how dangerous it had been. With all the government agents from all around the world, if they had been caught, it would have meant certain death. The rebels trying to bring back rock and roll music weren't fooling around anymore but neither were the governments, as if they ever had been. Again, a thought occurred to him as he watched Melissa's childlike excitement.

"Melissa, how old are you?"

Melissa stopped to turn to look at Damien with wide eyes.

"I told you. I'm twenty one."

"I don't think so." Darmien was blunt. 'Now tell me the truth. How old are you?" Damien's tone of voice warned Melissa that she had better tell the truth.

"Seventeen." She mumbled. "But please don't tell anyone and don't send me back." Setting her chin, she continued, "I won't go back! There is no way you can make me!"

Damien sighed. Deep in his heart, he had somehow known that Melissa had been lying about her age. Yet, now that he had gotten to know her, it didn't matter. To tell the truth he was falling in love with her.

"Don't worry. It will be our little secret." Damien reassured Melissa. He crossed the room and took her face in his hands. "Just don't lie to me again. All right?" Damien looked deep into her eyes as if he was willing her to answer the way he wished her to.

"All right." Melissa whispered and she meant it. Their private moment was broken by the entrance of other people but the feel of Damien's touch still burned on Melissa's face even though he had pulled away.

Robert glanced at the couple that had quickly parted when they had walked in and smiled to himself. When Damien had first arrived with the two girls, Robert had had misgivings. It was obvious that the girls weren't as old as they were saying but the two had quickly proven themselves. One day he promised himself, he would get the whole story about them.

Beth saw the look that passed between Damien and Melissa and silently cheered. She knew that part of the reason that Melissa had come to England was so that she could be near Damien. Now it appeared as if something was going on between them. Just as Melissa had hoped.

Through her joy for her friend, Beth felt a twinge of sadness as she mentally compared herself to Melissa.

Melissa was tall with long auburn hair and green eyes. Beth was short with dark brown hair and brown eyes. Beth had always felt plain beside her glamorous friend and today was no different. Sighing to herself she prepared herself to be overshadowed by her more gregarious friend unaware that someone was watching her very intently.

Cedric watched Beth with hidden admiration. Ever since that day in the coffee shop, where he had first met her, Cedric had been drawn to her. Since they had started CIO, Beth had proven herself to be committed to the cause. Granted so was her friend but Beth went about it in a more quiet way seemingly avoiding all recognition. She was just the type of woman that Cedric liked though he just didn't know how to tell her that.

Seeing that everyone was here, Robert quickly called for their attention.

"Today we did well but that is only a start. The leaders of the government agencies are gathering together so now I think it is time for us to join forces with other rebel organizations around the world. I propose that a few of us make a trip to the United States to talk with Kaya More and her people. Is there anyone willing and able to come along?"

There was a silence for a few moments as people made up their minds.

"I'll go." Angus volunteered.

Damien and Melissa also agreed to follow Robert on this journey but Cedric and Beth said they would stay to keep any eye on things here. There were no other volunteers in the group though everyone wished them the best of luck.

Two days later, the four British rebels boarded a plane bound for Los Angeles, California.

"How do you know where she is?" Melissa asked.

Robert smiled quietly.

"I can't be sure but I just have this feeling that that is where she is. Something or someone is telling me to go there."

"Where do we go once we get there?" Damien said aloud.

"I don't know." Robert shrugged. "We'll cross that bridge when we come to it, I guess." The others settled back in their seats, not sure about trusting their future to a man who was leading them by feelings and nothing else but it was too late to turn back now.

CHAPTER Thirty-Five

Kaya was walking restlessly around the restaurant, trying to figure out what was bothering her. She had this distinct feeling that she needed to be somewhere but she had no clue as to where. Attempting to shrug off this mysterious feeling, Kaya went into the kitchen to make herself a sandwich and faintly heard a plane overhead. Then everything fell into place. Forgetting about the sandwich, she grabbed her purse and keys then went out to the car and drove to the airport.

Once in the airport, Kaya was again drawn by unexplainable feelings. Without thinking, she walked to the gate where a plane from England was just disembarking. Uncertain of what she was doing here or what she was looking for, Kaya searched the faces of the passengers disembarking. Nothing flickered inside of her and she was just about to give up when the situation changed.

A tremor shook her body so strongly that Kaya felt her knees go weak and grabbed the rail in front of her to regain her balance. Although she logically knew that she had never before seen the four people walking towards her, a deep-rooted feeling that they were what had drawn her to the airport flooded her entire being. Stunned, she stood there for the longest time, not seeing the people around her milling about. It was if the world had vanished except for herself, these three men and the young woman with them.

Robert was walking along with only blind instinct leading him. The feeling that they were near their goal was unmistakable but it was also frustrating. How could they know what to do? Was he foolishly leading the others on a quest that would have no satisfactory result? Almost as soon as he thought this, Robert saw the woman with the platinum blond hair standing behind the barricades staring at them as if she was in shock. Somehow he knew that this was the person they were looking for and had traveled across the ocean to see.

Kaya was mesmerized by the four people approaching her. She felt as if something great was about to happen. Then her eyes met Robert's. An electrical current flashed through both of her and Robert at the same time. Something was going to happen: Something that would change their lives and the course of civilization forever.

"Kaya More." Robert had now drawn close enough to Kaya to voice his statement softly. Kaya was startled back to reality and she smiled.

"Yes. And you four must belong to CIO. Am I right?"

Angus was quick to answer.

"Yes. But how did you know?" Kaya switched her attention to the tall, dark haired man.

"Let's just say that I had this feeling. I think that we should leave if you people are ready to go." Kaya turned and led the way for the others to follow her to her vehicle.

Behind the group, a man quickly hurried to the phone.

"Judah Arnold." The man stated to the receptionist who instantly recognized his voice.

In a few moments, Judah came on the line. Without preamble, he got straight to the point.

"What information do you have?"

"Miss More met four people at the airport. Their plane was from London, England."

"Do you know where they went?"

"No should I follow them?"

"Yes, but don't let them see you." Without another word, the phone conversation was ended and the mysterious man hurried out of the airport.

Kaya pulled into the parking lot of the restaurant. Everyone got out of the car and followed Kaya inside. There Kaya led them immediately downstairs. Needlessly checking to make sure that no one was near, she revealed the secret doorway to the hidden hotel.

"Wow" was all that Melissa could say. Kaya and the others had fixed up the lobby of the hotel, going by old pictures found in the library, of what it used to look like. Damien also was astonished to see the hidden hideaway.

"This is quite the place. If someone didn't know it was here, they would never be able to find it. Did you build it?"

"No, we didn't. At least not entirely." Boyce had been sitting in the lobby, unseen by the newcomers. "It was built many years ago." Boyce then went on to explain some of the history of the old hotel, holding his listeners enthralled.

"That's quite an accomplishment" Robert admired. "And the story is the thing that legends are made of."

Boyce looked at Kaya, a definite question in his eyes. He still hadn't been introduced to the newcomers.

"Sorry Boyce. This is Robert, Angus, Damien and Melissa. They are from the CIO organization in England."

Boyce greeted the newcomers then looked at Kaya again.

"Why didn't you tell me they were coming?"

"I didn't know. At least not until an hour ago." Kaya's nervousness made her speech rapid. For some reason, ever since she had seen Robert, she had felt guilty concerning Boyce. What was going on here?

Boyce, however, seemed to accept her explanation without further discussion. He offered to go upstairs and find everyone something to eat; an offer that was gratefully accepted.

Then Kaya led them to their rooms where they could stay while they were here.

Robert and Angus were sharing a room. Though some of the rooms were fixed up, not all had been revealed and of those that had, not all of them were completed so there was a shortage of available space. However, the room was furnished with two large beds and was clean. The two men found everything they needed there. Robert was quiet though, as if something was on his mind. Wordlessly, he unpacked his things. Angus kept glancing at his friend, trying to see if he could determine what was on his mind. Finally, he gave up trying.

"Robert. What is bothering you?"

"Nothing." Robert's answer was short, indicating that he didn't really want to discuss it. But Angus was persistent.

"Bullshit I know you better than that. You have to tell someone and why not me? You know that I can keep a secret." Robert smiled. Angus was right. He had to tell someone and Angus was the best choice.

"It's Kaya More."

"What about Kaya? I thought that she was quite nice." Angus saw the expression on Robert's face and groaned.

"Oh no! You haven't fallen for her, have you? From what I could see, that Boyce fellow and her seem to be together and I wouldn't want to mess with him!"

Robert sat down on his bed.

"I know that those two are together but I just can't help it. When I saw her at the airport, it was like I knew that I had known her forever. Then, when our eyes met, there was a feeling of electricity."

"Just stay away from her!" Angus warned. "Remember that the most important thing here is the cause. If it wasn't for that, we wouldn't be here."

Robert nodded as he ran his fingers through his long dark hair. His green eyes were troubled as he looked at his friend.

"I know. But I just don't know if I can survive and be around her all the time."

"Don't worry.You will." Angus promised solemnly though he was worried about his long time friend. He had known Robert for years but had never seen him this way about a woman before. A chill ran along Angus's spine as a premonition of future danger flashed through his mind.

In another room, Melissa and Damien were also unpacking.

"So what do you think of Kaya More?" Melissa asked. Damien took a moment to answer. He sensed Melissa's jealousy so he knew that he had to tread very carefully.

"I don't know." He shrugged. "I know her reputation and the accomplishments she has achieved with LUPO and she is good. She's beautiful, I guess, but not really my type. All in all, she's nice though."

Melissa let her breath go in a sigh of relief. From the first moment she had seen Kaya she had been worried. Logically she knew that her worries were irrational since Damien cared for her very much. But that green-eyed monster didn't listen to logic. Melissa had been impressed with Kaya's kindness though. Almost immediately Kaya had made the strangers feel welcome and at home.

"I think she's beautiful. And she is really nice. What do you know about her?" Damien sat down on the bed and patted a space beside him indicating that Melissa should also sit down.

"Did you know that Kaya's father was killed while setting up LUPO?" He began. Melissa shook her head.

"From what I've read, Kaya was eight years old at the time. Boyce is the son of one of the other founding members of LUPO, Brent Mitchell. According to rumor, Brent and Kaya's mother, Wind, now live together. I think that they are also here in California, since no one has seen them in New York, but I'm not sure.

"LUPO was originally set up in New York. For years after Kansall More's death, Kaya had nothing to do with LUPO. I doubt if she even really knew it existed. Then, when she was about sixteen years old, she got into a fight with a teacher regarding the censorship of music. She never went back to school. There were rumors that a good friend of hers, who was the daughter of the third founding member, was raped. Some say that PARR did it to her but, of course, that was never proven.

"Since that day, Kaya has belonged to LUPO. She has planned and executed many demonstrations and escapades that have been very successful. I guess her most dramatic was when she rescued Gleven Andrews and other members from the jail. I mean she didn't do it all alone, but I heard she planned it or at least a lot of it. Did you know that she is also wanted for killing a PARR agent?" Again, Melissa shook her head but this time asked a question.

"How do you know all this?"

"I have been against censorship since I was a kid. My parents also thought it was wrong. Between the literature that seemed to constantly be around and the other rebels that came to visit, I picked up a lot. Of course, some of this is public knowledge and some of it is just rumor.

"It never occurred to me, though, to actually do anything until I saw that article on Kaya and LUPO in the paper. It suddenly hit me that, if I want to stop this censorship, then I have to do something to fight it."

"So that is why you went to England."

"Yes. I thought that Robert would be open to my idea of fighting the governments. You see none of my friends in Switzerland were interested. They are all rich kids and are more interested in skiing, partying and having fun. So I went to England." Melissa snuggled against him.

“I’m glad you did." She whispered. Her hand ran lightly along his back and Damien caught his breath.

"You shouldn't do that Melissa." He warned. Melissa's eyes twinkled but she didn't stop. Instead her hands became bolder, touching places that aroused Damien to the point of no return. Just what Melissa had in mind all along.

Boyce and Kaya were having a very heated discussion.

"How could you do something so stupid? " Boyce hissed angrily. "You went to the airport, without telling anyone, and picked up four strangers! Christ! You didn't even know who they were!"

Kaya bristled.

"Yes I did! As soon as I saw them, I knew that they were fellow supporters!"

"And how did you know that?"

"I felt it."

Boyce rolled his eyes in exasperation.

"Kaya! You can't always rely on your feelings. How many times have I told you that? They may not always be right."

Kaya's silver eyes flashed dangerously.

"Excuse me, but my feelings have saved many LUPO members from being harmed, including yourself. Presently my feelings are what we are basing LUPO on. You may joke about my premonitions but without them Gleven and many others would be dead and LUPO wouldn't be where it is today."

"Perhaps that is so." Boyce conceded. "But what if you're wrong, what then? How many lives are going to be forfeited so that your ego and your damn feelings don't have to be questioned?"

Kaya's voice turned cold, the heat of the argument leaving her as her rage took over.

"That's a very stupid thing to say, Boyce. Is it too difficult for you to realize that the increased sensitivity of my feelings is what gives me an extra edge over PARR? Or are you just so jealous of that that you wish to destroy it and my confidence in them?"

"Kaya, I think we had better stop this now before we both say something we are going to regret."

"Or before we get to the truth."

At that moment, Gleven walked into the kitchen, having overheard much of their argument.

"I think it would be better for all concerned if both of you would just grow up a bit." He snapped harshly.

Kaya and Boyce looked at him, astonished by the severity of his words.

"I don't know what you mean." Kaya stated stiffly.

"Boyce, you are concerned about Kaya and you are trying to tell her so but you also don't understand the depth of these feelings that Kaya has. From what I have seen over the years, Kaya can't help but act on them." Kaya looked triumphant until Gleven spoke his next words.

"And Kaya. You have been acting a little high and mighty lately. And you tend to be overly reckless, as if you feel that nothing can ever hurt you. Boyce has a point; what if you're feelings are wrong? What then? I think perhaps it would be in the best interests of all if you attempted to restrain yourself some. It will do none of us any good if you get yourself, and others, killed with one of your escapades."

Kaya looked suitably sheepish then laughed.

"He's right you know Boyce. We have both been acting like idiots. What a stupid thing to fight about!" Kaya wrapped her arms around Boyce's neck to give him a big kiss. Boyce was slightly mollified but didn't feel he could let the matter drop without a final warning.

"Just promise me that you will be more careful in the future. I don't want anything to happen to you or to LUPO. Understand?"

"I'll try. I promise." Kaya gave Boyce another kiss to seal her vow.

Gleven quietly left the room satisfied that he had been able to stem another potential problem before it truly got started.

The mysterious man from the airport drove around in frustration. He didn't want to have to admit to Judah that he had lost the rebels but that was what had happened. Ansel Young swore softly to himself. To make matters worse, it was now evident that his brother Larret was actively involved with LUPO. For years his family had been convinced that Larret's escapades would lead to serious trouble and now it looked as if they had.

CHAPTER Thirty-Six

Jared and Larret walked along the street, looking in shop windows.

"What will you do with all the money you make?" Larret asked.

Jared looked puzzled for a moment.

"What money?"

"Well, after rock and roll is once again legal, we will be rock stars. Just like the ones they had in the old days. Then we will have money, fame and lots of groupies. It'll be great."

Jared thought a moment then shrugged.

"I guess so. It's really strange though. For my whole life, I've never done anything worthwhile until this came along. When those guys first came to my door, I thought it would be a good way to get closer to Kaya and have some fun. I never thought for a moment that we really had any chance of sticking it to PARR. But after a little while I started to get caught up with the cause and to see that PARR isn't infallible. The only thing I want now is to see rock and roll music being played by all its fans. I want people to be able to choose for themselves and, if they don't want the music, that's fine. But at least they will have the choice."

"Wow!" Larret remarked. "That was quite the speech from an ex-no good trouble maker and womanizer. But, and don't you dare tell anyone I said this, I happen to agree with you. For me, it was a lark at first. Something to pass the time but after seeing how committed Kaya is, it sort of rubbed off on me. Now all I want is to see the music brought back." The two men walked along in silence for a few moments, each lost in their own thoughts about how they had changed. The shop windows went by them barely noticed. Suddenly, Larret walked a little faster.

"Hey! What's up?" Jared asked as he tried to keep pace. Larret's face wore a grim look as he answered.

"My brother was in that cafe."

"So?"

"Ansel is a PARR agent. You see, my family are all good, upstanding citizens and I am what you could call the black sheep of the family."

"And you don't want Ansel to see you because he might ask too many questions. Right?"

"Right. I have a feeling that he already knows about my activities. After all, we haven't been too secretive lately."

"Larret! Wait!" A voice called from behind the two men.

"Shit." Larret swore softly. He said in an undertone to Jared. "You keep going. I'll meet you back at the restaurant."

Jared started to protest then thought better of it. He kept walking without a glance behind him.

Larret turned to face the accusations that he knew were coming from his brother.

In New York, Judah and Gary sat in Judah's office. Judah was becoming suspicious of Gary. Ever since they had come back from England, Gary had been different. He was no longer overly enthused about PARR activities and though Judah couldn't prove it he felt that Gary was beginning to sympathize with LUPO. A situation that could not exist.

"You are being transferred." Judah's order was short.

Gary raised his eyebrows a bit but that was the only reaction that he showed.

"Where am I being assigned to?"

"Los Angeles. We have confirmation of rebel activity there and we wish to have you at that location. You will leave tomorrow."

Gary didn't say a word. What could he say? Though his mind was churning with possibilities. In Los Angeles he would be farther away from the headquarters and the major decisions but he would be also be closer to the brain center of LUPO. And Kaya.

"Am I to take Krista with me?" He asked.

"That is your decision though I think it might be beneficial. We have reports that Gleven Andrews and Kaya More are there and she might be able to lead you to them."

"It didn't work last time. What makes you think that Gleven and Kaya will trust Krista anymore now than they did a year ago?" Gary was stepping over the line by asking his superior a question that doubted the superior's judgment and he knew it.

"Don't question the decisions of your betters." Judah bellowed. "We know best."

Gary lowered his eyes, appearing to be properly chastised but in reality not regretting a word of what he had said. Ever since England and his introduction to rock and roll music, Gary had felt the need to question more and more. No longer was Gary Shane willing to follow others blindly. Especially since he no longer understood why they were doing what they were. What was so wrong with the music? He wondered that constantly to himself. Not wanting to break his vow to PARR, he had searched through all the documents for some valid reason to support PARR's actions but had found none. It was true that teenagers had committed crimes and suicide in the past but could that really be attributed to the music? It could also be blamed on the society that existed as well as a lack of guidance in the child's youth. And though the teenagers had rebelled against authority, great things had come about. Now, with all the rules and regulations, it seemed as if the great minds of today had been stagnated. Most people were afraid to try something new for fear of prosecution. The people weren't like animals; they were little more than robots. Gary knew that it wasn't right.

"I shall start packing right away." Gary stood and waited to be dismissed.

With a wave of his hand, Judah signaled that their meeting was over.

Gary walked into his apartment and sighed. Krista was once again doing her nails. He wondered about her reaction to being told that they were moving to Los Angeles but he didn't really care. If he had his way, they would no longer be together but PARR deemed it that they be a couple so that was the way it had to stay for the moment.

"We're moving." He stated shortly.

Krista looked up in surprise.

"Where?"

"To Los Angeles. You had better start packing and only take what is absolutely necessary .We will have the rest shipped. We leave tomorrow," With that, Gary went to pack his things.

All the members of Mystique II gathered in the forgotten concert hall, along with Wind, Brent, Gleven, Margaret, Steven, Robert, Damien, Melissa, Angus, Andric and many other LUPO supporters. It was time for their first performance before other people. Nerves were stretched as the musicians took their places. Could they do it? Would they be any good? As one, they all took a deep breath then began to play.

With the first note, much of the nervousness went away and the newly formed members of Mystique II were lost in the music. The spectators were astonished. It wasn't exactly like hearing the original Mystique. The new Mystique had a style all their own and they were a long way from perfection. But they had heart; soul and everyone seemed to have a natural aptitude for the music. After the first song, everyone was silent for a moment then the cheers began.

"You guys were great!" Andric loudly exclaimed.

"Better than I have ever heard before." Brent joined in.

"This is going to set the world on their ears!" Robert was quick to add.

Kaya and Boyce exchanged glances.

"I think," Kaya began, giving the other members a meaningful glance, "that it is time for us to make our entrance." Her announcement was greeted with positive nods. The explosion was about to begin.

CHAPTER Thirty-Seven

The next day dawned bright and clear. The perfect day for what LUPO was planning. From a garage of a LUPO supporter, a large flat bed truck emerged. It was cleaned and then driven to the restaurant. Hidden away, LUPO members started outfitting the truck for its mission later that day.

Boyce and Andric went to the local high schools to spread the word that something was going to happen later that day. Finding the contacts they had previously spoken to, whispered conversations were held. Then small packages were distributed to the teens.

Kaya and Robert went to the local nightclubs to speak with the respective owners. These were owners that Kaya knew were sympathetic to the cause. After all, the revival of rock and roll music meant more business for the nightclub. Pamphlets and CDs were handed over to these specific owners.

Back at the restaurant, those LUPO members not involved with outfitting the truck were busy. Brent was organizing those that had volunteered to go out to the beaches. They were handed pamphlets to distribute. Once the population on the beach grew, these members were to go out and hand out the pamphlets.

At the airport, Gary and Krista were just landing. They had spoke very little as Gary mused over his present situation. It had become obvious to him that he could no longer stay with PARR but he also knew that Kaya would never trust him so there was no way he could actively join LUPO. His mind was confused about which direction to take. While walking through the airport, he happened to see a pamphlet lying on the ground. Picking it up, he read intently.

> THE TIME IS HERE
>
> "The time has come for supporters of rock and roll music to be more vocal! Tonight, just before the clock strikes ten, the members of the band Mystique II will be showing the public what they have been missing all these years. If you are interested in hearing what the government has taken away from you, be in the area of the government buildings tonight. There we will show you just how unjust the government has been and what you have been missing.

Gary read with excitement. This was the chance he had been waiting for. If he could go there and perhaps stop PARR activities, then maybe he could convince LUPO that he was serious about joining their cause. Krista, who had been reading over Gary's shoulder, said,

"Gary! Here is your chance to make it big with PARR. Just show them what you found and then they will surely give you a promotion!"

Gary glanced at Krista.

"I'm not going to do that. But I am going to be there tonight."

"And capture Kaya all by yourself. Won't that impress the superiors at PARR? "

Gary didn't reply. For some reason, he wasn't comfortable sharing his change of heart with Krista. Perhaps it was because, every time the name LUPO came up, she was very vocal about her opinions. According to Krista, LUPO was an organization that should never have been started. Gary chuckled to himself as a thought crossed his mind. Krista and Judah would be perfect for each other! Except Gary wasn't sure that Krista would be able to handle Judah's reputed sexual eccentricities. Still thinking his own thoughts, Gary and Krista left the airport.

In the local high schools, at a set time, all the PA systems went on. However, it wasn't for a principal's announcement. The packages that had been passed out earlier had contained, among other things, CDs. At precisely 3:00 PM, just as school had been let out, the illegal rock and roll music sounded across various hallways. Sentries were posted at each and every exit and, as each student passed, they received the pamphlets that Gary had seen at the airport. Teachers and administrators hurried to the office to try to turn the music off but the doors were locked. No one had seen anyone go into the office and no one had seen anyone leave. Until they could find a spare key to the office, since the janitors' were missing, the music would continue to play.

It was night, the darkness helping to hide the movements of several LUPO members. At a planned time, many of the radio stations were being illegally entered. The plan was to switch the music for rock and roll at the precise time that the arranged nightclubs were going to start playing it. DJs and technicians were held hostage while the members put in the illegal music. They were going to wake this city up.

At precisely 8:30, the members of Mystique II gathered in the place where the truck was hidden. On the large flat bed, all their equipment was already set up. They warmed up for a half an hour, and then Andric, who had volunteered to drive the truck, got into the cab. The CIO members were also along; Robert, Angus and Damien sitting with the members of the band while Melissa sat up front. Brent and Wind were going to follow in another vehicle with Gleven to keep an eye out for danger. In front of the moving concert, were a number of LUPO supporters also trying to avert danger. It was a risky venture but Kaya and the others felt it was well worth it. Larret sat at his drum kit, worried about the upcoming event. His talk with his brother was what was bothering him. According to Ansel,

PARR knew every movement of LUPO. Of course with the pamphlets being given to everyone, how could they not know about tonight?

"I'll just concentrate on my music and whatever happens, happens. If everything is finished for LUPO tonight, at least I've had one hell of a ride!" He thought to himself. Having thus reasoned it out, Larret felt calmer than he had in days.

Kaya took a deep breath as the truck started to move. This was it. Finally, after all the rehearsing and careful planning, they were going to make their move. Kaya just hoped that the band was good enough.

Jared closed his eyes for a moment to center all of his energies on the moment. Whatever happened, he could not let the concern that they might be caught enter his mind. He had enough to worry about with just making sure he played right.

Boyce fingered his guitar and glanced over at the other members of the band. They were good enough for this, of that he was sure. But what about stage fright? As far as he knew, no one with the exception of Kaya, had ever played in front of a large number of people before. Mentally he crossed his fingers that everything would go well.

Robert looked around him in awe. This was really going to happen! He couldn't believe that, within such a short time of their arrival, something of this magnitude would be happening. Just as he had been astonished and slightly in awe of the underground hotel, he found this to be difficult to comprehend. Was this the day that rock and roll music was going to make its comeback or were they all going to end up in jail? Whatever the case, it was exciting.

Damien was also slightly taken aback by the turn of events. He made a mental note to suggest to Robert once this was all over and if it all went well, to phone Cedric and Beth in England and get them over here as soon as possible. This was too exciting to miss.

Angus was a little bit jealous that all this action was taking place in the United States instead of England but he soon reasoned it out. LUPO had been around longer than CIO and rock and roll music had been born on this side of the ocean. Having thus made peace with himself, he settled back to enjoy the ride.

In the cab of the truck, Andric and Melissa were both too keyed up to speak. What would be the outcome of tonight's activities was the thought that occupied both their minds. It could be the rebirth of something great or it could spell the end of them all. Whatever the outcome, they were both happy to be here.

As the truck drew closer to the government buildings, a cheer could be heard. As one unit, the musicians started playing. The cheers from the bystanders grew as they heard the music approaching. When the buildings came into view Kaya's heart swelled with pride when she saw that over a thousand people were there. And all were cheering wildly in approval as Mystique II drew closer. Kaya also noticed that there were

PARR agents standing nearby. But because of all the people surrounding them, they didn't move. Somehow Kaya had known this would happen. Glancing over at Boyce, who was giving her a nod of approval, she signalled for Robert to increase the sound. The night air was filled with the sounds of Mystique II and the crowd loved it. As they drove on, everyone knew a battle had been won for LUPO.

Kaya's eyes swept over the crowd then she stopped. There was Gary Shane and he seemed to be trying to give them some sort of signal. Kaya's eyes hardened when their eyes met but soon softened when she read the message there. Gary seemed to be asking for forgiveness. Was that possible? Kaya didn't pause to think of it, just kept on playing, trying hard not to remember that horrible night in New York. Soon they were traveling farther away from the government buildings but the crowd of people were following them. More and more kept joining the followers, eager to hear the music. The traveling concert was more of a success than anyone had dared hope it would be. Now came the problem of getting out of sight.

The band stopped playing on cue. The lights that had lit up the vehicle and its passengers went out instantly. Andric gave them a few minutes to make sure that they were secure then sped up. Through the deserted streets they traveled until they made sure that no one was following. Then they went in the direction of the restaurant. At a crossroads, Brent, Wind and Gleven pulled up alongside them. Brent immediately got out of the car and went up to the dark vehicle.

"Everyone all right?" He asked. Once everyone had assured him that they were fine, he continued.

"Well, that was some show. None of the PARR agents followed you so you should be safe. Why don't we hide that truck, get the equipment stored away then discuss this evening?" Everyone agreed and then proceeded along the highway.

Back at their hideaway, everyone was talking excitedly, adrenaline flowing from the evening's activities and their accomplishment. That is, everyone except Kaya. Boyce, noticing Kaya’s silence, leaned over to whisper in her ear.

"Are you OK? You seem too quiet."

Kaya shrugged. “I'm fine. Just thinking."

"About what?"

Kaya looked up and determination showed in the set of her chin as she made her decision. In a strong clear voice, which silenced the room, she spoke. "I think it is time that we made a trip to the Canadian Rockies."

CHAPTER Thirty-Eight

A few days later, five notorious Americans, holding false passports and in disguise, disembarked the plane in Calgary, Canada with three men carrying British passports. One of the Brits rented a vehicle and the eight people casually left the airport, headed for Banff.

The drive was silent, each occupant of the vehicle lost in their own thoughts about the dangers of their upcoming mission. They found a nondescript hotel on the western edge of Banff and rented two connecting rooms with two large double beds in each.

"So what next?" Larret asked Kaya when all were settled in their respective rooms.

Kaya checked the list she had made before leaving Los Angeles.

"Is it all set up to get the dirigible balloon?" She asked.

Jared nodded.

"Called the fellow this morning. He says that he has it waiting just outside of town. In fact, it probably isn't too far from here."

"Damien, Robert, you know what you're supposed to do?"

"We drive to the border, switch vehicles then meet the balloon in a field outside of Billings, Montana." The two men said in unison. Kaya nodded.

"And Angus?"

"I take the rented vehicle back to the Calgary airport then catch a plane back to Los Angeles where Gleven and Brent will pick me up, take me back to the hotel and there I wait for you."

"OK. Now it is just up to we Americans to free Mystique." Boyce said.

"Right." Kaya breathed a sigh, mentally crossing her fingers for good luck. "As soon as it's dark, we will leave."

Darkness fell quickly and silently. Just as quickly and silently the members of Mystique II left the hotel and trotted steadily towards the field where the balloon awaited them. Robert, Damien and Angus had left some time earlier in order to carry out their part of the plan.

The balloon was just where Jared had said it would be and carefully everyone got in. Confidently, Larret went to the apparatus that propelled the vehicle while Kaya raised her eyebrows in question. Jared, seeing the question in her mind, grinned.

"As he has so often said about me, don't ask." Restrained chuckles softened the atmosphere as the balloon lifted from the ground and Larret directed it towards the prison that the daytime sun had outlined on the mountaintop. Thankfully, the night was cloudy, the silvery moon hidden. Though the lack of light was a hindrance to the mission, it was also an aid.

Without the moon and stars lighting their way, the rebels found it more difficult to navigate yet, without the illuminating light, the balloon appeared to be another cloud in the sky.

With extreme caution and silence, the balloon was landed on top of the prison. After being anchored securely, the five rebels lowered themselves to the roof. All stood silent for a moment, waiting to hear if they had been detected. The only sounds to be heard were those of the night creatures that resided in the mountains.

An air vent shaft was right where the blueprints that Boyce had found had said they would be. Breathing a silent prayer, he lowered himself into the metal pathway, followed by Larret, Kaya, Brian and then Jared. Silently, hardly daring to breath, the five rebels worked their way along a route earlier memorized.

Boyce suddenly stopped, the others, alert to his movements, stopped also. Through a grill ahead of them, the five could see a guard sleeping at a desk. Craning his head, Boyce checked the surrounding area but could see no one else. Neither could he see any cameras that would register their movements. Obviously, PARR and the other authorities felt that this place was too well hidden to be broken into.

Greasing the edges of the grill to prevent accidental noise, Boyce worked it out of its frame, one eye constantly alert for any movement from the guard. The guard however remained sleeping, oblivious to the events taking place above him.

The rebels slid through the opening with ease and crouched low as they quickly moved towards the key rack. Quickly scanning the labeled pieces of metal, Kaya soon gave a silent signal of victory. In her hand, she held a key marked Mystique. Pointing to a cell number marked above the now empty hook, she pointed to the door leading out of the guard's office. Nodding their heads, the four men lead the way out the door and went down the corridor in the direction where they thought the cell might be.

Pressing their dark clothed figures against the wall, the rebels attempted to blend in with the shadows and to make it more difficult to be noticed. As they went along, walking as softly as possible and bending low when they came to a glass partition, they silently read the numbers. Finally, they came to the number they were looking for and Kaya slipped the key in the door that soundlessly opened.

Inside on five narrow, hard cots the objects of their search lay sleeping. Each rebel crept to a bed and silently shook the sleeping form in it awake. Motioning for them to be silent, the rebels, with Boyce in the lead, led the musicians out of the room.

The ten people, five rescuers and five soon to be freed captives, moved silently through the corridors. Recalling the blueprint that was so engraved on his memory, Boyce came to a stairwell that led up to the roof. More quickly now, but just as quietly, they all moved in unison to the roof.

Bradley Mitchell contemplated his predicament with awe. After all these years in captivity, he was being rescued but by whom, he couldn't tell. The blackened faces of his saviours lent no clue as to their identity though one of the forms obviously belonged to a woman. Whoever these mysterious saviors were, they were assuredly welcome.

Cal Jensen blinked rapidly; tempted to pinch himself to make certain that this wasn't all a dream. They were being led to the outside world and to freedom. Being led by five unknown freedom fighters that he blessed with every ounce of his being.

Daniel More followed the female figure in front of him, somehow totally at ease with the situation. Though he wasn't sure how, he had known that the members of Mystique would not die within these stonewalls and that feeling had been unbearable today. Something had told him that they would soon be rescued though he wasn't sure who was doing the rescuing.

Ron Stopford walked surely and steadily up the stairs, uncertain of what was happening here. He gazed at the black figures around him and hoped that they meant well and were not taking Mystique to their execution.

Rick Young walked out onto the roof and took a deep breath of the clean, mountain air. For the first time in thirty years, he felt the life and energy of hope surge through him as he followed the rest of the group into the balloon.

Once the balloon was high in the air and being propelled south, Kaya broke the silence. Turning to the musicians who were gazing around them with astonishment, she smiled warmly.

"We are members of an organization named the Let Us Play Organization also known as LUPO. We have been fighting to bring back rock and roll music for years and we might be close to doing so."

"We have also started a band called Mystique II" Jared drawled. "And though we are not as good as you were, we may be getting close."

Bradley Mitchell's eyes twinkled merrily. "Is that so? Now tell me, who in the hell are you?"

Jared laughed.

"I'm Jared Jensen, that is Larret Young, Boyce Mitchell, Brian Malloy and the one and only Kaya More."

"One and only?" Daniel inquired.

"Yup. Her father started LUPO and then Kaya came along and, in the last five years, has managed to give PARR enough headaches to last them a lifetime."

"What is your father's name?" Daniel asked quietly.

"Kansall." Kaya stated proudly. "He was a great man."

"Was? Are you saying he's dead?"

Boyce joined in the explanation at this point. "He was murdered by PARR while in the process of getting LUPO off the ground. My father, Brent Mitchell, was with him at the time. Kansall, another man by the name of Gleven Andrews and my father, originally started LUPO in New

York. After Kansall was killed, Dad went to California and set up the Western Chapter of LUPO."

"Then Kaya ran into some trouble in New York and had to leave the city. She went to Los Angeles and joined the two chapters." Larret added.

"Then she found us and talked us into forming another Mystique in order to bring back rock and roll." Jared threw in.

"And since then we have been harassing PARR and turning the people on to rock and roll. It's been the most fun I personally have had in a long time." Brian finished.

"Sounds like it." Ron remarked then paused to study Brian closely under the blackening he wore. "What did you say your name was?"

"Brian Malloy."

"How old are you?"

"Twenty nine, almost thirty. Why?" Ron didn't answer the question instead asking another of his own.

"What is your mother's name?"

Brian answered. "Fiona Leigh Harris Malloy." Tears began to fill Ron's eyes.

"Do you have an older brother named John?"

"I did. PARR took everyone away one night and I have never seen them since. Why?" Brian answered hesitantly. The other rebels were curious as to where this exchange was leading but the members of Mystique knew. Through his tears, Ron smiled warmly at Brian.

"Because that makes you my son."

Brian was filled with emotion at this revelation and stood motionless, unsure of what to do.

Kaya, sensing his turmoil, pushed him gently towards his newly found father. As the two men embraced, every occupant of the balloon felt the emotion well within them. They had gotten more than they had bargained for when they had rescued the members of Mystique.

The balloon landed in the field outside Billings, Montana the next morning where Damien and Robert were waiting with a passenger van. The air travelers, who were still riding on the adrenaline rush from the rescue, bounded into the van and hastily made introductions.

"We rented four motel rooms with large beds." Damien commented to the new passengers. "We figured you would want to get cleaned up and relax before moving on."

"Good idea." Bradley assured him. "You don't happen to have any extra clothes that we could change in to, do you? I would use my credit card but I am fairly certain that it is useless after all these years."

"As if it wasn't useless thirty years ago! " Cal joked in an undertone. The other occupants of the van chuckled then Robert turned to Bradley.

"We did get you some new clothes. I can't guarantee the style or fit, but at least they're clean."

"And not prison garb." Rick added.

After everyone had showered and changed, Robert returned to the motel with several large pizzas and two cases of beer.

"I'm told this is what you Americans like to do." His purposely exaggerated cockney accent eliciting smiles from everyone.

"Right now, anything besides that slop we have been served for three decades would do." Ron said. "But this is fantastic."

"So how are we all related here?" Brian asked his mouth full of the piping hot pizza.

"Well, Daniel is obviously Kaya's great uncle." Bradley offered. "If Brent Mitchell is Boyce's father that would make me his uncle. Brent is my younger brother."

"Since I never had any brothers or sisters, the closest I can come is that Larret is a cousin. My parents had a whole mess of relatives." Rick volunteered.

"And Cal, you have to be the uncle which my grandparents would never, ever discuss." Jared commented. Cal laughed.

"That sounds about right. I was the black sheep of the family before PARR became powerful so I can just imagine how my parents felt when I disappeared."

The relationships settled, everyone sat back to eat their pizza, drink their beer and hear about the escapades and achievements of LUPO.

CHAPTER Thirty-Nine

When the van pulled into the parking lot of the restaurant a few days later, the members looked at their surroundings, puzzled.

"Wasn't this the sight of the Rocker's Paradise?" Ron asked.

"Yes." Kaya answered. "As you know, an earthquake demolished the place after PARR raided it. A LUPO supporter built his restaurant on top of it.

Jared filled in a bit more information.

"There is a legend that says the hotel will reveal itself when those who are worthy to bring back the music, are present."

"How does a story get known as a legend in only thirty years?" Ca1 asked, sarcastically.

"I don't know," Kaya retorted. "How does a band, whose music has been outlawed, become a legend in thirty years?"

Daniel chuckled as all departed from the van and stretched.

"She got you there, Jensen."

"Yeah, she's definitely related to you Daniel." Cal said.

The LUPO members took the band inside the back door of the restaurant and straight downstairs. Larret walked over to the concealed doorway and opened it, revealing the hotel that the band had last played in. As the Mystique members walked into the auditorium that still housed their musical equipment, all stared around them in awe. Ron closed his eyes and started to recall that evening so long ago.

"It was a big crowd, the biggest this place had ever seen." He began. "The fans were wilder than I had ever seen them before and you could feel the energy from the audience." Everyone was silent as they listened intently to Ron's recollections.

"The evening started out perfectly .The opening band, Raser, put on the best show they had all tour. I couldn't believe how they fed from the crowd but the more hyper the fans got, the more outrageous Raser became.

"We were on that night! It seemed as if nothing could get us down or damage our performance."

"And then PARR showed up." Bradley interjected quietly. Ron's eyes opened and the sadness there was heart wrenching to see.

"Yeah, PARR showed up and everything went to hell. They came in swinging clubs and shooting. Suddenly the joy of the fans turned to fear. People were running every which way and screaming. We tried to get as many fans backstage as we could but PARR was already there. They slaughtered the fans on sight." Ron went silent, reliving the pain and horror he had lived that night.

"But PARR didn't kill you?" Jared said.

"No, they didn't and we have never been able to figure out why." Daniel commented. "For some reason, PARR figured that we were better off being humiliated. The musicians and others that have died in that prison, without any shred of human dignity is a tragedy. I would much rather have been killed when PARR stormed the concert hall then to have had to die in that prison. They didn't even have the decency to bury, the bodies. Instead, the dead were put out in the woods so that the animals could destroy the remains."

"If someone were to travel through those woods, they would find numerous bones and some partially eaten corpses. It makes me shudder just to think of it" Rick commented.

Jared shuddered. "So much for getting something to eat. There goes my appetite." Everyone laughed nervously, the horrors of the narration still foremost in their minds.

"Enough of the past." Ron stated sternly. "Tell me, how did you find this place?"

Relieved to have the topic changed, Boyce began to tell the story, with Kaya filling in her parts.

"Here's the letter you wrote, Daniel." Kaya took a frame from the wall and handed it to the keyboard player. Daniel smiled when he saw it and passed it along to the other band members.

"So that's when you decided to start another Mystique?"

Kaya nodded.

"Actually, I decided then to also make some changes in LUPO. Like combining the two chapters to form an even stronger unit here."

"And it's worked?" Daniel asked.

"So far," Boyce replied for Kaya. "We are converting the teenagers to rock and roll as well as initiating the club goers to it."

"And they have even managed to plug the music into the local radio stations." Brent commented as he walked into the room. "You men must be Mystique. I must say that it is an honor to meet you."

Bradley turned and saw his younger brother. From what he had been told on the journey here, he realized that his brother's memory had been tampered with. Yet Bradley searched the man's face hopefully for some sort of recognition from the sibling he had once been so close to.

For a few moments, Brent looked puzzled as he stared at the other man's face. Deep inside his memory, something stirred then came forth with a rush. Recollections of watching his older brother practice, of playing ball with Bradley and of Bradley comforting him when he was troubled. He remembered when Bradley had landed the position with Mystique as the guitarist and how they had celebrated. Eighteen year old Bradley could have gone partying with his friends but instead, he had decided to spend the evening with his thirteen year old brother. And just two years later, that joy had turned to horror when PARR had gained power and Bradley had just disappeared off the face of the earth. Beneath the permanent tan Brent wore, his face was ashen as he slowly approached the man who looked older than his fifty years.

"Bradley. My God! How could I have forgotten you? How could I have forgotten what you meant to me?" Brent's voice broke with emotion as he put his arms out to his older brother. "I'm so sorry!"

"Hey," Bradley choked out. "Don't sweat it, Shit happens!" The somewhat blasé response lightened the tension a bit as Wind, Gleven, Margaret, Steven and the other present LUPO members came in to be introduced.

"Jared." Cal began. "You were boasting about the talents of Mystique II earlier, now let's hear just how good you are."

The members of Mystique II shrugged and went on to the stage. Brian walked up to the microphone and looked at his father.

"Well, I just hope that I do this right, Dad."

"Just do what you feel like doing. Do whatever the music tells you to do. That is what rock and roll is all about." With a smile of gratitude at these words of encouragement, Brian turned to Boyce and the sounds of Mystique II filled the room.

CHAPTER Forty

"How in the hell did they accomplish that?" Judah screamed into the phone at Gary. "Weren't there any PARR agents around?"

"Yes sir. We had a lot of them around but there was also over a thousand people there. If we had have moved to stop LUPO, they would have torn us apart. You should have seen the way they were enjoying the music."

"I don't give a shit about how much they were enjoying the music!" Judah snapped. "I want LUPO stopped. Last week, someone broke into the Canadian Rockies Hideaway and freed the members of Mystique. I know it was LUPO and it is time for drastic measures. In fact, I'm coming out to Los Angeles. I want you to schedule a rally for next week."

"Yes sir." Gary answered dutifully. Without further conversation, Judah hung up the phone. Gary did the same then sat back at his desk, thinking.

Kaya and the others were still high from the events of the last few weeks. With the instruction of Mystique, the band was becoming even more proficient on their instruments in a very short time. Nothing seemed able to stop them now. It was an exhilarating thought.

This morning, Robert had called Liverpool and told Cedric that he, Beth and whoever else wanted to come should catch the next plane out here because things were beginning to happen. They had promised to be on the next flight and then Cedric had said that he had a surprise for Robert and the others. Robert wondered what it could be.

Judah placed a long distance call to Scotland Yard in England. When Lester came on the line, Judah quickly explained the problems they were having. Lester promised that he, and the other representatives from around the world, would be in Los Angeles by the time of the next rally. All were coming to meet in the City of Angels for, perhaps, the final showdown between the government and the rock and roll rebels.

Gary was wondering the streets of Los Angeles in search of the LUPO members. He didn't wish them harm. On the contrary he wanted to warn them of the upcoming rally and the fact that Judah Arnold would be there and that he was inviting the government officials from around the world. It spelled troubled unless LUPO could plan something spectacular to avert attention from PARR's activities. It would be a confrontation to surpass others in the past. Gary was really hoping that LUPO would win this fight and soon. Every time he had an opportunity to hear the music, he felt more and more drawn to it. It was something that he knew had a right to be here. For hours he walked in search of a LUPO member he recognized.

Just as he was about to give up, Gary spotted someone that looked like he had been on the truck the other night. Gary hurried to the man and took his arm. Robert glanced down at the hand on his arm and then up at the face in alarm.

"Hey! What do you think you're doing?" Hidden panic making Robert's British accent even more prominent. Gary was quick to answer.

"Listen I know that you were on that truck the other night so don't bother to waste both of our time by denying it. " Gary's voice was barely above a whisper. "I want to meet with Kaya, it is time that I got on the right side of this fight and I have some information for her."

Robert was immediately suspicious.

"I'm not taking you to Kaya, if that is what you want. How do I know that you won't hurt her?"

"You don't. But I will give you a phone number and you can talk to Kaya and the others. Arrange a meeting wherever you choose and I will be there. I must talk with Kaya." Gary slipped a piece of paper into Robert's pocket and then let go of Robert's arm and vanished into the crowd before Robert could ask any more questions.

"What did this guy look like?" Boyce asked.

"He was average looking. Tall with auburn hair and gray eyes. His hair was cut short in kind of a military style."

"Gary Shane. " Kaya stated.

"The thing is, " Gleven began "why does he suddenly want a meeting? And what does he want?"

"We could be walking into a trap." Brent warned.

"I don't think so." Kaya mused.

"Why? And don't tell me it's another one of your feelings."

"Well it is." Kaya retorted, "I saw Gary at the government buildings that night and there was something about him that just told me that, for some reason, he was able to be trusted."

"Kaya's feelings have never been wrong before." Andric reminded everyone.

"But there's always a first time." Boyce muttered though everyone ignored him.

"I think we might as well call him. I, for one, am curious to see what he has to say." Jared mused. "If we arranged it right, Kaya would be in no danger whatsoever. And I could use the thrill of it all."

"So could I." Brian surprised everyone by announcing. He blushed when he noticed all eyes were upon him. "Well this is more fun than I can ever remember having. The last few days have been great."

Kaya laughed and looked at the others.

"So what will it be? Are we going to arrange a meeting with Gary

Shane or not? Let's see a show of hands. All in favor raise their hands." For a moment, only those who were overjoyed at the idea raised their hands but soon everyone had signaled their agreement including Boyce.

Later that night, Gary received a telephone call, informing him to be outside on the street within twenty minutes. Gary, anxious to meet with the silver haired rebel, hurried to the street.

Men in a dark van sat across the street from him and watched the surrounding area for a few minutes, making sure that no one was around. When all seemed to be clear, a huddled form strolled past Gary and handed him a note. After reading the note Gary walked around the corner where the van was already waiting for him. Without warning Gary was hauled into the van before it rapidly sped away. No one followed.

Gary sat in the van, staring at the men in dark clothing and with hoods obscuring most of their faces. One of the men motioned for him to stand, which he did, and quickly searched him for weapons.

"Nothing." A deep voice growled when the search had been completed. Another figure, obviously in charge of the situation, nodded then handed over a hood. Gary's hands were then tied, not too tightly, and the hood was put over his head, the blackness was all Gary could see in front of him. During all this, and the ensuing ride, not a word was said either between the hooded figures or to Gary.

Gary felt a twinge of panic as the ride extended on. Though he felt that LUPO never killed unless they were forced to, he was hoping that LUPO didn't see any valid reason for his termination. Just when Gary's imagination was fantasizing all sorts of horrendous instances, the van stopped.

Gently but firmly Gary was led to his feet and directed down from the van. The hood still on, Gary couldn't see anything and had to put his trust for his safety in his captors. He was directed to a seat and then the hood was removed. The muted lights didn't shock Gary's eyes and allowed them to adjust to his new surroundings fairly quickly. He scanned what seemed to be an empty warehouse. He listened intently and could hear the faint sounds of the ocean in the background, which really didn't mean a lot. His heartbeat quickened as he saw three figures walk across the concrete floor towards him. The lights, though dim, reflected off the silver hair that could only belong to Kaya More. As she stepped into the light where he could see her clearly, Gary felt a rush of adrenaline. He waited for Kaya to speak first.

"You're here. I'm here. Now what did you want to tell me?"

Kaya's voice was soft and melodic, giving no indication of any anger only curiosity.

Gary swallowed as his eyes were locked with those of the rebel leader.

"Judah Arnold will be coming out to the PARR ra1ly next week and he's invited leaders from all over the world."

"And?" The man who Gary knew was Gleven Andrews asked.

"And I feel that if LUPO could plan something really exciting, it would not only humiliate Judah in front of the world, but it would also strike a real blow for LUPO."

"And why would you want to help LUPO? You have been trying to end us for years." The tall, blond man asked.

Gary took a deep breath and glanced at Kaya, whose face was expressionless, waiting for an answer.

"When I was in England, " Gary began, "I had the opportunity to hear some rock and roll. I never knew what I was fighting against before but, now that I do, I realize that we shouldn't be banning the music. I want to be able to choose the music I listen to. I want others to be able to make their own choices in life, no matter what."

"Good answer." Kaya said. "It could have come straight out of a LUPO handbook, if there were such a thing."

Gary felt strings of panic begin to course through him. It has never occurred to him before that Kaya might not believe him.

"I'm telling you the truth." He cried. "I don't feel that PARR is right anymore. "

"Then why don't you leave the agency?" The tall, blond man spoke once again.

"Because," Gary explained patiently "I feel that I can do LUPO more good if I am on the inside. If you want proof, I will tell you something that you may not know. PARR has been using Regonol to confuse the people."

Kaya smirked. "That's not news to us but the question is, are you going to stop the use of it?"

Now it was Gary's turn to look smug. "I already have. Even before I heard the music, I started to wonder about the long term effects of it on the people. So I substituted the orders with plain drinking water. The people have had fairly clear minds for a little while now."

"And how do we know that?"

"You don't. That is one you are just going to have to trust me on."

Kaya and the others were silent for a moment.

"Fine. Do you have anything else you wanted to tell me?"

Gary shook his head, still not sure if Kaya trusted or believed him. Kaya turned to the men who had brought Gary here.

"Take him back. Just make sure you don't hurt him and that he doesn't know where he has been." Once more the hood was placed over Gary's head and he was led back to the van.

As the vehicle started moving away, Gary wondered if any of his words had been believed. He would just have to wait and see.

CHAPTER Forty-On

"So, did you believe him?" Kaya asked everyone now seated in the underground hotel.

Jared shrugged, still in his black outfit from transporting Gary. "He didn't really say anything that was too top secret but then again he didn't really tell us anything anyway."

"But, should we do anything for the upcoming rally?" Kaya persisted.

"It might be fun." Jared lazily commented, hiding his excitement with the expertise born of practice.

"I don't see why not. " Brian added.

"It might be helpful to the cause." Larret said.

Others in the room quickly agreed that something should be done. That is everyone except Boyce. Everyone looked at him expectantly, waiting for an answer.

Boyce returned their gazes then threw up his hands in defeat. "What the hell? Why not?"

Kaya hugged him tightly before speaking. "Great! Then it's settled. Robert, when do the rest of your people get here?" Kaya was once again the leader and in control.

"Tomorrow morning at six." Robert habitually glanced at his watch to check the time. "And are they ever going to be surprised."

The next morning, Robert stood with Kaya and Boyce at the airport. The plane they were waiting for was late. Anxiously Boyce glanced at the other people in the airport lobby but none of them seemed to be watching the group of rebels any closer than the others. Still he found it hard to relax. He would be glad when Robert's people got here and they were able to go home.

Scanning the people that were disembarking from the plane, Robert suddenly smiled. "There they are!' He whispered to Kaya and Boyce. He was disappointed to see that only Cedric and Beth had elected to come but they were better than none. As soon as they were near enough, Robert rushed to them.

"It is great to see you! Wait until I tell you all that has been happening here."

"If you mean about the rock concert on wheels, we already know about that. It was in every newspaper and on every TV station. What a feat you guys pulled off." Cedric was quick to praise though he was slightly jealous that he hadn't been there. Then he quickly corrected himself. It had been his decision to stay in England and, besides, he had more important news to tell Robert.

Robert, not forgetting Beth, enveloped her in a hug. As he pulled back to look at her, he noticed something.

"Beth! Is that an engagement ring you're wearing?" He turned to Cedric. "You little devil! Is this your surprise?"

Cedric nodded happily. This was the important news that he had had to tell Robert and the others. And though it wasn't as earth shattering as the news of LUPO's accomplishments, it was still very important.

"I think we should go now." Boyce suggested. "I get a little nervous standing in public areas like this."

Robert quickly agreed so the little party left.

Back at the restaurant, everyone was busy introducing him or herself. It seemed after a few moments, as if they had known each other for all their lives. The newly arrived British rebels were thoroughly impressed to be meeting the legendary Mystique whom they had assumed were dead. Everything was coming together as it should. Now all that was left was to plan their activities for the upcoming PARR rally.

Judah Arnold sat in his luxury hotel room, feeling ill at ease, as if someone was watching him. At his demand, securities had been increased so that there was no way that anyone could break in to the room and harm the international officials.

He sighed to himself. He wouldn't admit, not even to himself, but he had the feeling that Kaya More and LUPO had beat him. They and their associates were destroying everything he had worked for in his life. With a sickening feeling, he remembered the vow he had made to Kaya in his apartment. Where he said that rock and roll music would come back over his dead body. Suddenly, he felt that the hotel room was too hot and went outside to the balcony. Breathing deeply and trying to relax himself, Judah was unaware of the figure standing on the other side of the balcony.

"So, you have arranged this final showdown have you Judah?" Kaya asked quietly. Lowering herself down from the balcony above was easy and so would be the quick escape she knew was necessary. Balancing on the railing, waiting for Judah to venture out to the night air had been the difficult part. Judah's face hardened at the sight of the young woman he had tried so often to eliminate but hadn't accomplished.

"Cat got your tongue? I have never known you to be silent before." Kaya taunted. "Or perhaps it was because you once told me that rock and roll music would only be revived over your dead body."

Judah's eyes widened as he misunderstood her meaning.

"Oh, don't worry!" Kaya laughed. "I have no intentions of killing you. I promised you that I would destroy you and your ideals and that is what I am doing. I would say that we have done quite well, wouldn't you say?"

"You have managed to do better than I would have ever thought you would." Judah admitted grudgingly. "But the war is still not won.

Tomorrow will tell the story."

"Yes. Tomorrow justice and freedom will once again win out." Having said her piece, Kaya gave a tug on the rope around her waist and slowly she began her ascent to the floor above her.

"See you tomorrow, Judah." Her voice carried to him on the wind. Surprisingly, Judah didn't move to have her taken into custody. Instead, he stood there looking over the lights of the city and reflecting on her words. He would never let her win.

Gary Shane helped Kaya unfasten the ropes then led her into the hotel suite he had rented, under another name of course, for the evening. Going to the small bar, he turned to Kaya and smiled."Would you like a brandy?"

Kaya nodded then took the offered glass with a look of speculation in her eyes.

"Why did you do all this Gary? After all, if we were caught, you would be in more trouble than I would. "

Gary took a chair near Kaya and shrugged. "Well as I told you before, I really believe that you were right all along. Not only that, Judah wasn't going to do anything nor could he do anything."

"Why's that?"

Gary grinned mischievously as he sipped his brandy. "Because when Judah ordered extra security, he had to do that through me. And I sort of, conveniently, misplaced the order."

Kaya chuckled.

"So how much security is actually here?"

"Counting hotel security?"

Kaya nodded.

Gary's brow furrowed for a moment as he thought.

"Almost nil. I made the reservations in different names, of course, and the hotel figured it was going to be a slow night without any important visitors. So they cut back on their security tonight, saving them for a more important night, and left a skeleton crew on."

"Oh that's priceless." Kaya laughed. "So I wasn't in that much danger at all."

Gary turned serious. "Except from Judah. Whatever possessed you to attempt something as risky as visiting Judah on his own turf?"

Kaya smiled confidently. "Actually this is the third time he has received a visit from me. The first time was when I was eighteen years old and getting really involved with LUPO. I broke into his apartment knocked him out with ether and handcuffed him to the chair. Then I warned him to drop his vendetta against rock and roll. Not that I honestly thought he would listen." Kaya stopped to take a drink and Gary spoke.

"I remember that. You called the PARR offices in the morning and let us know where he was. I was one of the agents that were sent to free him. Judah told us that intruders attacked him. Why didn't you kill him then? It would have saved you a lot of trouble."

Kaya shook her head.

"I never intended that LUPO should be a violent organization. I never intended to kill anyone. Not even that agent when I kidnapped you. That was an accident."

"I know that, and that agent is alive and well in New York. I think I knew it that night as well. Which reminds me. Do you remember, just before someone knocked me unconscious, you threatened to shoot my genitals off?"

Kaya laughed and nodded.

"Well, I'm curious. Would you have really done it?"

Kaya smiled. "I honestly couldn't tell you. That night was so crazy and I was actually more frightened than I would have admitted that I think I really would have shot you. Though whether in the genitals, I'm not sure."

Gary shuddered.

"You really know how to hurt a man, don't you?" He paused to take a drink then continued. "But tell me about the second time you paid the illustrious Mr. Arnold a visit."

"That wasn't that long ago. In fact, it was just after Gleven's rescue. I had returned to New York and..."

"Returned? Do you mean that you had left New York after kidnapping me and when the road blocks were still up?"

Kaya nodded.

"Tell me. How did you guys accomplish that?"

Kaya grinned.

"Does this ring a bell? Maybe you heard about it." Kaya slouched in her chair and donned a dreamy expression. "Peace man. We're on our way to California, the land of sunshine and sinners to bring the word of God. Or something like that."

Gary howled with laughter.

"A fluorescent painted van with five people in it, two of them an older couple."

Kaya nodded.

"Yup. Andric, the guy whose wig fell off that night in the park, Boyce, Gleven, his wife and myself. We almost broke up laughing when we realized that the PARR agents were falling for it I hope you realize that many of your agents are not the brightest people to ever walk the face of this earth."

Gary grinned ruefully.

"I'm fully aware of that fact. But tell me the rest of the story."

Kaya paused a moment to collect her thoughts then continued.

"Anyway, I had returned to get mom and Brent out of the city and to form the new LUPO. I broke into the PARR buildings and went upstairs to Judah's office. I removed the fuse for his office so he would have to leave and, when he got back, I was there waiting for him."

"Let me guess, you stole his gun and tore out the alarm button."

Kaya looked surprised.

"Yes. But I left the gun there, didn't you guys find it?"

"Where did you leave it?"

"I threw it down the mail chute outside the senior offices."

Gary laughed.

“That’s the garbage chute! So someone probably found it and is walking around New York with Judah's favorite weapon."

Kaya shrugged all that beyond her control now.

"Tell me about Krista.” She spoke softly.

Gary thought for a moment.

"I have never been able to figure her out. Even though it was PARR that caused her so much pain, it is LUPO she hates. And in particular, you."

"That's because LUPO and I represent the cause of those actions. I know she blames me because I had a vision that day and knew something was going to happen. She blames her father for starting LUPO in the first place and she blames LUPO because, if it wasn't for that, she would never have been caught in the middle."

Gary stood up and started to pace around the room.

“Krista is so different. Sometimes, very rarely lately, she can be the sweetest person I've ever seen. But then there are the other times when she is self absorbed, self indulgent and bitter. I just wish that I knew how to fix whatever is causing her to make those drastic changes. More and more she is the selfish bitch that helped me capture her father. Did you know that she didn't even feel any regrets over that?"

"If only you had known her before the rape! She was a sweet, funny person. She cared about the little things in life, like whether the bum on the corner was getting enough food. And I think she did have some regrets about turning her father in."

"Why do you say that?"

"Because she saw us. Just as we were leaving the prison, she was standing there. She didn't say a word although she could have alerted the guards to us. She just moved aside and let us pass. I think there is still some good in her, at least I hope so." Kaya glanced at her watch then smiled wearily at Gary.

"I had better go now. Please don't tell anyone about what I did tonight. I am already getting enough flack about taking risks."

Gary nodded then silently watched the young woman leave.

CHAPTER Forty-Two

Judah sat in the back of the limousine with Gary.

"Are you sure that everything has been arranged?" He asked for what seemed like the hundredth time.

For what seemed like the hundredth time, Gary reassured him that it was. The only thing Gary didn't tell him was that he hoped that LUPO also had everything arranged. If Kaya had actually planned to do something outrageous, then he was certain that today would be very exciting.

"I just hope that LUPO hasn't planned anything. They could ruin everything." Krista spoke from where she sat.

Judah glared at her but, since she was concentrating on making sure that her hat was straight, she didn't notice.

"I must tell Gary to get rid of that woman." Judah thought to himself savagely. "She has outlived her usefulness."

Krista, oblivious to these thoughts, smiled brightly at Judah then transferred her thoughts to her nails.

Gary rolled his eyes. He hadn't wanted Krista to come along but she had insisted. When Krista insisted there wasn't much that anyone could do.

Kaya and the others were once more readying the truck for a moving concert. But this time there was going to be a difference. Music was going to be played from all angles of the park. There was no way that any person in the crowd could avoid hearing it. As she worked on setting up her keyboards, she suddenly had a chilling feeling crawl up her spine. A vision of Boyce and Gleven lying bloody on the makeshift stage flashed through her mind. She looked over to where they stood, talking to one another and a previous vision flashed through her mind. The one of her father lying dead. This time Kaya was going to stop it. She hopped off the truck and ran over to where Gleven and Boyce stood.

"You guys can't go!" She insisted. Boyce was shocked, as was Gleven. Gleven though, caught the meaning of her outlandish statement quicker than Boyce did.

"You had a vision, didn't you?" Kaya nodded and Gleven continued. "I don't know how Boyce feels but if that is the way it's supposed to be then so be it."

"But you have to stay behind. You have to. I can't lose you two as well. " Kaya was frantic, remembering her father.

Boyce glanced at Gleven with concern. He had never seen Kaya this upset. Usually she was the calm one.

"Babe, this is something we have to do. Just like it was something your father had to do." Boyce's voice was soft and gentle with understanding. "And maybe your vision is wrong this time."

Kaya shook her head.

"They have never been wrong before. Why should they be wrong now?"

"Kaya." Gleven spoke sternly in an effort to calm the young woman. "Now you couldn't stop fate from taking your father and you're not going to stop it from doing the same to me if that is what it has planned for me today. So quit worrying about it. I'm going and that is the end of the discussion."

"So am I." Boyce echoed.

Kaya threw up her hands in disgust. She knew by the tone of their voices that there was no way that she was going to talk Gleven and Boyce out of going. So she went back to what she had been doing previously, trying to push the concern from her mind.

LUPO members that hadn't stayed to help Kaya and the others were at the rally well before it started. Hidden around the platform and in the trees were various CD and tape players. As a joke, one had even been hidden in the podium where Judah was to make his speech. This one was, as were the others, remote controlled. Therefore, the LUPO members could switch them on at a distance without being seen. There was a general feeling of excitement in the air, almost as if all the bystanders already there could sense that something major was going to happen. Would this be the final showdown between PARR and LUPO? And, if so, who would win?

The moving stage was ready to go. Everyone was counting the seconds until the departure time. As if in a single movement, the rebels started to move. The musicians to their equipment, the drivers to their vehicles. This was the moment they had been waiting a lifetime for.

Though the LUPO leaders had had some misgivings, the members of Mystique had insisted on being in on this escapade. So, the five older men were seated on a makeshift, raised portion of the flatbed behind the band. They took their seats in the bolted down chairs regally. For the first time in thirty years, they were able to show their faces with pride.

Judah took the stage with a solemn grace, surprising for his ever-growing size. Stepping up to the microphone, he cleared his throat.

"Ladies and gentlemen, I would like to thank you for being here today."

"It was either that or be jailed!" Someone yelled from the crowd.

Judah stopped for a moment then decided to let the comment go. "We all know that rock and roll music is evil and that it must never be allowed to resurface."

"Says who?" Another voice yelled.

This time, Judah decided that it would be wise to answer.

"Psychologists around the world have deemed it to be so. As you can see, I have representatives from every country here today that can attest to that fact." Judah waved his hand behind him, indicating the numerous gentlemen that sat beneath the flag of their respective nation.

"But how much are these people being paid to say that?"

"Or have you threatened them?" The crowd was turning unruly, expressing their own opinions and questioning those of PARR. Worse still, they were making PARR look like fools in front of the entire world.

This was not the reaction that Judah had expected. Never before had people dared to defy him. He fought to keep his temper under control as he continued.

"These rebels have to be stopped. And the only way we can do that is with your help." Pictures of Kaya, Boyce, Wind, Brent and Gleven appeared on the wall behind Judah.

"If you happen to see any of these people or anyone you know is directly involved with LUPO, report it directly to the nearest PARR agency. This rebellion has to be stopped."

"But why? I was at the government buildings last week and heard this so called evil music. I saw nothing wrong with it. In fact, it made me feel good." Comments were now coming from the crowd so fast that Judah and the others on stage could no longer understand what was being said. Judah was appalled at the extent of the rebellion here. He glared at the members of PARR that stood on the platform with him. It was their entire fault. He went to take a step towards them but stopped as he heard something in the distance.

Obviously, the traveling rock concert that had so disrupted the order of things the other night was once again making an appearance. To the cheers of the crowd in front of him. As if on cue, music from other sources started playing. In horror, Judah realized that some of the music was coming from his podium. He turned to the PARR agents standing near him and shouted.

"Well, don't just stand there. Do something!" A few of the agents jumped to obey his orders but more of them laid down their guns. Stopping one who happened to be walking by, Judah demanded to know what was going on.

"Face it man. You've lost, there is no way that we can stop it. And not only that, I kind of like this music. Hell we have been supporting this agency for years, believing all of your lies but we never knew what we were outlawing. There is nothing wrong with this music. I say that rock and roll will never die!"

Enraged, Judah picked up a nearby gun. As the young man was walking away, Judah yelled at his retreating back.

"What kind of agent are you? We never lose!"

The young man turned to face his former leader and was astounded to see the gun pointed at him.

Gary, who was standing near the park, caught sight of this and moved in to help the young man.

"Judah. What do you think you are doing?"

"Bringing things back under control." Judah was deathly calm about the situation now; unaware that there was no way he could master the situation any longer.

"Judah. Look around you. The people are enjoying this music and they aren't going to stand for you or anyone else telling them that they can't have it. You masterminded this showdown and you lost. Judah. Look!"

Unwillingly, Judah's eyes went to the crowd. It was true. The people were dancing and singing along with the band. It didn't seem possible but he had lost. He turned to the other government leaders that were sitting on the stage and was horrified to see their looks of sympathy. Throwing down the gun, Judah fled the stage to escape his shame.

Gary walked over to the government leaders. "I'm sorry sirs. It seems as if Mr. Arnold has left the scene. Would you like me to arrange some transportation back to your hotels?" One by one, they all shook their heads.

"Mr. Shane." Lester began sadly. "I think we are finished. Once word of this day's events gets out, and that shouldn't take long, there is going to be no rest at all in our respective countries. Tell me, when did you change sides in this fight?"

"I guess I started to change sides years ago, when I first realized the determination that Kaya More possessed. Much of this," Gary waved his hand over the chaos in front of him, "is her doing. But I think I really saw the light when the rebels interrupted the meeting in England. Then I knew what we were doing was wrong."

"Yes, I can see that." Lester sighed. "The only thing I can be happy about is that it all happened without any bloodshed."

Gary thought about Kansall More and the thousands of others, both PARR agents doing their job and LUPO members fighting for a just cause, who had died in this struggle.

"Not true, Mr. Aran." He commented softly. "Not true at all. There was too much bloodshed in this fight." Lester looked at him in surprise but didn't question the young man's strange reply.

Krista sat in the crowd and glowered at the people on the moveable stage that had now stopped. Every time she turned around, Kaya More was doing something to destroy her happiness and ruin her life. Well she had had enough. Withdrawing a gun from her purse, she made her way through the crowd towards Kaya.

Boyce was having the time of his life. He really liked the fact that the people were enjoying the music so much, not that he ever doubted they would. This is what he had been fighting for. He more than liked it. He reveled in it.

Out of the corner of his eye, he saw Krista approaching. He recognized her from that day in the prison and he wondered what she was doing here. Then he saw the gun in her hand. Horrified, he followed her eyes to her unsuspecting target. Kaya. Without thinking, he hollered a warning to Kaya before throwing himself in front of her. The gun fired and the shot missed Kaya, instead hitting Boyce. The crowd, enraged at this turn of events, quickly grabbed Krista and held her there until an officer arrived to take her into custody.

Kaya wept over Boyce. Why did all her visions have to come true?

Boyce stirred restlessly.

"Ow! Damn that hurts!"

Kaya stopped crying and looked closer at Boyce.

"You're alive!"

"Disappointed? I don't think it is that serious. I told you that your feelings would be wrong one day."

Kaya laughed merrily and gave Boyce a sound kiss. Relieved, Kaya looked out over the crowd and saw the people talking among themselves and with the now unarmed agents. Some agents had even removed their uniforms and were now walking around in their underwear. The relaxed expressions and sense of freedom was something that Kaya had never really seen in her life. Joyously, she realized that the fight was over and LUPO had won. This day had brought about the rebirth of rock and roll.

CHAPTER Forty-Three

A great earthquake once more shook the place where the restaurant stood. This time, the restaurant disappeared and the remains of the hotel and auditorium emerged. A great wind blew, almost as if the gods were sighing with relief that the music had been reborn.

CHAPTER Forty-Four

Three days later, ten people got off a plane at the Calgary International Airport and rented two vehicles in order to drive to Banff. This time when Mystique II walked into the airport, a crowd of cheering fans greeted them. Proudly, with heads held high, the musicians talked with the people before leaving in their rented cars.

On the road to Banff, Alberta the visitors saw signs and posters along the way. All of the written greetings welcomed back rock and roll and the people who had resurrected the music.

Up the mountain road they traveled, followed by many other vehicles with occupants all wanting to witness this piece of history. At the prison, the political inmates had not yet received the news that PARR had been defeated. But they would soon enough.

The Americans gracefully exited their vehicles and walked up to the iron door that had served to keep the men and women inside imprisoned for so many years. Ron Stopford lifted his head to the skies and, in a voice that boomed over the area, he praised the heavens.

“Thank you God. Rock and roll has been reborn, LONG LIVE ROCK AND ROLL!" An ensuing cheer from the music fans that had followed the liberators deafened any comment that others may have made.

In one of the cells, a rock musician who was one of the first to be captured and whose stubborn hold on life was slipping away looked curiously on the scene below him. A tear coursed down his cheek as he realized that the prisoners' dream had come true. Rock and roll had been given another chance to flourish. Feeling the energy seep from him, he lay on his cot and listened to the sounds of rejoicing throughout the prison walls. Smiling for the first time in over thirty years, the musician slipped into that endless sleep.

Another musician heard the noise and wondered what was going on then he saw his cell door open and anxiety took over. It quickly disappeared when the door stayed open but no one entered. With a caution born of years of fear, the musician walked carefully out of the door. He looked around him in wonder when he saw the jubilant prisoners dancing in the corridors. One, who noticed that he was standing alone, enveloped him a big bear hug.

"We're free!" He cried. “PARR has been beaten and we can rock to our hearts content." The stranger dashed away, reveling in his new freedom, leaving the musician alone again. Confused, the man returned to his cell and closed the door. On his cot he sat, wondering what was going on until someone came and led him out into the sunshine.

A former female rock star stood in the yard with tears running down her face. Although she was overjoyed that the freedom to play whichever style of music you wished was brought to the people, she knew that she couldn't live in the normal world again. She gazed at her scarred and crippled hands through the mist of tears and realized that she could never play the piano again. Her hands went to her face and felt the ridged scar tissue there and her heart broke a little more. One of the first things that PARR had done to her was to permanently destroy any sort of beauty she may have had. She felt the damage was too extensive for plastic surgery and she also felt that it was impossible to face the world like this. Unnoticed by the revelers, she walked to the edge of the mountaintop, stared at the world below which she had waited so long to see then stretched her arms wide and leapt from the edge.

The walls of the prison couldn't contain the jubilant political prisoners that were now going to be set free. The PARR agents inside wisely decided to open the gates then vanish. It was evident that, although they had received no official confirmation, PARR and its ideals had been defeated. None of the agents assigned to guard the prisoners believed enough in the agency to risk their lives to continue its tyranny. So they stepped aside and allowed the prisoners to walk free.

Many of the musicians in the yard spoke of again exploring the industry. It would be so different now. It would be like when rock and roll had first started. To the majority of the listeners, everything would be new and fresh. There would be few, if any, jaded listeners. Yet, they all knew that it was all talk. Never again would their crippled, abused and mangled bodies perform in front of an audience. But there were many things that needed to be done besides that. Perhaps this time they could stop the industry from becoming too corporate, too money orientated. It was the music that counted and this time, they would make sure the entire world was aware of that.

Kaya looked around her at the delightful chaos and smiled. Now, more than before, she knew that her mission had been accomplished.

After everyone had left the mountaintop and deserted the area, the prison went through an amazing transformation. One by one, the stone walls started to disintegrate. Slowly at first then gathering more speed, the walls started tumbling down.

At the bottom of the hill, Kaya happened to take a final glance at the mountaintop as they were driving away.

"Oh my God!" She gasped. "Jared, stop the car!" Jared stopped immediately, struck by the urgency in Kaya's voice. Kaya, hardly waiting until the car came to a stop, got out and stood staring at the sight above her.

"Jesus!" Daniel muttered as he came to stand beside her. "What's happening?" Boyce answered for all of them.

"Damned if I know but, man, isn't it a beautiful sight?" The Americans, the now freed political prisoners and all the supporters stood at the side of the road and gazed up at the spectacular, unexplainable sight on the mountain. They stood there and watched until the dust had settled and the prison was no longer in existence.

When the vehicles had started again, Daniel leaned close to Kaya.

"I know you have the gift." He commented then asked hesitantly. “Did you see what I saw?" Kaya was silent for a moment.

"I thought I saw figures dancing in the ruins. They were transparent, I could still see everything behind them but I could also see them. They were so happy."

Daniel sighed in relief. "I think," he began "We saw the rock stars that died up there. And of course they were happy. No one ever has to suffer in that prison ever again."

EPILOGUE

The concert hall was packed with people, all coming to see the first rock concert in years. The excitement was electric as people greeted one another and speculated on the upcoming event. All knew that they were participating in a part of history.

The auditorium was decorated with pictures of LUPO members who had died for the cause over the last thirty years as well as posters of numerous rock bands who had existed over time.

On the upper balconies, hundreds of freed musicians sat and watched the commotion below intently. Subconsciously they were comparing the excitement to the days when they had played and, so far, they found nothing lacking. Everything was as it should be. Though these musicians, whose fame had once reigned supreme in the music world, were no longer able to participate in the strenuous onstage activities, they were going to be in the other areas of music. Recording companies were being established again as well as management companies. These men and women, with their knowledge and expertise in the business, would be guiding the newcomers. Not only would they be assisting them to overcome the pitfalls but they were also going to try to deter the business from ever becoming too corporate again. This time, the music must remain the most important factor.

The LUPO supporters that had managed to bring about the changes took the front sections. Directly in front of the stage, Wind, Gleven, Brent, Margaret, Steven and Calo sat.

Wind looked around her with pride. When her husband had started LUPO twenty-six years ago, this had been his dream. For the people to be able to enjoy the sounds of rock and roll. For the people to be able to choose for themselves. How she wished that Kansall had lived to see this day.

Brent, sitting beside his new wife, sensed the directions of her thoughts. He put gentle pressure on her hand to let her know that he shared her feelings though, in a way, he was glad that Kansall wasn't here. If he were, Brent would not be married to this wonderful woman who had been through so much and had survived.

Gleven sat stoically, trying not to let the noise behind him disturb his thoughts. For so many years he had lived for this day. The day when the world was once again be free and now it was being celebrated. The only worry on his mind was the fact that Judah Arnold had not been seen since the day of the rally when LUPO and Mystique II had the showdown. Gleven worried that Judah hadn't finished with Kaya and LUPO.

Margaret sat comfortably, marvelling at the changes around her. Throughout their entire courtship and marriage, Margaret had supported Gleven in all his endeavours. Now, she was just so pleased that it had all worked out. And that she hadn't lost Gleven in the process.

Calo sat uncomfortably in the seat. For a man his size, these seats were just too damned small. He shifted then settled down. His thoughts were on that day when Kansall had been shot. He should have known then that Kaya was meant for big things and, now, she had proven to the world that she was headed for greatness.

Steven pondered his present situation. After his restaurant had been swallowed by the earth, (and that was a shock to return home to), he had been at a loss on what to do with his life. Then the idea of running the Rocker's Paradise had occurred to him. Though the first few months had been spent restoring the auditorium so that they could hold this concert, within the next six months, the hotel would be returned to its former glory and he would be open for business.

Gary was standing at the front door, handling security for the concert. When Krista had tried to shoot Kaya, he had known then that she was beyond help. Though the women's prison she had been sent to might be of some help, he doubted it. Sighing at the tragedy, Gary just rejoiced that everything had worked out right in the end.

Behind the stage, Kaya and the rest of Mystique II were warming up. Kaya glanced over at Boyce and smiled. In the time since the last PARR rally, she and Boyce had been growing apart. Perhaps only the excitement and danger of LUPO had been keeping them together. In her heart, Kaya knew that their relationship was going to end soon. Somehow that didn't bother her that much. Of course it made her sad to think about it but that was life.

Boyce had his eyes on one of the girls that had come to help out with the concert. Though, technically, he was still with Kaya he knew it wouldn't be long before they broke up. He glanced over to where she was and smiled. But they would always remain friends, of that he was sure. They had shared too much over the last few years.

Robert looked at Kaya with new admiration shining in his eyes. Through her guidance, he had managed to form his own band. He thought back to even a year ago when none of this would have been possible and silently thanked the powers that be for making this come about. It was a dream come true.

The cheers of the crowd increased as the original members of Mystique walked onto the stage. Though the men still showed the effects of the life they had been forced to lead inside the prison walls, they were beginning to resemble the musicians who had inspired a revolution.

Ron Stopford approached the microphone, his walk and stance reminiscent of the vocalist who had won so many hearts. When he spoke, his voice rang loud and clear over the stilled crowd.

"It was on this stage, over thirty years ago, that PARR destroyed rock and roll and took away our freedom of choice. Therefore, I think it is only fitting that this concert be held here.

"We can't forget all the people who died in this fight nor can we ever forget what PARR has cost us over the years. If it wasn't for all those people who had the courage to fight for what they believe in and make a stand, we wouldn't be here tonight." Daniel More took his place at a nearby microphone.

"This is a very important night; the eyes of the world are on us. We have to prove to our critics that rock and roll does have a place in our society." Once more the fans began to cheer and those onstage waited for silence before continuing.

"So, on this night," Ron began "we will prove to the world that rock and roll will never end. They almost beat us once and we came back!" The entire band spoke in unison,

"Long live rock and roll!"

Daniel shouted above the noise of the people's cheers, "And now, let's welcome some of the people that are responsible for this evening!"

Backstage, Kaya glanced at her watch and signalled for everyone to join her. "Almost time to go on." She reminded everyone. "Does anyone have anything to say?"

"Yeah, I do." Jared began. All eyes turned toward him and he grinned. "Let's kick ass!" Grinning, the opening band trooped onto the stage.

Kaya stood there, watching Robert's band, and worrying about her own time to go on. It was the recognizable feeling of stage fright that she would have to get used to. Suddenly, she felt a warm comforting feeling wash over her. Then she heard a familiar voice in her head.

"Nice going Starlight. I couldn't be prouder." Then the feeling was gone but Kaya retained those words as she went on stage.

Through the cheering fans, there was one person who was silent. Judah Arnold watched Mystique with hatred.

"I will get you for this, Miss More." He vowed silently. "If it takes me to my dying day, you will pay!"

-the end-

Karen Magill comes from a family of writers. Her paternal grandmother, Katherine Magill, was not only a published novelist but also supplemented the family income with articles. Karen has written from an early age and past writing credits include poetry, a monthly column on music, a weekly newsletter on music and numerous other little things. If you look around on the Internet you will find her name here and there.

It wasn't until Ms. Magill was disabled by Multiple Sclerosis that she began to pursue her writing career more seriously. Her first novel, ***The Bond, A Paranormal Love Story*** *was published in 2004 through Lulu.com. Presently Ms. Magill lives in an eclectic area of Vancouver Canada.*

Visit Karen at www.karenmagill.com where you can join a free newsletter and win prizes as well as keep in touch with what Karen is doing. To email Karen write to karenmagill@karenmagill.com